THE RISE AND FALL OF THE

go:FIGHT MEKAOTSKO

23

**11 PULSEBLACK 11

The Rise and Fall of the

MekaDisko

by Jim Marcus

November, 2024

This book is set in Lato Regular 9/13
Titles in Lato Heavy 16/20

Cover:
Entertainment

by Jim Marcus 2024

Edited by Janet Valle

ISBN 979-8-9917282-4-9

Based on the Album "MekaDisko" by Go Fight

THE FOLLOWING PAGES ARE TAKEN FROM THE JOURNAL OF LLORONA, THE FIRST SPEAKER.

Elements may be flawed and not true to her actual experiences.

GO·FIGHT

"One day you will ask me which is more important? My life or yours? I will say mine and you will walk away not knowing that you are my life."

-Khalil Gibran

ONE

He wasn't going to stay and I wasn't going to force him to.

This was what I said to people who asked me why I didn't tell Leo I was pregnant.

And then people ask, "How do you know?" and I just have to say I know. I think people know. I think women know. You can call me an unreliable narrator, but not for that. I was deadly accurate about that.

When you're carrying a genius your body rebels against it. There is something in the root directory of the brain's software that knows you are carrying something better than you, smarter than you.

And that's a dangerous thing on this planet.

I was sick for about eight months and then spent the last two in the hospital. I missed the early days of the food riots, scarfing down green jello and asking them to wheel my bed over to the window.

I missed much of the widespread pandemic deaths that dramatically reduced the population of the US and many other countries.

I missed that destructive second term of the president that no one thought would ever be elected, much less twice. More and more the argument that came from people was one bound in a little suit of nihilism. "It's okay if it all falls apart." and "It's a good thing for us to start all over." But people don't start all over. They just sit, hypnotized by the flames until they can't feel their feet anymore.

But after the botched assassination attempt left him the leading candidate, people got in line, they felt somehow like he was the one to make it all better. And the fact that someone had taken a shot at him riled up his base to vote. And they did.

I lived through that.

I was alone when Ithad was born but he managed most of it himself. His apgar score was ten and that was better than I had done on any test. Most of my jokes are self-deprecating. You can thank Leo for that. It was the only way to get him to laugh, putting myself down.

But this I did alone and I did a great job if I can say that.

So, look, this is the full deal. I may jump all over the place and if I AM unreliable it's just because there are big parts I honestly don't know. Important parts.

For example, I have no idea how old I am.

I can't believe I'm telling this story again, but at least now it has an ending. And if you let me get to it, I promise you that there is some kind of payoff.

Okay, I have a son in New York City. It would be a few years before Mikah came along so the two of us were pretty thick. He started walking almost right away. He was talking in full sentences by the time he was a year or so old. What does a year old child even have to talk about?

It turns out everything.

He was fascinated by technology. He loved electricity. And every time something shocked him, he would feel it again - that emotional distress.

Why would electricity hurt him so much when he loved it?

This was THE big lesson. The things you love can hurt you. I had to remind myself over and over again that he was a genius but that had nothing to do with physical or emotional maturity. There were days when he had trouble controlling his hands and couldn't stay awake. And it frustrated him and he cried. There were days when his beloved technology bit back.

And he cried so hard.

And I picked him up and got to be mommy. I got to be special and important to a genius. I got to make silly jokes and dumb faces and watch him turn into a baby again, like some kind of street magic trick.

I got to sleep next to him and be there when he woke up confused and forgot he was smart, because that happens sometimes, I shit you not. I got to experiment with doing all the things my parents never did to make me feel important, but to do it to him. I closed my book when he spoke up. I turned off the television. I put my phone down. I made sure he knew that his words were the oxygen in the room for me.

And he grew up mine.

That is what happens when you are a single parent sometimes. You are the primary satellite to their sun. You revolve, face pointing toward them and watch and they are yours. You stabilize their wobble. You help manage their tides.

But you are their moon.

Ithad was three years old when the maps started coming out.

These were maps prepared by the local alderman. At first it seemed like they were fighting back against the system. Each one detailed parts of town that would no longer get any government services. The buses might not run, no sponsored food repositories, no ambulance or EMT response. Soon it became clear that these maps were not formative arguments against a government that had stopped caring, they were a round of ammunition in a war that many people seemed to support. A war that was meant to remove the poor from sight, area by area.

I wasn't necessarily poor. I've worked in IT and data science for most of my life, ever since I noticed that computers, mostly, do what they are supposed to do. That was a wakeup call, let me tell you. And I loved what I did. And I could work remotely. I found myself talking out loud to Ithad every day as I worked. He didn't understand me yet for most of it, but he was absolutely in love with the big technology words.

Some people just love a four syllable word.

But, again, I wasn't rich. We were now a year into this president's third term and he had declared martial law in many of the cities run by the opposition so he could implement "austerity programs." One of these was killing overtime pay, which, for me, was generally about a third of my paycheck.

The maps got bigger and were more forcibly worded. They seemed to be blaming the poor in various areas for "stealing" the government resources needed to keep business in the area. Our NOHO apartment complex was in a blacked out area in the most recent maps. I confess, at the time, I didn't know exactly what that meant. Until the streets got dirtier. And garbage and sewage workers visited less and less frequently.

The maps were part of a program called "City Forward" and they were all about creating areas of opportunity for businesses to come in and provide private services.

For a time Wal-Mart was our waste removal company, charging every month for services.

This was supposed to kickstart the economy and deliver huge boosts to Wall Street and the private sector. The private companies came and went and by the time Ithad was five years old we'd had about ten different ones.

Some of the companies required a down payment for premium services, which we discovered included removing wet waste.

Which meant that if you didn't have premium and it rained the night before pickup you were on your own for getting rid of your garbage.

I learned that one through trial and error. I have all these diary entries in front of me as I write this so I can juxtapose some events from this time. Sometime around Ithad's seventh birthday, the president died and one of his sons took over almost immediately. There was no election or opposition. The country was focused on fighting the recession and getting back on track. No one wanted to spend money on an election or really cause any waves.

The City Forward program had evolved to creating massive structures downtown. These big windowless buildings went up seemingly overnight and no one really knew what they were. It was the era of business leader cooperation. The new president got on television and said that just as the Japanese had pooled their corporate resources to create JVC - Japanese Victory Corporation during world war II, over one hundred businesses would create what they were calling a "corporate overlap" and merge for the purpose of efficiency. This giant corporation would manage privatized services, from prisons to sewage and more, leaving the government to focus on getting the country back on track.

The corporation would be called MekaCorp.

I remember thinking how friendly the big "M" was.

I grew up in a fairly apolitical household. My mother was from Cuba and my father was from the Dominican Republic. I used to joke that it just made me a New Yorker. But there is a lot of truth in that joke. A lot of people like me, second generation kids living in the US, were so anxious to fit in, to assimilate, to be a part of it all that we didn't ever bother with the politics of it. My parents never spoke Spanish at home and I never learned it. Looking like I do and having a name like Llorona, I certainly had people speak it to me on the street. But every time I would shake my head graciously and shrug. I didn't speak spanish.

No hablo español

In hindsight, you are asking yourself why I wasn't part of some political movement to stop any of this, especially given who I am. But I WASN'T political and didn't even really know what the talking points on any side were. At this point in history it just looked like people agreed that this was how it had to be. I was focused on my son.

I was trying to make our little family work.

There is a lot to tell and I can never really figure out how in-depth to go into it. Our building had been around for a long time. It was called the Delroy and it had a history as an arts and entertainment center. There was even a small musical studio on the first floor that I would sometimes walk by on the way to pick up ice from the machines there. Lately I had taken to giving myself a little break and visiting the first floor so that I could clean up the mounting wave of garbage accumulating there.

I don't know who was on the floor and what they were doing, but they weren't cleaning. It was satisfying picking up some of the garbage and cleaning the hallways up on the first. I found myself doing that in front of the building and in the courtyard as well.

And then I discovered it was actually someone's job.

Noel was the doorman and de facto maintenance guy. I discovered this when I ran into him around lunchtime on a Tuesday when I chose to clean up a bit of trash. Ithad was sleeping late and we were going to do two school sessions that day. This was sort of a treat for him. He liked to "binge" on schoolwork and then ignore it for a few days. He was developing so fast that I didn't want to stop him from doing these things his own way.

Noel brought an extra bag for me for garbage. From then on, he tried to meet me while I was picking up garbage. I appreciated the company, especially since the building would sometimes get creepy. I guess I didn't know how creepy.

Nothing you know about me is going to help you see how I could be raped that way. Nothing you think is true about me is going to help make that a believable story. But one day the power in the building went out and I sat there, without an elevator or lights, and tried to not field the awkward advances of Noel as he pushed me up against the wall.

He had the good sense to disappear after that. Although, not the good sense to NOT leave me a card that said "I'm sorry" lodged under my door.

Because he was so sorry.

Ithad stared at me while I tried to rip that card into its atomic components, tiny pieces of confetti spilling all over the floor soaking into the rug, leaving lesions in the skin of the room. He curled up in my arms afterward and asked me, his mother, if I wanted him to read me a book.

I cried and shook in that corner and hated myself for not seeing Noel as a threat. And then hating Noel more for forcing my son to have to be the grown up, even for only a few minutes. In my mind, this person had made my beautiful son, this genius in my arms, do something that I had fought against for the last seven years of his life.

He made him have to be my support.

At that moment, I would have killed that pig.

And if that sounds more like the person you think I am, maybe it is. Maybe it was the start of me becoming that Llorona.

Over the next few months, my journal entries are short and pertain only to work and, in some cases, Ithad's school work. Home schooling him seemed to get easier as he got older but that meant that we rarely ever left the house.

When summer came, I planned to fix that, taking him to art shows, openings, anything that a normal eight year old would love, too, but mostly things that they really would not. He was devoted to me. And despite the fact that he was with me every single day, nearly all day, it was the check out girl at a local supermarket, Carmela, who noticed first that I was pregnant.

For all that, Ithad seemed not to be bothered by the idea of having a brother or sister. Somehow I had missed the part where he understood how all this worked as well as I did and realized that getting a termination was no longer really possible in the existing political climate.

I would have expected him to be angry, I suppose , once he came to realize that there would be another baby around, but to him, three of us would be even stronger than just two of us. He came up with silly names to make me laugh and talked about what we might do if the new baby were smarter than all of us or, conversely, what if it turned out to be dumb but lovable and we'd have to hide from it just how dumb it really was.

This was Ithad's unique ability in the world - to make me feel like I could handle things, no matter what. He acted in all ways like it was obvious I would have everything under control so wouldn't it be fun if some craziness happened.

He drew pictures for me of what would happen if the new baby was a fish person. Or if the new baby had laser eyes. Or what if, and he tried to explain this elaborately, the new baby could teleport all over and only spent half the time in my belly which is why I felt pretty good this time around.

I saved his pictures and thought maybe we would make a book for the new baby.

But I still couldn't bring myself to name him.

The president's son, who had taken office, seemed to disappear, to be replaced now by the president's other son. Everyone acted like this was just a normal state of affairs. And, I guess it was. During my pregnancy Carmela visited me a lot. She brought food from the store and books, showing me that she had been studying to be a midwife.

I was grateful for all of it. It was hard to get a doctor's attention and my work no longer offered health care at all. Soon Carmela was there every other day, with a handful of goodies, and a book to make me feel better.

It had enjoyed her visits. She seemed to have no problem sitting with him and drawing pictures of flying babies or half-robot babies or space alien babies for the fridge. We were getting closer, he thought, to figuring out what was going to make this one so special.

"Because he will be, because he comes from you."

That's what he said. Those were the actual words he said to me while I was seven months pregnant, big as a house, miserable, half-wanting to jump out the window. That was how he showed me that it was all worthwhile.

Carmela rubbed my belly and did her best to help me stretch so that I wouldn't tear. She listened to me. She brought me anything I asked for. And she cuddled with us on the couch while we all watched every single romantic comedy that netflix had ever made.

Netflix was a company that delivered movies to people at home, on their television.

Our building was bought that year by MekaCorp. They were doing a program called "build everywhere" where they actually bought buildings and built sub basements in them where businesses would operate. So the Delroy eventually had a coffee shop on the 4th floor and a doctor's office on the-8th. This was unexpected and it actually served to keep us in the house more and more every day.

Mikah came just one day before his presumed birth date, while I kneeled in the bathtub and Carmela assisted. Ithad held my hand and was as serious as he had ever been. He ran for water, he patted my forehead. He looked to Carmela for what to do next. I was so incredibly proud of him I barely had time to yell out in pain or anything.

And then he was there.

The four of us stayed on the bed for the entire first week, it seemed. I tried to work from the bed, but without Carmela there would have been no way. She started getting books on IT, proofing, fact checking, all of it, just to help me.

She was not a network administrator or an editor or anything I needed to be, but I loved her. She was just this amazingly good person who helped remind me that this existed. She got me an appointment to see the building doctor and came with me. This is how we discovered that Mikah had Diabetes and would need insulin.

The company I worked for was in publishing. I actually wore a few hats already. As expected, the demand for actual books was going down dramatically. It was clear I would need to find other ways to earn money. Carmela admitted to me that she had been seeing an older man who was giving her money to spend time with him.

It was hard for me to see her like that. The Carmela I knew wasn't a sugar baby, not a kind of sex worker. But she asked me to open my mind and I tried.

I did.

I tried looking at her like the world might. She was naively attractive. She had an open, inviting face, ready to laugh, prepared to listen, easy to look at. She was lovable, she was desirable. Her mop of reddish hair looked like she had always just gotten out of bed and her life lived in belly shirts and yoga pants made her seem lithe and eager, sexually accessible. Of course men wanted to spend time with her.

Of course they were willing to pay to do it.

I had grown up like everyone else did here, aware of the attention, cognizant of the effect women had on men. But I liked to remove myself from the equation. I liked to think of myself as a mind, as an intellect, and it made me see the women around me that way, too. And when it hit me in the face, I ignored it. I wondered if I had done Carmela a disservice by not seeing clearly just what a desirable person she was, above and beyond the kindness she had always shown me,

She moved in and gave up her place. That's how I met Jorgen, the older man who gave her money for her exceptional company.

Jorgen came to dinner and brought wine. I was working very hard to breastfeed so I passed, but I did drink some of the grape juice he brought for Ithad.

Both my children seemed less judgmental than I was. So I learned to let it go. They were consenting adults. If this is what they wanted, good for them. I queried my own brain, much like a database search, to see if I had feelings for Carmela that would make this hard for me. It turned out I had feelings but they weren't exclusive ones. And they didn't preclude her from having fun or taking money from a man she liked. I thought I had time to figure out what, exactly, those feelings were.

So I like to think that I made it easy for Jorgen to connect with Carmela. And that meant that he was around more often. He worked in finance and he was very in the know.

Jorgen is how I first learned about the ships.

We all sort of knew that the government had worked with private industries to reignite the space race. Carmela had said, when we were alone, that they were pouring more money into other planets than they were into this one, which wasn't a lie. But I had no idea that we had established colonies.

A number of human colonies had been built within the solar system. A couple, like IO and Titan, were on moons of Jupiter. And that seemed to be where the hyperwealthy were migrating. In my head, a space colony was a dark, cold, bleak place, but Jorgen said that wasn't true. He had fistfuls of pamphlets in bright colors, printed on glossy stock, showing these beautiful and opulent getaways.

The colonies seemed focused on hiding the fact that they WERE colonies. Rooms filled with plants and waterfalls, both possibly as artificial as the air. But the guides and spaces were stunning and Jorgen seemed anxious to go.

He seemed anxious to move there.

Ithad was captivated with space, as you might imagine. He poured through the pamphlets and asked Jorgen to bring more, but to focus on the technology ones He wanted to know how the ships worked. He wanted to know how the habitats worked. He wanted to learn all of it.

By the time Ithad was ten I had stopped really having to home school him. He led his own education and he had outpaced me in nearly every way. Handing over the job of managing the technology in the house to him was a strange thing, given what I did for a living. But he was good. And he wanted it. Soon he had the wireless connection running faster, using the wiring in the building. I still read with him but now I focused on love stories, romances, human stories. And immediately afterward, I heard him read those same books to Mikah.

One day I woke up to Ithad acting out Romeo and Juliet as a one man show, in front of a giggling toddler. Ithad made me love Mikah harder. He accepted everything about his brother. And despite the circumstances of his birth I started to think of Mikah as mine, too.

For a time, we were a family. Many of you reading this are just learning now, again, what a family is. It's people who love each other, united without questioning. It's people who don't think about being a group anymore, who don't care about anything outside this space and don't really believe that it will ever change.

It's who we are when we're not alone, really.

I even believed, I did, that Jorgen counted in that group. I would have done anything for him. When he was sad, I helped cook for him. When he was exhausted, we told jokes. And when he said that he wanted to leave, to go to IO and take Carmela with, I tried so hard to be happy for her.

I stood in front of the mirror and made my face be happy. I forced myself to buy her a nice dress and wrap it carefully with pictures that the boys had drawn, to hold the package close to me and try to put myself in it so she could tell that it was real, not just me not caring.

I made myself love her enough to let her go. Because that's what you sometimes have to do.

We went to the spaceport. It was October and Mikah was nearing three years old. It hadn't really gotten cold since he was born, and this October was no different. The sun glared down and darkened the windows in the autonomous taxi Jorgen had gotten so we could see them off. I told him to take care of her as though I were some kind of former suitor warning him to be on his best behavior or he might have to deal with me, but I knew there was little chance I could ever see them again.

The migration ships were expensive and most people who had secured a spot in the colonies stayed there. Only the wealthiest came back and forth. Truth be told, I had little idea HOW much money Jorgen really had. But I knew what my gut was telling me and it was saying I would never see Carmela again.

The boys and I had the car for another couple of hours, a gift from Jorgen, so we rode around the city, watching the incredible disparity between downtown's huge sweeping cadres of skyscrapers and the run down depressed areas surrounding it. It almost seemed like the wealthy areas were leeching vitality from the rest of the city, a city too afraid now to fight back. Jorgen had left another gift for us in the back seat. I was almost afraid to open it, as though it would make all of this real. The card said it was from Jorgen and Carmela. This was the first time I saw their names together and I realized I knew so little about what was inside their relationship. What were they like when they were alone together? Was there humor, passion, did they fight? Did they love to touch each other? Did they cuddle?

It was just another thing I was blind to. It was another thing I knew nothing about. I took my key and I slit open the tape on the package. There were two things in the package. One was a picture, in a frame, of all of us together. Somehow, I knew that it had come from Jorgen. I sense that he wanted that last little bit of emotional closeness, that last bit of feeling like a family. That was his drug, I guess. That is what he paid for.

Because the other thing I knew came from Carmela. It looked to be about a year's worth of Insulin.

My eyes filled up with water. This was the Carmela who had sat up reading books on being a midwife so she could take care of me. This was the Carmela who brought food and diapers and cased the building for resources, set up doctor's appointments and filed paperwork for me. This was someone who understood how hard it would be to pay for insulin for the next year and probably went out herself, with money requisitioned from Jorgen, to buy the ampules, along with the little red refrigerated case they sat inside. This was how she showed love. It was real. It wasn't a picture. It was her.

This was every Carmela I knew.

I was suddenly very alone but I wasn't. I was a single mother with an eleven year old genius and a three year fishbaby.

He wasn't a fishbaby.

Life was quieter without Carmela. And it was harder without Jorgen. I had forgotten how often he had given Carmela money to manage things, to take care of us. My job was winding down and so I supplemented it by taking on another job at the publishing company, in the editing department. Realistically, I knew I was now working two jobs for the same company in two different departments and giving them the chance to not have to onboard a new hire, but I was still grateful for the work.

Being taken advantage of is sometimes better than being forgotten.

There used to be large art sculptures in front of the Delroy. They were slowly morphing into structures that supported advertising. Much of the art all around us had been privatized. The city website claims this is a good thing as it raises money to make the cities more "productive and prosperous." Those two words seem like they are constantly said together now, despite the fact that they don't seem to actively describe ANYTHING, really, certainly not the city I live in.

I started cleaning up outside again, taking the boys with me. They seemed to enjoy getting out. The trains don't stop at our stop anymore so we are feeling, admittedly, a bit trapped, unable to get around.

Ithad came to me with an argument he had written on index cards, asking if he could spend time with friends if he kept his phone on at all times. It's hard for me to say no to the index cards, honestly, or to him. As scared as I am, I say yes. And now, every day, he's gone for a few hours at least. I asked him what he's doing and he tells me he's playing soccer some time, while others he is building things with other tech-focused friends. The latter is very easy to believe.

I don't think he would lie to me.

More and more now, we are hearing about the wealthy leaving for the colonies. I heard a story about Brad Pitt, past his prime now, preparing to leave. I imagined him as Benjamin Button growing younger and younger eternally on some distant space colony, ending up as a wise but sweet-faced little baby under the giant red belly of Jupiter as he spun around its surface on a tiny ball.

We've resorted to wearing masks again, not because of the virus, but because of the air quality warnings. The air seems thick in the constant heat now and our plans to celebrate Mikah's fourth birthday at a park fell through as the parks were closed.

Now they close on the weekdays every week.

I count insulin bottles. We are months away from running out, but I am concerned that I still don't have a lead on a reliable place to get more. I think about what a phenomenal gift it was, this box, and how I've come to rely on it.

But what happens when it's gone?

The doctor's office in the building is now a container store. The maps in this area are still blacked out and I can't find another doctor's office. There is a pharmacy in our building but it seems open only by appointment and I can't find a way to make an appointment.

One night, I had a panic attack. What would I do if I ran out? I started only giving Mikah insulin when he seemed sick. I could tell, though, that it was taking its toll on him. He wasn't as rambunctious anymore. He wasn't bouncy. He stayed in bed longer in the morning rather than jumping up to climb into bed with me,

That's how I found myself in the sublevel of the building with a hammer in my hand, standing in front of the pharmacy, waiting.

The rolling blackouts across the building had become more aggressive, I remembered the first one I had endured, with the pig forcing himself on me, in the pitch black on the first level. I stood outside that pharmacy and held my breath.

If it wasn't that night it would be the next.

Or the next.

When it finally happened, a scream ripped out of my throat. I pulled the hammer back and smashed the pharmacy window. I hadn't anticipated the explosion of glass as it scattered across the open hallway. I reached in and opened the door, climbing over boxes placed in front of it, avoiding the glass.

I stole almost four hundred dollars worth of Insulin that night. But I would never be able to do that again. '

And it wasn't enough. Not nearly enough.

Crime and protests during the blackouts soon called for a curfew every night. Ithad was good about making sure he was home before dark. I gave solent thanks that he was logical, reasonable. Mikah seemed determined to get sicker.

Out the window I could see the protests gathering. But I couldn't find any information online or on the news about it. It's almost like they didn't exist, but I could see them, in front of me, with my own eyes. I had no idea what they were about.

Ithad came and went out the back door, but still I was worried for him every day. I toyed with asking him not to leave, but he was so committed. I don't know what to do. He says that he will tell me everything soon.

But I don't know when "soon" is.

I feel incredibly lost. We celebrated Ithad's birthday inside, as well. He was in a hurry and admitted that he had to meet a girl. He said I would meet her before too long.

Mikah is losing weight but his face looks puffy. We can no longer access websites outside the country and no one seems to know why. I discovered these two things on the same day.

From my Journal | October 12th:

Mikah is sicker every hour. I haven't slept in a week now. I can't find insulin anywhere. There is no mention of a shortage online. In fact the news just keeps getting better and better.

The woman across the hall says the new maps are online. I'm afraid to look.

The woman's name is Julianne. I talk to her every once in a while. She is as confused as I am. She is a pretty girl with blonde hair who used to be a model or something. She only recently began living here in the building and the first time I visited her it occurred to me that she might be squatting.

I may just record my journal entries for that time.

Jounal Entry| Nov 1st:

The last two weeks have been a blur. Mikah Died on October 16th and his body is still in the basement waiting for the city to come pick it up. I sit on the floor next to it sometimes. The blacked out areas on the maps mean no city services for the foreseeable future. That means ever.

Journal Entry | Nov 20th:

The little body was picked up. I am dead, too, I think. Ithad is finding food for us somewhere and I don't want to ask. I am afraid to ask anything. I don't want to know anything anymore. The city set the burial for December and I don't know why it's so far away. I don't understand why it can't be sooner.

It doesn't get cold anymore. Which is strange, because I can't see the sun. It's all just fog and gloom. Ithad is taking care of me. Suddenly I think of Noel and how he forced Ithad to be my support, my little superhero. I feel angry again and it feels amazing. I love the feeling of anger right now, welling up, propping me up, giving me a reason to fold my fists and sit upright. This is how he continues to hurt me. And all the pain is now converted, for a moment at least, to rage.

It makes me want to find him and rip his head off.

When I finally get out of bed, I see that Ithad is making a grilled cheese sandwich for me and it makes me angry all over again. But not at him, never at him. I see that he is hurting so badly. My son who takes care of people, my son who dreams about the people he loves and promotes them and makes them bigger than life. My son who dreamed his brother a beautiful life and drew him with laser eyes and now has to watch him just descend into the ground like so much trash.

I held him and didn't ever want to let him go. Part of me wished he were still in my belly so I could take care of him. It's an absurd thought and it makes no sense. We keep the lights off and he tells me he's been building a spaceship with some friends. It sounds so unreal to me. He promises to take me to see it. He tells me it's a beautiful thing and he wants to name it after me

Ithad falls asleep and I get up and pull a blanket over me. If he's going to finish his ship, he'll need things.

He'll need money.

I start collecting everything I find I can sell and I put it into a box. I am in so much pain that nothing I put in that box, no matter how precious, can hurt me. I place my rings in there. I put the locket my grandmother gave me. Microphones, extra keyboards, synthesizers, hard drives. I will make this room white and clean if i have to. I purify the room with loss. I will purge this fucking room.

I will make sure he has everything he needs to leave this.

The funeral is for all the people who have died this quarter. I don't see his body but I am told it is in the middle of this mass grave.

Ithad has a girl come visit him when we get home. She holds him while he cries. I didn't realize he had a girlfriend. She works with him on the ship.

She is petite and pretty and Korean, I think, with green hair. She cries with him and holds my hand at the table as I stare straight ahead.

I tell her about the box and she promises to take care of it. I feel lighter giving her the box. The box was dead weight, full of lead and wood and pain.

It's almost Christmas. I try not to remember that Mikah loved Christmas. I try not to remember anything. Julianne helps me pack everything else I can find for a second box I give to Ithad's girlfriend. In my haze, I realize I don't know her name, although she's now been to the apartment over a half dozen times.

Julianne tells me that she will ask her name next time. I just can't feel like a bad parent right now. I can't take one more sign from the universe that I failed at this. I'm so grateful to Julianne I can't even speak.

This was the first time I heard the name.

She sat next to me on the bed and talked. I tried to listen but instead the words just washed over me. They felt good, like water, like a bath. They felt meaningless and hopeful and soft on my face, raw and red from crying.

She says to call her Julie. I hear that as though I'm in a tunnel, far away.

She says she works at the MekaDisko now. It's a giant club that is moving underground, getting bigger every day. Wealthy people go there to watch people dance.

She says I can get a job there if I want.

She says I'm pretty.

I heard the word "Pretty" in my head. It felt like it echoed, repeating over and over and fading but never to silence, almost like some kind of perpetual motion sound device,

And then, I threw up all over her feet. I don't know why.

The year ends

At the start of the next year, I lost my job. I guess print really is dead. It seemed as though the entire business went under but I'm not really sure what happened. Even under the best of circumstances, they were not great at relaying information.

Ithad's girlfriend's name is Jen. She is quiet and incredibly smart. But also very sweet. Watching the two of them do math together at the kitchen table is like watching world class figure skaters move around the rink. They are amazing. She's started to stay over. She was sitting on the couch for a while reading a book. Ithad smiled a little as he helped her up with a silly flourish. I looked at him. My son is a gentleman. I hold my arms in my hands and think about that, because I need it right now. I need to let it wash over me and insulate me from everything bad, everything evil.

My son is a gentleman.

He is kind and responsive to her and he defers to her. He says things that make sure she knows she is right. He reminds her she is usually right. He jokes with her but never at her expense. He makes a point to call out things he thinks she is better at. He picks an errant hair off her shirt, not to make her feel unkempt, but to make her feel cared for, watched…

To make her feel seen.

He looks taller every day. I see on his face that he survived losing Mikah and it makes me feel like I can, too.

For him.

The first time I went there was with Julie. There was an entrance about four blocks aways. We managed to dodge the protests, which had grown fewer and fewer every day. The city had begun to use robots to manage and slow them down. I remember that on the day we went to the entrance I saw my first body on the ground. It was a woman and she couldn't have been much more than twenty four, with long dark hair like me. She had marks on her arms as though she had been run over by one of the larger street robots. I imagined it was me, lying in the street, thrown away like bodies were now, like unwanted clam shell cases tossed aside out of enthusiasm for what was hidden inside them, carved out, taken.

Doesn't anybody haunt anyone anymore?

We walked to seventh street and saw it. It was a faceless building, relatively new construction. It had no windows like the raft of buildings that were being built downtown. It occurred to me that these buildings may well have been part of this as well. I saw the now familiar "M" shape on the doors and we entered.

The thing about new construction at the time was that it was all focused on building downward. Basements and sub basements and sub sub basements. Ithad had told me that the air quality was so poor all the buildings had to have their own air supply anyways, and the heat had gotten so bad that underground construction made far more sense than above ground equivalents.

The atrium of the building was huge. I never would have been able to tell from the outside. And it was bright and sunny, with nature and outdoor scenes fed all over the room to large monitors that were positioned to feel like windows. The illusion was so seamless that it extended to the elevators, looking like open air gazebos that flit between garden floors in some posh multi-level horticulturist attraction.

At the time it seemed to me I was overthinking everything, I'm sure as a panic response to everything that was going on. But it seemed to me that nothing in this building was real. But even more than that, everything here was built specifically to prevent the viewer from recognizing that. The floors, I realized, were not numbered, but named. We were on our way to the staging level and it was positioned, in the elevator, as the bottom-most level of four. But it was not clear that this equated to actual real world levels and the elevator, despite seeming modern and efficient, took such a variable amount of time between levels that it became clear that there was more in between each one, in some cases, much more.

As we descended, one wall of the elevator started to shimmer and the visuals of our descent through plants and natural waterfalls faded to a video of a handsome man with full dark hair with a river of white running through it. The text near his midsection said his unlikely name was David Midland Kelto. There was a bizarre sort of logo nestled below that using the letters DMK with a pompous little crown on top. Almost as though everyone now was expected to have their own logo.

He welcomed us to the MekaDisko and explained that we were now part of the biggest and most responsive company on earth. It occurred to me that the language he was using made it feel as though we had already been hired and I hadn't spoken yet to a single person. Julie looked over at me hopefully and I nodded back at her. I'm not sure exactly why I did that. Suddenly I missed Carmella and our physical shorthand and I felt the elevator movement in my belly.

David Midland Kelto was a smooth and eager speaker. He explained how the MekaDisko was meant to be a revolutionary business for cities all over the country. The complex was already the largest underground facility ever built and spanned three states. I remembered the buildings downtown without windows or doors and considered how these all fit together.

This is where I learned how many people had left Earth. The news wasn't reporting it, people weren't talking about it. But a full eight percent of the population had left for the Colonies. This was a few hundred million people. How could I have missed that? My head got lighter and I started to feel oxygen deprived, except instead of air, it was something else.

It was real information. I realized that I hadn't been exposed to much information at all. I didn't know anything about what was happening all around me. I screwed my eyes to the screen and listened to David Midland Kelto.

"This facility joins thousands of interconnected entertainment spaces all over the East Coast. Just as America used to be known as the Media leader of the world, we have now become known as the entertainment complex of the world. And Beyond. Today we partner with our sister company, MekaAir, to deliver shuttles to and from the interior colonies where thousands of people a day fly back and forth to enjoy the kind of entertainment that was previously reserved only for the 1% elite."

I made a mental note of the words here I didn't know. What was an "Interior Colony?" And MekaCorp had a space shuttle division?

What else had I missed?

He continued, thanking us for our part in making this all a reality.

The mathematician in me began to count seconds as we descended and evaluated the result based on a baseline median travel rate in a modern elevator of thirty miles per hour. At that rate we had gone our full six minute long elevator trip should have taken us nearly three miles underground. I had no idea that there was anything near that depth built in Manhattan. I remember hearing about track 61 when I was a kid, a forgotten section of subway that was deep underground, used now just for storage until people had descended to actually live there. Three miles below ground should have been unbelievably hot.

But I didn't feel it.

The people at the test were kind, but efficient. My first experience there was in a room full of women, asking us to disrobe, to dance, to talk for a few moments about this subject or that one.

They asked questions that would ordinarily have seemed invasive and without context:

> Q: How many sexual partners have you had?
>
> A: This one had made me sad ever since that night in the blackout. I tried to count up my "number" and then realized I don't care. I wondered what they would want to see. I decided that ten made me seem not slutty but not prudish. Questions like this would be easier if they just told you what they expected.

Q: Are you willing to groom yourself in ways appropriate to the terms of the various MekaDisko club environments?

A: I wasn't sure what that meant, honestly. So, I did what people who just needed a job have been doing since the dawn of time and answered ""yes"

All the following questions were answered much the same way.

Journal Entry | Jan 20th:

I tested at the MekaDisko. They wanted me to dance nude. I don't care anymore. I need to bring home food. I told them I would do what I needed to. I'm told a lot of people who come here are billionaires many times over.

I wonder what that feels like.

So many of the dancers here are beautiful beyond belief. And I fear for their safety, honestly. There are rumors about new "business friendly" laws that are permissive toward trafficking and other models of abuse.

And those aren't even the worst pieces of new legislation.

When I got back home, Ithad was there working on sketches in the kitchen with Jen. It lifted my spirits to see them immersed in their work so I slid behind them and made egg salad sandwiches to place on the table. I didn't want to interrupt them. I kissed Ithad on the head and he leaned into me.

Before I went to bed I checked in again. They sat in the living room area talking quietly but in an animated way. They were holding hands. I realized that I hadn't heard them laugh in the few months since Miikah had died.

I stood in the doorway and made some stupid joke about a frog. It had looked down and smiled like he always did when I told stupid jokes.

"Why did the frog wear his voice out barking all night? Because foreign languages, while rewarding, are often hard to learn and require repetition to master."

But I'll never forget what Jen did. She looked up at me like I was some kind of a superhero. She looked at me as though I had solved Fermat's last theorem and did it with a little joke, and she literally beamed at me. She looked at me like you look at a movie star and smiled and just said, simply, "I love frogs."

Her face told me so much.

Her beautiful face told me I was expected to die.

I was a mother who just lost her youngest son and no one really believed I would make it. Her face said that my fever broke, that I had risen from my coma, that I was in remission. It said that anything could happen now because the dead were walking.

I was grateful for her. I kissed her head, too before I went to bed and she touched my hand. I would never meet her parents, but I was suddenly their biggest fans. I went to bed lighter.

Things progressed quickly from there.

My badge to the MekaDisko was dropped off in the morning. Apparently I was hired. I looked at my phone and saw that they had deposited my first check into my account, just as they said they would when I was hired. My bank account had been negative by forty seven dollars so I did the math to see how much I had just been paid.

I closed my eyes and took a breath. I realized that we were going to make it, right then. We were going to survive. I wanted ice cream. I wanted a hamburger. I wanted to spend money on lunch.

I wanted to breathe.

Julie came bounding into the apartment and hugged me once I showed her the badge. She was excited to work together and I confess some of it was infectious. Jen and I thad congratulated me without really knowing much about it.

Later that night I tried to parse through the twenty or so onboarding emails I had received that day. Most of them were fairly standard but one hit me hard. On a list of recommended resources they suggested I take advantage of the free on-site services for a complete permanent infertility treatment.

Apparently there was a one thousand dollar bonus if I agreed to a hysterectomy. This felt like an invasive and strange clause, but I was in uncharted waters now. The email linked to a series of stories that detailed how the procedure had become more and more common for women living in the city. The article said that incidents of rape had hit an all time high and presented this as the only approved option to avoid pregnancy incurred via rape.

I considered what a thousand dollars would mean to me right now but also what another event during a blackout might mean. When Carmela was here, I might have had some option if I had gotten pregnant again, but with her off-planet, I had none.

If I got pregnant again, I would be unable to work. I would be unable to do anything, really. Suddenly the idea seemed not only appealing but obvious. And it wouldn't just be free. They would pay me to do it. I clicked the link and set the appointment up.

The emails included about ten other links and documents that needed to be signed.

I went through my wardrobe to figure out what to wear in the morning when I reported in to the facility. I put together two outfits and laid them on the bed next to each other. It occurred to me that I would be spending at least part of my time dancing in what I assumed would be little or no clothing at all. I wondered what it really mattered what I wore there.

And tomorrow I would be there for an entirely different reason - a medical one

I took a bath and followed the grooming guidelines, shaving myself completely bare except for a small tuft of hair right above my pubic area. It felt surreal and still somehow clinical but I realized it was the most self care I had engaged in in months. Looking in the mirror I saw my hair hadn't been cut in months and my skin regiment had been reduced to letting hot water fall on my face in the shower until it hurt.

I made a mental note to get the things I needed to take better care of my appearance.

My phone dinged and I lifted it up from the sink next to me. They had deposited the thousand dollar bonus from my decision to have the procedure already.

I was pleased to have the excess money, but I felt slightly invaded somehow by their feral responsiveness. I walked out of the bathroom and said "hm" to myself.

Ithad was in the hallway and he asked me what was up. I had no intention, really of explaining all of it, but I did ask him why it would bother me that this company would be so quick and responsive to pay me for things I just decided minutes ago.

If I ever forget that my son was a genius, I will remember that moment. He talked to me about something he had been noticing more and more. He called it the "watching mind problem".

We all grew up in a time when most of the decisions made for us, on our behalf, were made by human beings with access to data. So they took time. It took time for a bank to approve your loan or for a publisher to decide to publish your book or for a landlord to decide to rent to you.

But today, the proliferation of AI in key decision making positions meant that many of these decisions were made immediately. And the responses to them were made that way, as well. And when decisions like this are made so quickly it makes us feel like we are being monitored, watched.

It makes us feel like there is a dedicated brain overseeing the response to our questions. And that triggers our "stalker" response and creeps us out.

We went back and forth and even created, together, a sort of model for how to address that. Certainly it would make sense for AI systems to have some kind of a attenuation loop they could employ to pause and slow down their response a little. Not much, but to at least address the problem of it feeling "too fast." For not the first time it occurred to me that I was smarter when Ithad and I were talking. I was smart, he was a genius, but together we were something different

We were something really great. I kissed him goodnight and planned for the morning.

I wasn't sure if I had stopped dreaming entirely or if my mind was just preventing me now from remembering my dreams. Either way I was happy to be rid of them for now, I slept all night without waking up and wondering how I was going to pay for anything.

I just slept.

I woke up in a panic, realizing that I didn't know where Mikah's body was in that mass grave. I couldn't have pointed to the area. I ran downstairs and opened the doors to the complex as though I could just ask one of the anti-protest robots that sat immovable, like some egyptian monolith, in front of the archway to the street.

I'm not religious and I was never superstitious. I knew he was gone. I knew it shouldn't matter where his body was, but it was still a part of me, missing, lost, and it physically hurt. I tried not to remember his little body. How long his fingers were. How pretty his eyelashes were. How he would scratch his feet if I left him without socks. I made that body.

The street was empty. It was a few minutes before six and I stepped out into the road in front of the building in my shorts and a tank top. I had no business being outside dressed like this.

It seemed like it might have been about a hundred degrees already and the thickened air was gelling, dirty and toxic, seemingly rising from the earth to fill the entire rotting space of the city like a gray watercolor wash across a pre-filled cityscape drawn canvas. I screamed and it echoed from the building across the street, which I now noticed had been reconstructed just recently, windows removed, surface smoothed to a synthetic stone gray symmetry.

I walked across the street and touched it. It felt cool to the touch in a way that was wholly artificial.

I turned around and walked quickly back to the doorway and up the elevator to my apartment. As I entered, closing the door, I realized I had been holding my breath on the way up. I had two hours before I had to be anywhere and no one was up yet. I considered going back to sleep but that seemed like a trap. I considered going to Julie's apartment but that, too, seemed like a trap. Once I was ensconced at work, riding down that green-blue elevator, that would surely be a trap.

I considered climbing into bed with Ithad, but I knew Je
n would be there and he needed his space. I went back to my room, which now seemed hopelessly large and unsafe, grown beyond my expectations for security, with wilding floors and wide open walls that seemed to be spreading out away from me as I watched them. I couldn't go back to bed.

I walked over to the closet and dropped to the floor, crawling under the hanging clothes, past the boxes I had left unpacked when moving in, years ago, to a space on a black rug, half in darkness from the shadows of the dresser, half dimly lit through the slats in the closet door and sat down.

I worked for the MekaDisko. But not for a couple more hours.

TWO

I had gone to work for Roiz Family Publishing right out of college. If you had taken any advanced science classes in high school or college you probably find that name a bit familiar. We were responsible for most of the science textbooks at that level. My combination of a BS in math and a masters in librarian science actually made me a good fit as a proofreader and eventual editor for many of the heavily math focused tomes that we produced.

I ended up running IT for them as well because computers never scared me. You'd be surprised how many people in academia are terrified by functional technology.

And I was good at my job.

On my very first day at work, after my last round of interviews, I was meant to have a little introductory lunch with my boss in the cafe that sat at the ground floor of our building. It was called "The Artist's Cafe" or "The Artist's Nook" or something equally cute, and my boss, a svelte and erudite man in his seventies named Jeffrey loved it.

You could tell this was the part of the job he enjoyed the most.

Jeffrey was thin and balding and a little awkward. His mouth seemed to move a little oddly as he talked as if he were saying, in his head, "Jeffrey, move lips now," each time he spoke. He was brilliant, no doubt, but I soon came to learn that he had lived a life where people were conditionally secondary to his own interests, most of which included math in very large percentages.

He was a kind man and his face lit up when checks came on tiny floating carpets on cafe tables so he could majestically conjure up the requisite 35% tip Jeffrey loved to add to the bill without slowing his hand.

Sometimes it was 40%.

In conversation with me, he loved showing off how much work he had done in advance reading my resume and the notes from my interviews. He referenced my favorite books, my favorite classes, even my favorite foods, as I discovered when we went to order and he made sure that there were extra blueberries on the table.

Meetings like this were when a man who had grown up as an internal man - a person focused on his mind - surrounded by the common boisterous boys he had been peered with, could finally build family the way he wanted it. He invited me in and playfully tested my acuity, not as a boss might with a newly hired underling, but as a little boy might do tossing a ball back and forth with a newfound fellow baseball fanatic. He made math jokes.

Two kittens are trapped on a roof, which one falls off first?

The one with the smallest mew.

I mention this all because something interesting happened that day, and I want to remember it with enough detail to make it relevant here.

Immediately outside the cafe was a man, a taller man with longish brown hair. I remember that specifically because he had a face that looked very much like he might have had an aversion to long hair. This wasn't a man who wore his hair long freely but rather a man who had neglected himself for too long and tolerated the overgrowth.

He sat in the street with a sign. I stared for a moment outside the window, trying to read what the sign said, but he seemed disinterested in its general legibility. It pointed away from me, teasingly, bobbing back and forth as he fished in his soiled clothes for something, until finally it slid to his side, readable by no one.

I realized I had been so caught up with reading the sign that I had failed to notice just what he was fishing out from his clothing. As a man, dressed mostly in a green t-shirt and jogging pants moved into my line of vision to help him, he lifted his hand firmly.

And the man dropped dead.

At that point, I saw the rusted barrel of a sawed off shotgun in his palm. Screams went out from other people in the street and Jeffrey froze, unable to move.

I turned and saw the man lift his arm again and place a nearly perfectly round hole in the forehead of a woman looking at him with disbelief. She fell to the ground nearly comically, while I stood up.

Nothing in my body knew how to respond to this. The cafe window between us had rendered everything distant and foreign. I was used to watching television through a glass like that. I looked at the internet through a glass like that. A monitor glass.

Nothing on the other side of the glass was ever really real before.

I saw people in the cafe duck down under their tables and looked up again at the disheveled killer. I swear he looked directly in my eyes as he lifted the gun one last time and shot himself in the head.

He slumped to the ground like a pile of unworn clothing and I realized I needed to breathe in. The room began to swim and I almost blacked out.

I felt Jeffrey's fingers on my arm, paternal, aware, and it steadied me. Together, we walked out of the cafe and toward the dead man in the street. People were running in all directions and I heard a siren in the distance. I tried to do the math to determine how far away it might be by relative volume but I gave up once I saw the sign, lightly spattered with blood, lying face up on the ground.

I wondered for a moment about how iit had fallen that way. After its coy refusal to be read during the entire time the man had been holding it, it's as if the sign was tired of attempting to maintain its secrets and wanted to be finally, prone on the ground, clear about its intent.

I read it nearly out loud, my lips moving.

It said "This is the end of the world"

But still I stood there. Jeffrey stood there. Dozens of people gathered around and a squad of police cars began to drive up, all testifying through their bustle that the world went on.

Later, I learned that this man had lost his wife of forty years to cancer three months earlier. He descended into grief, then into anger, then frustration, then, finally into the apathy born from losing your rudder, your steering wheel. He fell into a kind of anhedonia that couldn't find the world anymore or really touch anything in it.

The sign should have read, "This is the end of MY world." and that would have been 100% accurate. Just like avowed religionists who can't imagine the world going on without their own identity as a lens to view it through, he didn't realize that there would be a world still.

Just not one with him in it.

Eight minutes down in the Elevator at the MekaDisko.

It smelled like fresh rain and ferns and I knew that was artificial, just as I knew that the visuals showcasing our descent through foliage and flora was a lie. I closed my eyes and let my stomach decide how fast we were going. The upward-rushing pit inside me suggested it was far faster than thirty miles per second and even conjured up, unbidden, some suggestion of sideways motion at times, as though our descent had paused and put us on train tracks moving us in a circle horizontally around the facility.

David Miidland Kelto was talking, in a subdued voice that the creators of this video may have thought was sexy, about the various entertainment facilities scattered across the entire complex. My phone service had ended abruptly as soon as we entered the facility. I pulled it out anyway and looked at its blank face offering up no service.

A bar irised open below David Midland Kelto offering cell service for a discounted rate for employees, service that would work underground.

I made a mental note to switch carriers and, almost as though it read my mind, the ad disappeared. I wonder if I had changed the look on my face, a look that had been detected but the AI interface in the elevator.

Julie was taking this opportunity in the elevator to change. There was another girl in there with us, with a shock of pink hair on the very top of her head, but it didn't seem to matter to her that Julie was stripping nude and putting on her tiny black dancer costume.

I hadn't seen Julie nude before and it occurred to me that she was young. She was clearly very pretty but it was a vulnerable beauty, an uncertain facade. Her breasts were small and perfect but they gave you the impression that they had sprouted not five minutes before and she didn't know what to do with them. Her outfit was playful and sexy but now just made me want to mother her. Where had the urge come from to throw a shrug over another woman's bare shoulders? What was that about?

I counted the time in my head since stepping into the elevator. And at the end of eight minutes, the doors opened to a massive room with ceilings nearly thirty feet above us. There was a low bass drone that seemed rubbery yet melodic, as though a song were playing next door that was all bass. It created a rhythm that was very hard to ignore. We found ourselves walking in lockstep to the rhythm toward the far gate.

There were a row of elevators behind us, affirming the idea that they may have moved laterally as well, since that same bank didn't exist in that configuration above us. They wrapped around the amphitheater like space making it hard to see where they ended. I later learned that this area was called the crown, predicated on its appearance when you stopped to look up. The shape and distribution of lights presented the illusion that you were inside a giant crown.

I want to say that I don't remember what it was like at first. But I do. I remember everything.

Julie pointed me to a row of rooms just off the periphery of the crown. She said I could go into any one of them for the placement test. She hugged me tightly and told me to just not think too hard.

In all honesty, this was the exact opposite of my mandate for the entirety of the rest of my life. I was born a person who thought too hard and I probably had thought too hard about that.

I saw that the rooms were color coded and, without any signage to explain why, the colors meant nothing to me. I began to exercise the sensible advice I had gotten from Julie and I chose a pretty one I decided was hunter green.

The room was empty but a monitor on the right side wall flashed an instruction to sit down. I looked around and took note that the room seemed nearly empty except for a small twelve inch tall column in the center. I moved toward it to sit and was assaulted by thoughts.

It was only one foot off the ground. If I sat on the column, it would be not much different than sitting on the floor. I would still need to cross my legs or find some other floor-seated model by which to rest. And I didn't really know the function of the tiny column-like platform. It seemed to me designed completely in such a way that sitting on it was not a primary function. It wasn't a seat, just a slightly raised structure.

I looked again at the monitor to verify that it was still flashing "Sit" and so I slid to the ground where I was and sat. I crossed my legs and leaned back waiting.

Once I did, the monitor stopped. I put my bag on the ground next to me and alternated staring at the door and the monitor. As I looked back at the door, it slid open and a man in his 40s in a black suit entered. He was handsome enough, in a corporate way, and he told me his name was Keen.

He used my first name.

"Can I call you Llorona"

"Sure."

"We're going to play a kind of game. It's going to help us determine where you might fit in best. Are you ok with that?"

"Yes," I said, not wanting to say "Sure." again so soon.

"I want you to talk to me and have a conversation while you obey what the monitor says. Is that clear?"

It was.

And that was the instruction I got. It seemed simple. I tried, again, not to overthink it.

Keen asked me why I chose this room. I explained to him that, in my head, I called this room "Hunter green" and the color interested me. I answered quickly. He smiled and asked me again.

"This time, I want you to invent a story. Nothing too far-fetched. Do what the monitor says and create a story about why you love Hunter Green. The ability to talk to new people and give them beautiful stories may be the thing that serves you the best here."

I looked at the monitor and it said, simply, "Stand."

I stood and told Keen about how I had gone on a trip once with two friends from college. We had decided to go camping and had gotten mostly lost in the forest surrounding our simple camping glen. When we finally found our way back the lantern mounted above our tent had rendered the entire area, in mostly darkness, as a sleek hunter green, the color of the room, our sanctuary, our little home to rest.

Keen asked me what we did once we got back into our tent. Out of the corner of my eye I could see the monitor flashing.

It read, "Take of your shirt"

I began unbuttoning my shirt. Reading the room, I told Keen about how I had been so tired that I climbed into my sleeping bag with my friend, pulling my clothes off as we slid into bed together. Her face nestled in my neck and I began to drift off.

Keen asked me what had happened then, aware that this was a made up story. The monitor flashed.

"Remove your bra."

I took a deep breath and continued. I suddenly felt incredibly tall and realized that I was at least a few inches taller than Keen. His eyes never moved from my face as I pulled my bra off and let it fall to the ground.

I told him that my friend had softly begun wetting my right nipple with her tongue, running it slowly over the tip of my breast just forcefully enough to keep me from drifting off to sleep. I began to feel excited and I reached around to the back of her head and pulled her closer, letting her mouth surround my nipple completely.

Or that's what happened in the story.

Keen stepped around me and placed his foot on the small one-foot-tall column in the center of the room. He pushed down and let go, letting it rise up again a number of feet. Just then I realized that it had an indented groove around it, an opening. It was a seat recessed into the floor. I shook my head as he sat down on it.

I turned to him, putting the monitor on my other side. He nodded pleased. I realized my turning to face him was the preferred action. This was the behavior he was looking for.

I tried to feel sexy as I told him my made up story of having my breast suckled on by a friend on my camping trip. He sat, legs apart, on the column and stared at me.

The monitor flashed again.

"Remove your pants."

I took a deep breath and continued my story, inventing details about the way her skin felt, the texture of her tongue, even how her lips tasted when she finally got the nerve to kiss me, full on, her hands curving around my naked waist.

I kicked off my shoes and pulled my pants down to my ankles. I stood there for a moment and tried to figure out how to masterfully remove my extremely tight black jeans. I stood in my black cotton underwear and tried to meet his eyes as I continued.

He smiled as I made a show of extricating my feet from my jeans. Not thinking was helping. So I let myself go a little. I started to whisper a little, playing up how my friend had pressed me into the ground to kiss me harder.

The monitor flashed, seemingly brighter, more aggressively.

"Sit on his lap."

I moved forward two steps and slid onto his knee. Keen was looking straight ahead, into my eyes. He was prodding me for more information about my imaginary camping event.

"Did it feel strange?"

In my head, it didn't. I imagined Carmela as my camping friend. I realized that, for all the times we laid down together, for all the times we shared our closeness, I'd never let her touch me like that. I had never kissed her. I suddenly remembered the times where it seemed like she'd wanted to. And I ignored them all. I knew that she wanted to be with me but I pretended we were just friends. And now she was gone.

His knee was bony and uncomfortable and I slid my arm awkwardly around his neck. I was nearly naked in a strange man's lap, talking about how badly I wanted to have sex with my friend. II knew I would be dancing and I knew it would be nude, erotic. I had imagined in my head that it would be like the week or so I had spent stripping during college. A time I could retire into my head and just move to the music. I didn't realize I would have to be so present.

The monitor glowed again and I knew what it said before reading it.

"Remove your underwear"

I rose up slightly on the man's knee and used my left hand to shimmy my panties down to the floor. I felt them fall under my left foot and I kept it steady, as though feeling where they were would help me feel more centered. I kept talking although, at this point, I honestly have no memory of what nonsense I said.

I was very aware that I was sitting directly on this man's pants with nothing between me and the fabric. Against my will, thoughts of Carmela had made me feel safe, nurtured.

I realized that talking about the girl on the trip as though it were her had made me a little wet. The monitor, as if in response to that, flashed yet another instruction. This one felt impossibly human. It made me feel, suddenly, as though there were a person typing in these words, not just an unfeeling computer logging time in a bizarre test of new performers.

These were typed in by people. Probably people who were watching.

"Spread your legs"

I inched my legs apart as I continued to speak. The man, Keen, asked me a question.

"How did she taste that night?"

To be clear, my story, so far, had focused on my friend touching me, licking my breasts, even kissing me. I hadn't gone further than that. It was as if Keen wanted me to fast forward deep into the story. He wanted me to amplify it.

"Spread your legs"

The monitor became more insistent. I spread my legs wider.

And I lied.

I told him that my friend had tasted like summer. She had tasted like the freedom you feel when you can do anything. I became grossly metaphorical and tried to remember the way Carmela made me feel. Maybe that would be the way she tasted.

And then it happened.

Keen looked into my eyes, smiling, laughing at my story, and he, without hesitation, inserted two fingers inside me.

The monitor flashed tirelessly as I gulped in a mouthful of air.

"Spread your legs"

The room went red. I stopped breathing. I stared back into his face where I saw no recognition that he was invading me, violating me. There was no conscious sign that he understood what this rape was.

But everything had changed for me. The sound of his voice had become impossibly grating. The air in the room was cold. I sat on his knee and felt my anger rise. Nothing about this was playful anymore.

I thought that this couldn't possibly be what the room wanted. He must be going further than intended. This is just him. I looked at the monitor.

"Spread your legs"

It blinked out five or six times and the monitor was black.

The man didn't move. I was afraid to move. He explained to me that it was a lovely story and that I was going to do very well here. He said I had done everything exactly right.

He pulled his hand from inside me and took out a handkerchief from his suit coat. He stood up, nearly quickly enough to send me toppling.

Then he smiled.

Staring right into my eyes, he wiped his hands off and returned the square of fabric to his pocket.

I stood there awkwardly as he began to leave the room.

He turned to me as I was gathering my clothes.

"How much of that story was true?" he asked in a flirtatious way. To me, it felt like how a criminal might ask for money from a stranger to put on his commissary. He had nothing to lose by taunting me and every pleasure to be gained.

I wanted to punch him in the face. I wanted to shove his head through the monitor. I wanted to kick at his head until he bled and passed out. I settled for lying to him.

"All of it. It was all true."

He made a sound, surprised. And walked out.

As I dressed, I looked toward the monitor. It remained dormant, dead. It had no instructions anymore. It had nothing to say. It had seen what it had seen and now it was satiated. It was satisfied. I stood up to go, anticipating one last wan commentary.

Nothing.

I thought about the cafe, with Jeffrey. I considered the shooter with the sign, his long hair spread out matted with blood on the ground.

I thought about how nothing was real usually on the other side of the glass

Until it was.

I didn't wait for Julie to get back home. I had scheduled the procedure for the next day so it would be about four days until I began working for real. As soon as I made a move toward the elevator I heard a ding, a notification, on my phone. Two notifications from the MekaDisko and one from my bank.

My pay would be increasing. This was before I even began. And, to assert that, a bank deposit of five hundred dollars. This was my incentive for coming today.

I was paid for that.

I remembered the man wiping his hands with a handkerchief, grinning at me as though he were some criminal taunting his pursuer in the back room of a procedural cop drama.   I was paid five hundred dollars for that.

I looked down at the other message. A schedule that had me working every single day.

I wanted to throw my phone across the space in front of me.

I belonged to the generation that destigmatized sex work. I didn't think less of someone for being a sex worker. Today, though, was an unassailable reminder that this wasn't just some replacement job, something that would occupy me the way that publishing had. I was a sex worker. And today's violation wouldn't be the last.

I shared the elevator ride to the surface with a number of other women and I tried to decipher their expressions to determine what their experiences might have been. But we were like a gaggle of office workers afraid to disclose our salaries to each other, not just because it was against some unspoken corporate rule, but because we didn't really want to know how little we were valued.

The woman next to me was looking down at the floor. She was slight, with a blue-tinged bob and a thin face. She looked to be nineteen or so. I took one step to the side and slid my hand into hers. She didn't look up but she began to squeeze my hand as though we were on a roller coaster.

It took eight minutes for the elevator to reach the surface. She squeezed tightly the entire time. Her hand was tiny and cold at first, but warm by the end of the trip.

I never saw her eyes.

Ithad had invited Jen over for dinner that night. It felt normalizing. I was surprised at how quickly I had come to think of her as a member of our little troupe. I made spaghetti and she brought over what looked to be about thirty very small chocolate cakes with various fillings. The idea was that after dinner we would test them all and get fat.

This is the kind of genius that Jen had.

Everything was a game for her. Everything was a procedural event to be savored with some joy. She didn't have dessert. She had a communal experience where we happened to eat dessert. Jen's special kind of intelligence seemed to be about making everything more interesting. Being around her made me feel like I didn't have to give up on the world and that was a precious feeling.

When she was around, we didn't talk about the simple failures of our day. Jen's conversation wasn't ever banal or small. I could see, too, by the way Ithad looked at her that he understood who and what she was. Tonight she had us discussing the rules of cartoons and trying to idealize ourselves as cartoon characters.

To her, I was the mathematician, the one with sacred, scrawled geometries spinning around my head, solving problems with pure math, divining, confirming, and she had brought me some glasses to wear to look the part. They had glass in them but they had no prescription. And when I placed them on the bridge of my nose, I confess that I felt smarter. It was surely my imagination but her swell of green hair seemed brighter in my new glasses.

After dinner, in the blue-tinted mirror in the bathroom, she put my hair up into an elaborate rise using a couple of chopsticks. The combination of the glasses and the hairstyle made me feel impossibly smart. I looked very much like the cartoon character of the math guru, and, in all honesty it didn't frame my face too badly. I looked like a beautiful scientist, she convinced me.

I was lovely, in an earthy, physical way, she had added, viscerally, but my specialty was idealized, pure. She painted me as a being of reserved intellect, someone who belonged to the higher planes even as my "bikini body" attracted baser attentions.

I WAS a cartoon character. And she painted a series of cells for me in my imagination that detailed exactly how. Just as Cinderella would dance around letting the birds and small animals around her dress her and send her off to the ball, I was a princess of raw numbers, no less visible in her cartoon world.

Iithad walked in wearing the white coat she had brought for him. He was the physicist, the jet propulsion expert... Dark, brooding, but expert.

The Rocket man.

They had become fascinated with the idea of leaving the planet, of being on one of the ships that sped off to the colonies. I realized how little I knew about the colonies. And Jen, with her lithe jade hair and open smile, wide cheekbones and slightly curved upward asian eyes, was the alien girl who called us all onward. She was the one who benevolently visited this planet and called us all onward.

She knew all about the colonies.

And even had the board game.

As she pulled the game out, I read the back of the box.

> *"The Three Exocolonies, outside the solar system, are dramatically far from Earth, between 38 and 44 light years away. But you can be there within a few days. Here's why:*
>
> *The 2035 discovery of the Harbinger Black Hole, right outside the solar system, was a powerful spark to our extrasolar capabilities. Because the Harbinger creates a stable conduit to Blessing Point, we are able to travel to the ExoColonies incredibly quickly. Ironically,*

> *it meant that we were able to colonize planets far farther from earth while ones closer to us, such as Proxima B and Ross 128 B require prohibitive travel time and remain unexplored."*

This hit me like a punch to the gut. Not less than a few months ago, I had been working for the biggest print science publisher in America. And I had no idea that anything I had just read had happened. How was I so divorced from what was happening in the scientific world?

There is a stable black hole right outside our solar system.

And it led to a place called "Blessing Point," which permitted access to the exocolonies. These were the colonies outside our solar system.

All of these were between forty and forty four light years away, a number so astronomical that I had never considered it outside science fiction. All three were unnaturally hot and the last two impossibly massive. But outgassing greenhouse gasses had thinned the atmospheres and made areas habitable. This, again, was something I had thought was beyond modern science,

The first, Gliese 12 b, is located 40 light-years away in the constellation Pisces.it's a bit smaller than Earth and close in size to Venus, has an estimated surface temperature of 107 degrees Fahrenheit . That's admittedly warmer than Earth, but cooler than many other observed exoplanets. Apparently, last year they found water and were able to let free enough greenhouse gas to drop the planet's temperature nearly 25 degrees.

Next, 55 Cancri is located 41 light-years away in the direction of the constellation Cancer and is visible with binoculars. The system contains a clutch of four inner planets that are separated from an outer planet by a huge gap. The second of the inner planets, though, has a surface temperature and atmosphere that, with some management, can support human life.

Then there is Majriti. It's a super-Jupiter exoplanet orbiting within the habitable zone of the Sun-like star Upsilon Andromedae A, approximately 44 light-years away from Earth in the constellation of Andromeda. It was only recently discovered and was the last exocolony to have visitors. It's considered wild and untamed.

How did all of this happen without my awareness? I thought about how hard it was to get information anymore and I suddenly felt starved for it.

Jen read aloud from the cards in the board game as we set up. Many of the other colonies, all within the solar system, were scattered across Jupiter's ninety-five moons. I had always thought that seemed like an ostentatious number of moons for any but the most narcissistic of planets. There was IO, of course, volcanically active and tumultuous, and Europa, one of the biggest ones, with its smooth surface and trapped water.

But the colony that had excited them both, the one on the poster currently on the wall of Ithad's room, wasn't a moon of jupiter.

It was a moon of saturn.

Enceladus, with a full day rotation just a little longer than 32 earth hours, was one of the first colonized worlds to be adjusted for human life. Strategically placed bombs had loosened water vapor into the upper atmosphere, which acted as a greenhouse gas, thickening the atmosphere and keeping the solar heat inside. Once the ice caps were minimized, the released water had turned the entire planet into a temperate, water filled wonderland.

As we played the board game, Jen tried to sell me on Enceladus. This is where she thought our little group, along with their friends, would be most comfortable. I think about the boxes that I've been giving her, things to sell, to fix to sell. I want to get her more money. Jen is controlling the fund to get the two of them off planet.

I think about the five hundred dollars I earned today. I fish for my phone in my pocket and I send it to her over Xoompay. I feel lighter being rid of it.

I feel somehow cleansed of it.

Her phone beeps and she pulls it out. She smiles and shows it to Ithad. It has nearly four thousand dollars in it now. I look over her shoulder and see the name on it.

It says at the top, playfully, "Ithad, Llorona and Jen get the fuck out of dodge."

My name is on it, too.

They want me to come with them. I never considered that. I never thought about leaving, just making sure that my son and the people he loved had a chance at something better.

I go into the kitchen and break down. Leaning over the counter I let the day out in my hands, crying and listening to teenagers laugh in the other room about how they might dress for going into space for the first time. I feel the glasses on my face as I nearly knock them off and for some reason they are impossibly precious to me.

I grab them and hold onto them.

The next day I meet Julie in the morning for coffee before we go for this procedure. Abortion is completely illegal now, regardless of circumstance, and if you already have at least one child, the hysterectomy is permitted. My concerns about rape amplified by the previous day, I confide in Julie that this is a motivating factor for me.

Julie tells me that she was raped last month on her way to work. She had let someone she met at the club drive her while he was still in town and to him, that was an invitation to assault her in the back seat while the car drove itself along a scenic path that gave him time to finish. At first, she was glad to have the company when he chose to sit in the back with her and let the car drive itself. But soon it became clear that he would be relentless, pushing, grabbing, prodding her, until finally she relented and let him relieve himself.

Those were the words she used. "Relieve himself." She painted a picture of a man who, when sitting so close to her, needed it, like a biological function. Just as he might need to go to the toilet, he needed to mount her and use her to satisfy himself.

Julie told the story without emotion over a cup of coffee and I reached for her hand. She made a motion as if to say "It's ok," and swatted my hand away. She was not telling me to unburden herself or feel better. She was telling me to urge me to feel better about this procedure - to treat it like a necessity, something that would prevent a crisis later. She was telling me almost casually, but she meant for me to be comforted by my decision.

We had decided to walk a bit before finding transportation to the entrance. Realistically I hadn't spent too much time outside recently and I now saw why. The protests near my building were minimal, just a few stragglers, but the police were all over. There were crowd control robots moving slowly through the thinning crowds and I could see people wait and then move almost as an afterthought when they passed.

As we moved closer to the 18th street entrance to the MekaDisko, the crowds had picked up a bit. Many of the robots were massive, seemingly alive and aware. They moved with a slow determined ferocity, much like television shows I had seen when I was younger depicting Elephants lumbering through human crowds, seemingly unstoppable.

We turned onto a side street just a few blocks from the entrance and found a street nearly empty and open. About a block away we saw a man with a protest shirt kneeling, seemingly tying his shoes. I tried to avoid meeting his eyes, especially given the conversations Julie and I had been having regarding men, strange or otherwise, but, as we moved a little closer, it became clear that his foot was stuck in the rubble.

We could see, moving toward the side street horizontally, two giant crowd control robots in some sort of intentional configuration. As they passed the street, one paused as the other one continued.

We stopped and watched. This couldn't actually be happening. The man trying to free his foot didn't seem to have noticed the Robot yet as it turned, seemingly willfully, to move down the street to approach the man. Julie's eyes were wide and she quietly pleaded with the man, under her breath, to get up and move.

"C'mon. Move. Get up. Move."

We could see the back of the robot now moving forward toward the man who was almost obscured by the massive frame of the red and black police-issued monstrosity. It moved at a steady pace, as though it didn't see the man, although it had clearly changed direction to approach him, rotating on its giant single wheel.

We could hear him now yelling out, waving his arms, while the robot marched forward, on a single axis, a ball-like sphere that kept it somehow gyroscopically upright. I focused on the wheel itself moving, rotating through the thick debris until, without slowing down, it rode over the man and collapsed his head into the pavement. I imagined I could hear a far away crunching sound as the machine moved on.

The panicked flailing of the man's arms stopped while the body twitched visibly in death. The robot continued on to the end of the street and turned, ostensibly to meet up with its twin and continue their patrol.

I realized that I had been saying out loud "Oh my god" and I didn't know how to stop. I don't know if it was a prayer or a mantra or some kind of invocation to make what I just saw not be true. But we both saw it. We both watched an innocent man run down by an unliving crowd control robot. I tried to remember if he had done anything threatening or illegal.

But the truth is that this machine had turned down the street with the seeming intent of murdering a man who was trapped in the rubble.

I picked up my phone but I suddenly didn't know who or what to call about what I'd just seen. I lifted it to take a picture but Julie's hand covered it. She slowly pulled it downward.

She was right.

I didn't want this picture on my phone.

I didn't want to have seen it

I didn't want to be involved in any of this.

I had nothing to gain and everything to lose by even knowing what had just happened.

As we stood in the elevator, I could feel Julie shaking a bit. She rode down the entire way without moving. She didn't change or speak until, about a minute left to go, she turned to me and told me that she was coming with me. She had taken the day off to be with me for the procedure.

I hadn't realized that she was doing that. I was suddenly a little overwhelmed. After Ithad and Jen had gone to bed last night, I had tried to prepare myself for this, to manage this alone. I was going to just try to shut down and do what I needed to do to make it through the procedure.

The fullscreen imagery all over the elevator shifted to a comforting white and blue professional space as we came to the medical floor. The doors opened and a stark white light spread out in front of us. The sign next to us reads "Women's services" and there is a blue arrow pointing forward.

It's hard to overstate how white everything was. I was reminded of a passage I had fact-checked years ago.

In the early 1900s, the color white communicated to patients the concepts of purity and cleanliness. Staff also found that it was easy to maintain white surfaces since dirt and residue was so obvious on their surface.

During World War I, a doctor by the name of Harry Sherman determined that white was distracting for surgeons. The high contrast between the white and the splatters of red blood was too glaring and prevented doctors from discerning the finer delta needed to recognize more subtle anatomical edges.

So, using color theory, he came up with the idea of using "spinach green" for scrubs, rags and some surfaces. It showed the blood but did it in a more functional way, one that didn't tire out human eyes so quickly.

For sixty years or so, Hospital white was peppered, across many important areas, with hospital green. And it reduced wear on the eyes of human surgeons.

It turned out, though, that AI, robots, machines, and other surgical devices, the ones that now performed most of the procedures, had no real use for subtlety and would not tire out from the high contrast blood splattered white surfaces. These new robotic surgical spaces reverted, again, to the purity of white, so pervasive that human eyes immediately clung to the small specks of color that they could find within the wash.

The signs were clearly designed for human visitors. We watched AI and fully robotic information and logistics devices move up and down the hallways without any need for them. They slid in and out of doorways, up walls, even into reset areas in the floor. The hospital area seemed, to my eye, like a hive built for the habitation of robots and we humans were meant to be infrequent and casual visitors.

This was an ecosystem built to serve humans without human involvement.

Which would have felt a lot more inviting if I hadn't just watched a robot kill a man.

I checked the notice on my phone and found the room, 334h. The sign on the door was in dark blue against the white.

"Please enter alone".

I ran through all the different ways, in my head, that could have been written in a less ominous way and encountered so many. The editor in me rose to the surface and shook my head. I looked at Julie who she seemed to have expected this. She patted my hand and told me that she would be waiting here when I was done.

She pressed a squarish indent in the wall right by the door. It sunk in a bit and then extended outward, as if on a spring. A surface shot out from the white wall, much like a bench, for her to sit on and wait.

I thought about the foot high cylindrical column in that other room. Did everyone but me know how these things all worked? I could see the cuts in the wall now around the back of the bench. This wasn't magic. This was just me not being familiar with how things worked.

I moved into the darkened room and the lights cascaded on for me. A monitor on the side wall told me to disrobe down to my underwear and get comfortable in the bed. My recent experiences with this method made me look around the room for cameras, for the person potentially typing the commands. But nearly anything recessed into the walls of that room could have been a camera. The room was not hurting for a lack of high tech looking gear. This, at least, calmed me a bit. It certainly looked like a competent surgical room. Taking a step back mentally, though, I realized it looked like a competent room to accommodate ANY technology. Nothing except the bed screamed medical. It could have been a clean room from a nuclear research facility or an antiseptic automated manufacturing center for high tech stuffed animals.

Iit could have been anything.

I ran my hands over the equipment to the side of the bed, I didn't really recognize much of anything. Again, I started to wonder about much of the science I was seeing around me. I wrote about science. I fact checked it, researched it, read about it on a daily basis. What was going on that I was so frequently surprised by it lately?

I pulled off my shirt and jeans and slid into the bed. It was actually not uncomfortable. I didn't remember the last time I was in a hospital, but this seemed to not be overly horrible.

The monitor on the wall flashed again, asking me to place my right arm in the groove at the side of the bed. I realized that I had missed the groove and had very nearly placed my arm there anyway.

I shifted a little and looked into it. I could see a series of sensors and holes running up and down the length of the groove. I placed my arm in it.

The bed seemed to come alive as it responded biometrically to my arm. A series of lights ran up and down the side of the groove and the monitor began to flash diagnostics. A series of straps slowly wound out from the holes on the sides of the groove and pulled taught on my arm, securing it in place. Another strap secured my wrist. I could feel the tension as the straps began to record my blood pressure.

Later, I think, it was obvious that the straps had encouraged me to focus on the tension to my arm, and I missed the injection.

That was likely the thing that put me to sleep.

I woke up groggy with my arm free of the straps. I looked down and could see the indentations up and down its surface. A tiny bit of blood marked the spot where I had been injected. The room was dark and the monitor held a tiny word in the center of it, different than the large font usually used when ordering me around. It simply read

"Maintenance"

I swung my legs around and stood up. The lights in the room didn't spring on automatically as they had before and I could see, along the bottom of the walls, near where they met the floor, a line of red that was illuminating the floor in front of me. This lighting was very different from when I had walked in, and it didn't seem normal. I wondered if there was a nurse or someone I could talk to.

I walked to the door and opened it.

The hallway was as dark as the room and the red light running across the lower edge of the wall was everywhere. It flashed and blinked slowly, as though it were trying to do something, to reset. Every thirty seconds or so, it blinked in succession, drawing the eye down the corridor.

I looked to the side of the door and saw Julie slumped in the seat. She had fallen asleep, too, and I considered waking her up. I didn't really understand what was happening so I thought I would let her rest a bit while I found a nurse.

I hadn't panicked yet and there was no point in making her panic.

The robots that had been scurrying around so prodigiously when we walked in seemed paused as well. It was almost like everything had shit down, into a kind of "stand-by" mode. The red lights flashed again and a chain reaction sent the wave down the hallway where I thought I saw a figure moving.

If I could find a nurse, I could figure out what was happening. I looked down. I was still in my underwear and t-shirt. As far as i knew i hadn't had the procedure yet. But there was a slight drip of blood down my leg. I walked over to the nearest bot and found a small white towel. I wiped the blood from my leg and looked at it. In the low light it looked dark, almost black.

I did some math in my head and there was no reason I should have been bleeding right now. I wondered if the automated bed hadn't done something to me. I didn't feel any different and I certainly didn't feel any cramping.

Could this be a side effect of the medication? That was a possibility, but what medication could make me start bleeding? I couldn't think of any. I looked again, down the hallway and was sure this time. There was a figure moving down the hall.

I looked back at Julie and let her be. This would be quick, I hoped.

I set off down the hallway past a suite of rooms just like the one I had come from. Most of the doors were closed but the ones that were open, even a tiny bit, showed the same thing that I had seen in mine - a darkened room with a rim of red lights against the floor.

I heard some pulsing from down the hall in front of me. Iit was reminiscent of a beating, like a heartbeat. The further I went, the more I saw them - these ridged white tubes that stretched from room to room, becoming more dense by the step. They all seemed to have the same destination. They connected the rooms together and bridged them with something I was approaching.

I saw a movement ahead, a figure dressed in white. This would be a nurse, I hoped. I was tired. I still hadn't recovered, I thought, from the sedative I was given and now I was beginning to wonder why I had left bed at all.

A flash of light in front of me, almost a spark, shot out from the opening to a room where the tubes seemed to feed. I stepped forward, forcing my legs to lift and fall in step. I leaned against the wall and felt one of the tubes. It was warm and undulating, like something alive. Instinctively, I pulled back. I moved forward a few steps and looked into the room.

At first, it was dark. It took my eyes a minute or two to readjust after the spark. But as I looked closer, I could see that the room itself was massive, large, and it seemed to extend far into the darkness. In it were what looked like pods, white and peach colored, with tubes running from them. I stepped into the room and saw the one closest to me. It was rounded and had what looked to be a monitor on top of it, facing me.

My breath was suddenly visible and I realized that it had clouded the glass of the monitor. The pod looked like a person, but without arms or legs. A round person. I wiped the condensation from the glass and saw it.

A woman's face stared back at me. These pods contained people.

The bloated face of the woman in the pod shook as her eyes opened. I could see that the respirator in her mouth was sutured directly to her skin and that skin stretched and split as she opened her mouth to scream. I could barely hear the sound of it through the pod.

It contained a woman - a pregnant woman.

I recoiled in horror. As I did I bumped into a cylinder directly behind me. An alarm rang out.

The alarm seemed to trigger a lightshow. Lights suddenly lit up the room, in succession, starting at my location and cascading deeper into the space. There were thousands of pods.

There were tens of thousands.

There were so many of them. As far as the eye could see. It looked like a cartoon step and repeat visual effect done with mirrors maybe. It went on and on.

I panicked and my vision started to close in.

I looked down. The blood was running down my legs into a pool on the ground. A gush of red seemed to empty me. It felt as though the sun was being pulled from my head.

My foot slipped out from under me.

I don't remember hitting the floor.

I woke up back in the room, lights bright, invading my head. My arm was back in the groove and the monitor was alive with lights. It said, simply, in the center of it,

"You are free to leave."

I pulled my arm and the straps gave way, receding into the bed where they had originated. I shoved the blankets aside. I was wearing a kind of thick pair of hospital panties. The t-shirt had been replaced and was white and starchy.

I put my clothes back on in a rush and grabbed the small pamphlet on the bedside stand that included instructions on care. In the hallway, I looked up and down and couldn't see Julie.

The robots whirred and slid up and down the hallway again and today there were people, as well. Nurses, patients, even a doctor was visible, interacting, moving from room to room. I stared down the hallway when I felt a tap on my shoulder.

It was Juliie, holding two cups of coffee. She had gone to get one for me once she heard I was free to go. She said she had a short conversation with the doctor who suggested I have a bigger than usual dinner and get some rest for a couple of days.

That seemed like a truly facile piece of advice from a doctor. No invocations to eat well, protein, green leafy vegetables. Just have a big-ass dinner and sleep it off. This was the advice of a cartoon marijuana dispensary clerk from the 2020s, not from a modern doctor.

I put my hand on my stomach and felt gingerly for anything unusual or different. Lifting my shirt I could see a small bandage where presumably the robot had gone in to do the procedure. There was no pain and nothing I could feel was any different.

Julie tried to keep my mind off the procedure on the way home. She took it upon herself to bring me to her favorite mexican place for a strawberry licuado. Despite everything, I had to admit that this was good. It was only strawberries, sugar, cream, ice, and a little cinnamon, but it was virtually perfect.

Nature may have invented volcanos, mosquitos and the Zika Virus but it also pulled strawberries out of its back pocket, I tried to remind myself.

That was a trade off you just had to accept.

Julie only remembered napping for a few moments before getting up to get coffee. I tried to work with her to construct the timeline but none of it really made any sense. She had no recollection of the lights going off or certainly hearing my scream from the other room.

Did I leave my room before the procedure? I can't say I was 100% sure that all of that happened. I considered telling Julie what I saw but then thought better of it.

I wondered if I could have a second drink and then reflected back on the doctor's wild hippie advice and ordered one for both of us.

I listened to Julie talk about how perfect this would be if they contained alcohol. Her laugh was explosive and simple, girlish and slightly wild. I could see myself getting addicted to it easily.

I remembered a joke I would tell Mikah when he would lay in bed with me, laughing like a demon. It was stupid and had a painfully stilted delivery. But I told it to her anyway.

A little polar bear comes home from school and asks his mom if he is really a polar bear. She says for sure he is. So he shrugs and goes to bed. The next day he comes home and asks if she and his dad are all polar bears. She says they sure are. So he shrugs and goes to bed. The next day he asks if grandma and grandpa are definitely polar bears. She says yes and asks what's wrong. He then tells her:

"Because I'm fucking freezing."

Julie laughs for a full minute and then starts again. The joke isn't that funny, but we are.

We're funny.

We made our way back home. I turned on the lights in the bathroom and pulled the tiny bandage off.

The hole was small. Just a tiny indentation. If it hadn't been covered by the bandage I might have missed it.

The area around it was slightly red.

I let my shirt drop and moved back to my room. I knew I had it somewhere.

Beneath the bed was a box of old textbooks. I remember one I had done fact checking for a million years ago. It was a biology textbook, something that was a bit of an outlier for the company at the time.

I remembered thinking that it was stretching my fields of discipline a bit. Something made me forget this box when I was considering what to give away for cash to spend on the getting the fuck out of dodge fund. I realized that many of these textbooks sold for over two hundred dollars when new.

Not only did people used to read books, they used to pay for them, too.

Under a dusty textbook about quantum mechanics was one called "Reproductive Care- complete surgical procedures guide" from 2032 by a series of doctors. The lead on the book was Doctor Agnes Court, MD.

I looked up the section on Hysterectomies. It listed five different types of Hysterectomies. Each one came with its conditions and the impact it would have on the body.

None of them left just one tiny scar on the abdomen.

In the section where it described a robotic assisted laparoscopic surgery it said:

> "Your surgeon inserts a laparoscope through abdomen incisions. They insert small, thin surgical tools through three to five other small incisions around your belly button. The surgeon controls robotic arms and instruments."

I read through it over and over. But none of them explained the blood from earlier or the single incision point.

Further down, It read:

> "Anesthesia will keep you from feeling pain during the surgery. But you can expect soreness and discomfort for a few weeks. Your surgeon will discuss your options for pain relief during recovery. This could involve prescription pain medication or over-the-counter (OTC) pain medicines like NSAIDs (non-steroidal anti-inflammatory drugs) or acetaminophen."

But I hadn't felt anything like that. I was feeling no pain right now.

Nothing.

There was no soreness, no discomfort.

I didn't feel any kind of generalized pain at all.

I sank into my bed and stretched out, looking down at the tiny incision mark on my belly. I closed my eyes and felt it with my fingers. It felt like an old scar, like one that had healed a long time ago.

I reached into the thick padded underwear I had been put into and touched myself. There was no pain there, either. I looked at my finger.

No blood.

Nothing.

What the hell did they actually do to me?

THREE

Jen carries a tablet with her everywhere she goes. When I lean in over her shoulder I see that it's full of books and reference materials on biology. This is her job in their group. She is focused on what it takes to keep human beings alive in space and in alien environments.

She's about life.

It's not surprising.

She's quick and silly and funny and charming and wickedly smart. Listening to the two of them talk is like being front and center at a tennis game of words and ideas, played by tennis masters who don't feel the need to hold back anymore. She is beautiful but my sense is that this is more an additional influence than a prime mover in their relationship. Ithad is tall and handsome, taller than me now by a few centimeters, and his voice, steady and soft, is lower and more resonant now. It's calming. I can tell that Jen is affected by the sound of it.

Her family is Korean and she lives with her grandmother now after the disappearance of her parents a few years ago. It's getting harder to find real information, but it's clear that this is not uncommon. I remember being very young and hearing amber alerts when people went missing. The police would look for them, they would care.

People would be found,

This really didn't happen anymore. I wondered what might happen today if I called 911.

She is fifteen years old, about five months older than Ithad. She would be a grade ahead of him if there were schools in session here anymore. We are now officially in a black zone on the maps so there is no school service. But I had been homeschooling Ithad long before that. And lately, I'd been making sure I was paying attention to Jen's development, too.

At first, my efforts were about working with him, finding texts that were age appropriate, reading with him, making sure that he met the requirements for the specific grade levels. But he had exploded those meager expectations a long time ago. My job as educator now was just to keep on finding more and more heady information, books, when possible, pdfs, documentation, etc. Much of it was about getting him out of his own head and keeping his education diverse.

Our home doubled as a learning center, with every day filled with some sort of acquisition of knowledge. Ithad and Jen let me pause their work to read from great literature, to talk about poetry, to even paint together and reflect on artists that were defining for their times. I had never been particularly immersed in the liberal arts but I was determined that they wouldn't grow up knowing HOW to do things with no idea WHY to do them.

I was determined that they would be happy.

I had two more days of recuperation before I had to return to work and I wanted to spend them doing something I would love. So I played art teacher for a while.

I had decided to wear my new prescription-free glasses whenever I played the role of teacher and that seemed to amuse Jen to no end. I had found a few thin pieces of wood when cleaning outside a few days ago and I figured we could paint on them. I wanted to paint aliens with them and explore, at the same time, the major influences of the artist Jean-Michel Basquiat.

I was grateful that they both were open to dropping their work and following my often stream of consciousness lesson plans wherever they meandered. I knew, in some ways, that it was a kindness extended to me, but I also recognized that they both seemed to really believe that I had something to offer them.

I appreciated that.

I pulled out the art kit from the cupboard and we sat around the table painting.

Basquiat seemed like an appropriate topic for a conversation about art with this group. He was a brilliant child. Before the age of seven, he wrote a children's book with a friend, illustrated beautifully. He was ahead of the curve in every way throughout the course of his life.

There is a recurrent iconography in his work that creates a kind of "Rosetta Stone" for human signage. It is a passion for the creation of shape meaning that seems to link hobo signs with children's games like hopscotch and skelly's court, with universal roadside drivers icons. It's a distillation of meaning that infuses his work and gives it a kind of all-human appeal. Symbols unite us. And there are universal shapes that ensnare meaning in ways that travel well person to person,

During the first great depression, almost four million people were displaced from homes, wandering, looking for work, for food. They would sometimes ride the back of train cars and came to be known, many of them, as hobos. To make their lives even harder, the elite classes persisted in targeting them legally just for existing. They had to create community any way they could under the watchful gaze of the wealthy, sure in the knowledge that the police were absolutely in their employ.

They, nomadically, roamed the countryside, taking jobs whenever and wherever they could, and never spending too much time in any one place, often asking for food or lodging from sympathetic families. When responses were good, it was helpful. When they were received badly, though, it was potentially deadly. Many were shot and killed just for asking for basic necessities.

So in order to warn each other, they created signage, icons, symbology, that communicated the important information. This was a good place to sleep unmolested. This place was aggressive. Etc. Basquiat was drawn to symbology like this and used icons like this in his work. Since he picked up this knowledge as a child, he assimilated it with the signage and iconography of various children's games, which had their own exotic import.

I talked a bit about his relationship with Andy Warhol and how the world famous pop artist and the street level neo-Expressionist became friends. It was a fun part of the story, a time when he was on his way to being recognized as a great artist.

But long before that, when he was seven years old, Basquiat was in a car accident. It necessitated him spending more time than he wanted in the hospital. His family was first generation Haitian living in the US and they spoke multiple languages at home. Spanish, French and Creole, as well as English were a part of his upbringing. They were invested very strongly in his education.

So, as he sat in the hospital waiting on a surgery to remove his spleen, his mother brought him a copy of Grey's Anatomy. This catalyzed a lot of what he was visually interested in. Anatomy, body parts, many reduced to iconography, symbols, these drove his work. So much so that while the subjects of his work may have been political representations of issues that impacted black America fervently, like police brutality, the visuals in that work were reflective of the iconography of community, what is universal in the human mind, coupled with the arcane art of anatomy.

We drew aliens in the style of Basquiat, the great signifier. They looked, for all the world, like cave paintings you might find on alien worlds. Like the cave paintings you might find on a world like Enceladus, if it had been populated, full of alien life.

Jen chose a small, round piece of wood and painted it densely. Hers was colorful and full of icons that spoke to me, symbols that looked like tiny people. It occurred to me that she grew up in a Korean family and may have been exposed to elaborate ideograms all her life.

It was a beautiful piece. She looked at her tablet and inscribed a small quote on the back of it with her tiny square pen hand.

I made a point to inscribe mine, too.

We all did.

We talked about what it would be like to live on that world, to be an alien ourselves, divorced from humanity by distance, able to build something foreign to Earth-like experiences. What part of humanity would we take.

What part might we leave behind.

We took Basquiat.

We all showered and got ready and I followed them down to the spaceport. They have a tiny area blocked off for their work but some days just watch the ships leave. Every day more and more leave Earth.

The first ships I saw leave were pendulous, massive, beautiful streamlined ones, looking for all the world like the product of an advanced civilization. As time goes on, the ships themselves look smaller, less grand. It's as if, as a matter of priority, the super wealthy left first, followed not long after by the less wealthy, then those even less so. And so on.

The air quality seems worse every time I leave the building. Today it was perceptibly worse than when Julie and I were out. It's thick and feels dead. Breathing in too hard hurts your lungs and it's even possible in some places, to see the air as a particulate fog, as living aerosol dirt. We wore masks today to try to filter out most of it.

We change our course a number of times to avoid protests and crowd control robots. Ithad is fascinated by the robots, who he claims are evolving in certain recognizable ways due to generative AI routines. He says he has been plotting the movements of many of the larger, more visible ones on the glass windows of the apartment, looking down at them.

At one point he calls the newer behavior "predatory" and I ask him what that means to him, in this context.

So he creates, for me, an example.

Let's say, for the purpose of argument, that the crowd control robots are given a directive, to maintain peace and order in certain areas. Now they are also provided with a generative AI, a learning intelligence. To us, it might "feel" like satisfaction to follow through on a programmed mandate. And the generative component seeks out satisfaction.

It is DRIVEN by a sense of accomplishment. So that is much like the human brain getting a little shot of serotonin. You did something, you got a reward. Let's call the robotic version of that, in the AI brain a "spark." That is robot serotonin. Now, remember, it doesn't get a spark just by seeing order. That wouldn't be very active. That isn't how you program a device meant to act quickly, to intervene. It is spark-reinforced when it MAINTAINS order. And because situations shift and change, that baseline may be one of the things learned by generative integration of its own awareness of the environment.

Every minute, it is relearning what "order" is.

Not just when people are peacefully protesting. But at night, during off hours, during the times when people aren't around. It's learning steadily, inexorably, how truly orderly things can be. A human, in this case, may run amok through their passion for the exercise of power. An AI may become equally predatory in its execution of the job through their ongoing assessment of what it takes to perform the task expertly.

And determine what order is.

So the Robots may begin to alter their behavior as time goes on. And a likely direction for that delta may be in the direction of "more order." At one point, an empty street may seem optimally orderly.

I considered for a moment about how a lone man, trapped and flailing in the middle of the street could easily seem less "orderly" than a dead body and a chill ran down my back.

Jen noticed right away and I smiled at her. There was no need to tell them what I saw. We were avoiding them anyway.

I did tell them both I had something very important to say, then forcefully reminded them that, once they made it to Enceladus they would, technically no longer be earthlings. They would be Enchiladas. so it was important to keep their cheese on straight.

Ithad shook his head and smiled, looking down. He refused to let me see him laugh at something so dumb. He had an image to preserve.

Jen just giggled and told us she was hungry.

Then called me the queen enchilada for the rest of the day.

We moved past the crowds to watch the smaller ships take off. They were more interested in the smaller ships regardless, and the mechanics of what made them work. The police and crowd control bots thinned as we got to the less visited parts of the spaceport. That worked for us, too, since we had no interest in interacting with them.

They were here every day, but this was one of my first visits. I remember back when this was an empty field near the airport, a place where cars would crawl up and array themselves around the trees, couples climbing on the hoods to stare up and departing planes all night, holding hands and wishing they were going, too, on that trip.

I couldn't tell if the spaceport had eaten the airport in its entirety or if the airport hadn't just expanded to encompass the entire area, channeling its new focus of off-world travel.

I was surprised at the dearth of colorful airline company logos, each one replaced by the somber and modern MekaAir logo.

MekaAir. We bring you worlds.

I don't remember when every company around me became one hyperinflated conglomerate corporation. I've clearly not been paying attention as the world decays and evolves toward....What?

I don't know.

I don't see a plan anymore. I just see people scrambling to leave. I see robots running over people. I see middle managers raping employees in empty monochromatic rooms and robots performing bizarre procedures on half-willing people while computer monitors bark commands in greenish white fonts.

What is the end here? Where is this all going?

We meet up with some of their friends to watch a test flight. There are two young girls and two boys. One of the girls seems impossibly young. She has a wide afro and a beaming childlike face. I'm told by Jen in whispers that her name is Latia and that she is a twelve year old genius in the field of water purification and renewal. Her designs were used in the processing plants of her school before it closed.

She seems happy. The stereotypes of child geniuses as sullen, depressed and often morose combatants fell apart for me a long time ago. I know that none of it is true. Genius is about wonder, about the joy of creation.

She lights up with ideas.

One of the other boys, Malcolm, is her big brother. His skin is even blacker than his sister's, almost blue black. He is seventeen, tall, and quiet but friendly. He greets Ithad with a big boisterous hug that makes me imagine them play-wrestling in their spare time, patting each other hard on the back, roughhousing like boys do.

I smile at all of them and shake their hands. The other girl, Pia, is curvy but studious looking and reminds me of Velma from the scooby gang, in a pretty and likable way. She talks a lot about food and weight distribution. And her companion, Virgil, is thin, Nigerian, I think, with glasses as well.

He is also interested in physics, from what I gather

They seem like a cartoon enclave of child geniuses, maybe setting out to solve crimes in a green bus or something. They look like people I would have enjoyed spending time with when I was young and a sudden wave of pleasure washes over me.

The ship being tested is called the Albatross. It is a similar design to what they are building with the same propulsion system. It uses Jet fuel to reach orbit then a light sail to do the heavy lifting in space, landing with the last of the jet fuel. For that reason, it's considered a hybrid device. Their ships are about equal size and are made to carry about ten people maximum.

Due to the boxes and transfers, I am, apparently, the primary donor to this project and for that reason alone, I think, everyone is kind to me. But after I ask one or two questions, I start to suspect they like me.

I listened.

Before the Albatross launched, across the spaceport, there was a massive ship launching, containing over six thousand people. It was called the Millenium and it was heralded as one of the most substantial ships to ever fly. It was far too big for a solar sail so it used a different technology to make it to IO once it passed the Orbital sphere. The sheer size of the ship actually helped. Most of the mass was behind, protecting the occupants from the billions of tiny nuclear explosions used to send the ship to its destination. It only used the laser links for guidance.

That's when I asked Virgil what a laser link was.

He looked like he loved talking about this.

The amount of sunlight that fell on earth was significant. This pushed photons that were needed to make the solar sails work. No problem, right? Until you got our past mars. Then the photon push lessened. Once you got near Saturn it was essentially intermittent.

It was dark.

So they invented the Laser Links.

Lasers mounted on earth and on various planetary bodies pushed photons back and forth. It was incredibly powerful. So, if you were flying under solar sail, you could ride the Laser Links to your destination, basically, with enough power to make some serious time. If you were in a larger ship, one with ion or nuclear drives, you could still use them to navigate.

No matter what, they are useful. Every single ship used the laser links, as soon as they escaped the atmosphere.

And for a tiny ship like the Albatross, the Laser Link from Earth to Saturn would be incredibly overpowered. Way more than was needed. So energy could be stored for landing, even if there wasn't enough liquid fuel.

I asked Virgil a question. I could tell Ithad was excited. Every one of them wanted to tell me.

It's the equivalent of 750,000 tons of TNT.

Ithad knew I needed numbers. Real ones.

3.15×10^{15} Joules.

To put this in perspective, when I was younger, that would have been about 0.5% of the world's total annual energy use.

But not now.

This was just for that little ship.

I tried to imagine what the energy requirements were for the Millenium. Even from across the Spaceport, we could feel the rumble. And we could see the tip of it. The ground was shaking.

I had to ask the question. But these were numbers unlike anything I had considered. I looked at Jen. She was a biologist. Surely these numbers terrified her. But she seemed calm.

She seemed happy.

So how fast does that get you?

Jen smiled. "Fast enough to make it to Enceladus in ten days, even with the demands of liftoff and landing."

Ithad looked up. "1% the speed of light."

I felt the rumble increase. It was like the world was exploding. It was suddenly as bright as if there were two suns. The noise was so loud that a part of my brain actually started to get angry. I let it wash over me.

That would be ten thousand times faster than I had ever considered traveling.

We were going to go Seven million miles per hour.

Compared to the Millenium, the Albatross takeoff was stealthy and somber. It made its way quickly to the tip of the atmosphere. Today's test was to reach the Laser Link but not use it.

I asked them if they were going to test the Laser Link.

Pia looked up and made a face.

We had saved up money for materials and for fuel, for all of it. But what I didn't realize was what was preventing this ship from leaving.

Every ship used the Laser Links. And there were many of them. There was more than enough room.

And every ship paid fifteen thousand dollars per use.

My stomach dropped. We had raised some money but we were far from that. If I wanted to help make this flight a reality, we needed to find over ten thousand dollars somewhere.

I needed more money.

I remember the rest as a bit of a blur. That day was a hurricane of ideas, numbers, emotions, all of it.

I know we never made it home.

I got a text from Julie as we left the spaceport. It said to meet her at a specific address. It was closer to the port than home, just a few blocks from our entrance to the MekaDisko. There was a video that came with the message but I couldn't make it out. It was dark, but it looked like the top of a grill, flames spitting out over coals.

We walked quickly to the address on the text. We got there in time to see a line of people moving furniture into the front door. The building was huge, larger than the Delroy. It was dark and gothic, with few windows.

Julie met us outside.

I wrote in my journal that night.

From My Journal:

The Apartment is gone. The entire building was leveled. They told us it was protesters, but how could they have pulled the entire thing down. Ithad thinks it was a robot and I think he's right.

We moved a few blocks closer to work. The building is just as destroyed as the apartment was. And I had to leave Mikah's things behind.

It doesn't matter.

We are all machines now.

Julie had gotten us an apartment in the new building. We slept there that night on the floor. I wasn't sure how she had wrangled this so quickly, but I suspected we were squatting. I didn't care anymore. I was still awash in wonder at what we'd seen that day. We wouldn't be there long, one way or the other.

I still had the next day off so I spent it going through the rubble of the old apartment. We didn't find much. I had the glasses that Jen had given me in my pocket. And I managed to find the circular wooden slab that she had painted on. Most everything else was gone. The remainder fit in a box I could easily carry to the new place.

The word "new," though, was kind. The apartment was bigger, but it was a mess. It was covered in dirt and mold and the floor was rotting through in one place. No one had talked to us about rent, so that was an interesting development. I considered how much more that left for the fund every month. In fact, this seemed to be the exact thing we needed. To minimize, absolutely, all expenses, and maximize income.

We all had one or two sets of clothes,

For the first time I was excited to work the next day. I felt fine after the procedure, and, in a strange way, a bit invulnerable. I knew what I needed to do and I didn't care about what it took. I would say yes to every opportunity and I would make the money needed to do this.

I scrubbed the living room and the kids' room. Jen was staying with us full time from now on, it seemed, and I wanted them to have a space where they could think and work. The rest of the place was spartan and, I tried to console myself, even a bit Japanese in its restraint. I found a single color black rug and a low-to-the-floor black table for the center of the room. We all took our shoes off and sat there. The lack of windows was fine, There was nothing to see out there anymore.

Nothing at all.

Julie's apartment was next door and it felt like we were living together. The door between our places was always open and she came and went as she liked. And that was good.

Most of the time, when she came she brought something.

A coffeemaker.

Some juice

A block of cheese.

Julie never talked about these things, she just did them. On my way back from the old place I had found a lamp that still worked. I left it in her place and saw that she built the room around it. She was grateful for me, but it couldn't have come close to how grateful I was for her. And starting that next day we rode the elevator down together to work.

There were literally hundreds of dance clubs that made up the MekaDisko in our area. Some were on different levels. Julie and I would wake up early to log in and reserve spots at the same ones. Even if we didn't see each other, working the same shift in the same room was worth missing a little sleep.

The very first day I worked there was at Julie's favorite place.

A club called Angelus.

Dancing at Angelus was a tier three paid shift. This was okay, but not the best. The clubs and services were broken down into six tiers. It was like this:

>
> **Tier six:** *Family establishments, waitstaff and host work*
>
> **Tier five:** *Bartending and serving drinks*
>
> **Tier four:** *Clothed performances, bikini dancing*
>
> **Tier three:** *Topless and nude dancing, stage services*
>
> **Tier two:** *Customer integrated Topless and nude dancing and mingling*
>
> **Tier one:** *comfort services, overnights.*

The last tier was definitively sex work. It was prostitution - escorting. But it wasn't called that. But it paid like that.

With tier one jobs paying the most and tier six the least. As tier three dancers, we would be nude but there would really be no physical contact with customers. I read through the customer FAQs for the club and was shocked by all of this. It seemed so normal and, at the same time, so bizarre. I was getting an idea of how large this entire structure was.

How did this get built?

The coffee shop across the street is missing a wall.

An entire wall.

And somehow there is a massive, multilevel nightclub right under it.

The first few days flew by quickly. It wasn't hard work and the men were not that difficult. Sometimes the club was only half full and that made the whole thing easier. It was fairly easy to zone out and listen to the music and dance.

At Angelus, the illusion was that this was a kind of heaven, filled with beautiful angels who stripped and danced erotically for you. There were expensive drinks and brilliant light shows and the occasional Electronic performer, maintaining the quick and steady dance pulse of the room. This was one of the clubs where effort was expended to make the experience feel beautiful - to make it cinematic and powerful.

The smoke from the machines left a light oily residue on my skin but besides that didn't bother us. And we started meeting people, although given the fact that I had been planning on leaving at that point, as soon as possible, I wasn't really invested in getting to know anyone.

Ithad said, back at the apartment, that there was a seat for Julie if she wanted it. There were only seven of us going. I was afraid to ask about Pia's parents, or Virgil's, or Malcolm and Latia.

Each time I met a young person whose parents had been killed by crowd control, lost in the city, or left via shuttle I got a little more sad. None of this was right. Kids shouldn't have to live like this.

I didn't know if Julie wanted to come. When we asked, she just smiled and looked grateful. It was so much to think about that she may have felt scared, afraid to talk about it. Maybe she didn't believe it. Sometimes I didn't.

I didn't know for sure.

I was curious about the colonies themselves, though. What would happen once we got there? If the laser links alone cost fifteen thousand dollars to use, how much could the colonies cost?

It turned out the answer was simpler than I thought.

Nothing.

Jen explained that the colonies had cost so much to terraform and build that the only groups capable of that kind of expenditure had been governments. And the governments provided them to live on at no cost. This is what had originally triggered the mass rush to migrate there. Once companies realized that the transportation was the only legitimate expense, they invested hard in that, forming MekaAir as a means to create massive surpluses, while countries like Finland and Norway and others funded the build outs across the colonies.

Once we made our way to Enceladus, we would be free citizens of Denmark. This was a fascinating turn of events. Oh, we would be asked to pitch in and help build along with everyone else. But that was hardly oppressive. We could live there.

We could really live there.

Scientists had spent the last few years releasing water vapor and other greenhouse gasses into the environment there, helping create a heat-containing greenhouse effect on the too-cold surface. And it had worked, the moon was temperate and was growing real plants, raising real animals.

Real people were living there.

I started looking for videos of the colony itself across the broken internet. We still were unable to access sites from out of the country, and most news sites and dot edu destinations were suspended.

But the clips we found were remarkable. There were empty buildings just waiting for residents. Wide, open hydroponic farms. I thought about growing my own food and it seemed too wonderful to be true.

We could be safe.

I remember sophomore year in college, taking the night off with my friends to visit a local strip club called Pole Katz. I thought, when we drove up, that I would be more comfortable there if they had proven to me they could spell at all.

This place was unique because they had an amateur night, one night a week where people who didn't usually strip could get on stage and show off what they could do. And the level of applause would determine the winner. Competitive stripping seemed like a stretch, but there were six of us in the car. I would have five automatic fans if I dared to get up there. When we walked in I was still unsure if I would, but once I saw the dismal turnout for the night, it felt possible. Like it was something I could do.

The prize, for the dancer with the most applause, was five hundred dollars. In college, that seemed like bagel and coffee money for the rest of the year. It was, essentially, free money.

On the way there, the guy sitting next to me, Paul, was my favorite work partner in my advanced calculus class. He liked to read about famous philosophers and do their accents to me during study groups. His Kant sounded like John Malkovitch, but I liked it anyway.

I caught him looking at me on a number of occasions, I knew he would applaud for me if I got us there. Two drinks in and I did. An old Prince song came on and I started moving.

I had worn a matching set of crimson red underwear for this occasion and I thought the color looked great on me. It was a stark reversal of my ongoing college trend of boy shorts and sports bras under shapeless shirts and baggy jeans.

I went up last of three and by the end of the first song I was showing my underwear set off, deep red under the reddish lights. The other two girls had been good. They were pretty, for sure. But something was making me feel like I could win.

The DJ went into a classic old Doja Cat song and I pulled off my bra, to a surprising volume of cheers. I was feeling sexy and the music was working on me, in ways I hadn't anticipated. My friend Lilly had told me how to end my routine if I wanted to win. It had been her experience that the dancers who ended this way traditionally won.

I massaged my breasts onstage and made eye contact with a few men in the front row who had come alone. Soliciting a volume of applause from them seemed my best bet. My friends were sitting in the back, Lilly, Paul, all of them.

I assumed I had their votes.

The third song began, something newer that I didn't recognize at the time. It was harsh and skeletal and raunchy, with a deeply resonant low end that shook the stage under me. I started pulling my panties off and left them halfway down my thighs, slowly grinding for the people up front to see.

As the song progressed I considered doing what Lilly said. I could see that I had their attention and It felt right. I don't know where I got the guts to do it. But if I could see my friends at all, past the lights, I'm sure I wouldn't have. I pulled my panties down entirely and let them fall on the stage. Kneeling down on the hardwood, I undulated back and forth, knowing that the men up front were close enough to see everything.

Then I tried Lilly's finishing move.

I turned around and bent over, laying my head on the stage and arching my back, exposing myself to the room. This pose was an invitation that women had been offering for millenia and it seemed to overpower men's reason.

The song ended and the room exploded. The applause was powerful and I could already sense that I had won. I stood and looked out to see my friends' faces but it was too dark in the audience.

I was paid in twenties and I bought a round of drinks. I still had over four hundred and thirty dollars in my pocket on the way home and everyone in that car was bouncy and excited.

Except for Paul. He was quiet and didn't meet my eyes.

This was not my first lesson on how to manage the expectations of men, but it was a good one. I could see that Paul had considered me "girlfriend material" and now did not. At one point, he thought I was for him. Now I was for everyone.

How do you manage the expectations of men?

You don't.

Dancing at Angelus was similar, in a way, to being at Pole Katz, except that I had no friends in the audience. That much was clear. At first, I tried to avoid making eye contact with anyone, especially the men. Throughout the night a few men, here and there, had pointed their phones at me for a second. I assumed that they were taking a picture, which, honestly, I had no idea was legal or not there.

Either way it wouldn't be my place to say, I guess.

My own phone was in my locker and I took a break whenever possible to check it, to make sure that Ithad and Jen were ok. On my next break I noticed some notifications.

They were tipping me.

Ten dollars here, twenty there. Somehow their phones were responding to my face or appearance and were tipping me. But without my own phone in hand, I couldn't tell. There was no way for me to know how much.

Some of the girls had strapped their phones to their legs - their upper thighs. I had wondered why, but now I knew. I needed to cultivate the attention of the people who tipped, and my phone could help me do that. I asked one of the other girls - Beth, I think, for a nylon strap.

Somehow I felt even more naked. I had on shoes and a tiny pair of wings with my phone strapped to my thigh, but wore nothing else. It felt perverse and disconcerting. But it worked.

This changed everything. It was like I had figured out the code to the entire job. My phone was set to vibrate on notifications. I could now easily see who was tipping me in real time and play to that. I could dance for the people who were being most responsive.

I thought about the ten thousand dollar differential between what we had and what we needed. Just that night, so far, I had made nearly four hundred. This was on top of my Tier three pay.

I could have this money in a month and a half if I pushed myself.

And I was willing to push myself.

The kids were asleep when Julie and I got home.

I could see they had been working. There were notes, some handwritten, scattered all over the tiny Japanese table. I kneeled down and considered organizing them, but thought better of it. They would expect them to be in the same place in the morning.

I read the notes and it was comforting. I was suddenly back home, in an environment I understood. There were numbers all over the pieces of paper, some scrawled quickly, some methodically, with purpose.

Absent friction or any semblance of an atmosphere, something you experience when you have mass, speed is a state, not a behavior. That was important to remember. It took energy to change states, to speed up, to slow down, to stop. But the interior of the trip, the constant state of forward motion, was surprisingly thrifty and energy efficient. I thought back to my own physics undergrad classes. My professor had tried to get us to think about it not as a human being- a creature of intrinsic mass, but from the other side.

As massless things, photons have nothing weighting them down. They have no choice but to travel at the speed of life, In fact, a photon is technically a verb. It's not A PHOTON as much as it's PHOTONING.

As a massful thing, a particle like an electron has no choice but to work to move. It is definitely a noun.

For a moment I thought about a romance between a photon and an electron. One, unable to consider the ground, hopelessly in motion, never able to be contained or tied down, the other established, set in its ways, requiring energy to move. But once in motion, capable of staying that way.

It would never work.

Mixed marriages have their own challenges.

Every connection has its own challenges.

The next day, I met Per.

Julie and I returned to Angelus for our next shift. I had switched my service to the one approved by MekaCorp a week earlier and my phone now worked even in the elevator. My service below ground was actually better, in many ways, than above.

I began the night in a white skirt, looking like an angel. Julie was wearing a white dress split down the front and a small white thong. My phone was on my thigh and I was prepared to test my hypothesis and see if I could just put my head down and earn money tonight.

It was in that headspace that I met Per.

I had found a small stage area near the back bar that had a reasonable amount of traffic. It was visible from seats in all directions which seemed to be a recipe for gathering tips. At the beginning of my shift I was gathering up tips in thirty and forty dollar increments from people sitting around that stage, even while I kept my tiny skirt and white underwear on.

The stage had poles on either side of it that I could hold onto while dancing. The way it was arranged actually made me feel a bit like a professional. And the lights from the ceiling were flattering, I thought.

I was wearing a cropped shirt that left my belly exposed and I felt like I looked good. My focus, again, though, was on how much I could make tonight.

As if in response to that thought, Per appeared.

He was tall and nordic looking. He looked to be in his late forties and his hair was trimmed closely. My bet was that he was balding a bit and was cutting it closer and closer until he finally embraced it. He wasn't someone I would have actively sought out as a partner but he wasn't ugly. His eyes were the lightest gray I had ever seen, though, which was fascinating. It made him look innocent somehow, wide open to the world.

He wasn't.

I remember that he had tipped me the night before when I was fully nude in this exact place. But he had done it from afar, from the seats around the bar. Today he walked right up to me and stood there watching. Tall as he was, his head hovered around my belly button due to the platform I was on. He pulled his phone out.

The room was loud and I stared directly in his eyes. He pointed his phone at my belly and a kind of blue laser shot out, illuminating the number "250" across my abdomen. I looked down and he seemed to meet my eyes with a querulous dip of his head.

It was a negotiation.

He pointed to my panties. I made a tiny nodding motion and his hands rose to my waist. His fingers were cold as he placed them inside the elastic band and slowly pulled them down.

I continued to dance.

My phone vibrated with the newly acquired tip

He maintained eye contact as he slowly pulled them from my legs and then he reached out for my hand as I stepped out of them. He dropped the panties onto the platform and I shifted them into the clothing receptacle where they would be kept safe until later.

He smiled and turned, pulling up a seat behind him and sitting.

From there, he could very clearly, I guessed, see up my skirt. I imagined I was completely exposed to him while dancing. He seemed happy. I imagined that I might be able to make more money from him in a bit, possibly removing my skirt.

It was amazing to me how quickly I was getting used to the idea of taking men's money to promote their sexual gratification. Every dollar was earmarked and even if I felt like I needed a shower, it was still money.

I convinced myself.

I saw him again toward the end of my shift. He was standing near a hollow cylinder in the back of the club. He handed me his card. It read:

Per Manon

Radion Systems

IO colony

I smiled at him and motioned to the fact that I wasn't wearing anything at all anymore. I had no place to put his card. He laughed and took it back. He took one step forward and I instinctively backed into the hollow of the cylinder. I was new enough not to understand any of the protocols. And while I wasn't afraid of him I was more aware than ever, nude, walking around in that space, of my own physical bubble and the need to maintain it.

What he did next I didn't expect.

He slowly dropped to his knees in front of me. I looked around the room and no one seemed to notice at all. He fished his phone out of his pants and flashed a blue number, laser-like, on my inner thigh, right at the crux of my legs, where they met.

It read "$500"

I had a vague understanding of what was happening but this certainly wasn't a perfectly informed negotiation. He looked up at me quizzically again, almost childlike. I could tell he was trying to act harmless, in order to get what he wanted. I felt a pit open in my stomach and a million conflicting emotions. I nodded almost imperceptibly and felt the vibration as the money was sent to my phone.

I leaned backward with my back and held onto the sides of the cylinder. He crawled forward about a foot and gently put his mouth between my legs. I half shut my eyes and tried not to panic as his tongue began working on me.

I knew that I wasn't aroused and I hoped that he couldn't tell. He put his hands on my waist and began licking and sucking on me in earnest. There was nothing necessarily wrong with his technique, but I was nothing if not absolutely conscious of the circumstances. I tried to imagine it as some kind of medical exam, something that was essential and invasive but not particularly pleasant. It was something that had the outward appearance of a joyful act, maybe, but was just pushing me further back into my own head.

The girls in the club made a point out of courtesy to avoid looking. But I could see some of the men becoming aware of what was happening and beginning to wander over. We hadn't gotten much of a download on what was permissible here and I confess I really didn't know, but no one stopped us.

No one stopped him.

It was a few minutes before I realized that I was in charge of the arc of this act. And so, for the first time since college, I faked it. I put my hand on his head and shook quietly. I moaned. I pulled back as if to suggest that I was now sensitive.

I breathed heavily.

I looked down at him and he seemed satisfied. He leaned back on his haunches and smiled at me. Then he stood up and held out his hand, making a show of helping me step out of the cylinder.

I wanted to run. I wanted to find Julie. I wanted to get out of there. I had another break and I took it. Julie met me at my locker and hugged me. I suspect she had seen at least part of that. My phone buzzed again unexpectedly. I pulled it from the strap and searched the notifications page.

The MekaDisko had paid me for today as a tier one worker.

I showed Julie. She took my hand and read the phone, considering, like I was, the implications.

The club was aware of everything we did.

And we would be rewarded for going that extra mile.

In the mornings, we had gotten into the habit of eating a light breakfast and then going to the spaceport. That day was the first time I stepped inside Ithad's ship, the Huimang. Jen had named it. Huimang was Korean for "hope" but it also, in English, sounded almost exactly like the word "Human."

That sort of word play amused her.

I had transferred almost two thousand dollars to her from the last few days of work. It was certainly not what I wanted to be doing but it was well worth it. When I thought about the events the night before at the Angelus they seemed unreal, as though I had dreamed the entire thing. None of it made sense to me at all and none of it felt like a story I would be in.

They had enough to make some test flights. I watched Virgil and Malcolm go up for a bit and then come back down. It seemed simple and uneventful. They had used up four hundred dollars of liquid fuel but that was just par for the course. Test flights were necessary and not free.

If I was feeling more "Huimang" it's because there seemed to be a path I had a goal and we had the means to get there. I could see a way to get to the amount of money needed and it wouldn't kill me, even though it wasn't pleasant.

But once we left, all of that would be wiped away.

We would start with a new slate.

Ithad pulled me aside and asked if I wanted to go on a test flight in a few days. The idea was remarkable to me. I hadn't even gotten there yet, in my head. To go up in a spaceship with my son.

I checked my phone and made sure that I had the morning off that day. I had signed up for more shifts. I can make more money in private dances and even overnights with wealthy patrons. I didn't care anymore at this point.

We need this money.

I had talked to Mel, one of the girls at the Angelus, about overnights. She said that the facility itself would pay for the room and then send men according to your and their specifications. She had done it a few months ago to raise money quickly for some work she needed done on her home. And she was thinking about doing it for a month straight to raise the funds for a starliner ticket.

When she said it like that it didn't seem bad. The term "overnight" was deceptive, really as most of the men only stayed for a short time. The girl, however, got access to the room all night.

Again I wondered why and how this was legal. I didn't remember a news story that discussed how prostitution ws now effectively legal. And if it was, what else was legal?

What were the laws?

I wondered about what might happen if someone hurt me. Or if I asked someone to leave and they stayed. Mel didn't really have an answer.

No one did.

The ship was breathtaking.

It wasn't large. The entire interior was about the size of our living room. Everything was smooth and much more padded than I imagined it would be. Most of the ship was composed of the external shell that was about twenty feet deep on all sides, filled with gravity gel, meant to cushion inertia and prevent any sense of impact that might disturb the precious cargo.

There were surprisingly few controls and the ones there were seemed distributed across most of the chairs. There was a pilot but it was the responsibility of the other passengers to attend to their own areas of interest. Jen's seat was covered with anime stickers and seemed focused on life support systems, breathing, etc.

Ithad was one of two pilots and his chair was dark, leather, black. It was simple without too much embellishment. But on the display, near the front of the armrest, was a picture, a tiny one. I recognized it immediately. It was a shot of Mikah taken at his 4th birthday party. He was wearing a paper hat and grinning ear to ear.

So much was obvious in that picture.

Ithad was leaving the world that killed his brother. And he was trying desperately to bring everything good with him.

He never despaired, he never gave up. He never stopped trying or believing. I saw it all in that picture.

He was committed to living.

I realized that Mikah was one of our threads. I had tried so hard to be a good mom and he had so effortlessly and with so much intelligence and playfulness and humor and with every skill he had at his disposal just been a good brother.

It seemed to me that it had been easy for him. But maybe it wasn't. Maybe he had to fight through his own feelings.

Maybe he had to rise above them.

Maybe we needed to talk when we landed where we landed. For a long, long time.

The idea of just sitting with my son and talking about our feelings felt like peace to me. It felt like the most remarkable gift I could think of.

And so I reclined in the middle of a homemade spaceship, surrounded by a deep cushion of high tech gravity gel and felt, for the first time in months, peace.

I removed my name from the list that night for overnight stay. My full immersion into sex work would have to wait a day. I tried to be as flippant about that as I could be. After all, I was an avowed feminist. I certainly believed in the rights of people to do that if they wanted to make the money. And everything we DO for a living is selling our bodies.

But I didn't have any illusions that I was free from all the cultural baggage I had when growing up. And simply, selfishly, I didn't want to share that kind of intimacy with people I didn't know,

People I didn't at least like.

So, I think, in my head, I convinced myself that I liked Per. He was kind. There was something kind of sweet about his halting and reverential demeanor. I made myself think that I wouldn't mind it so much if it were him.

I could deal with that.

The problem is that I didn't have any way to contact him. I considered for a moment how I had returned his card to him, having no place to put it.

Since Julie had been there for a while and now I had done tier one work, we were given more options where to dance. We had chosen the temple of Bast for our shift that night.

It looked pretty on the schedule.

It was an Egyptian themed place that had a series of very high priced custom drinks, infused with various drugs. Statues to Egyptian gods were all over and the costumes we were given to wear were more elaborate. Stripping them off would get us more tips.

In general it was a higher class of customer.

With more money

I texted Julie but there was no response, She wasn't in her apartment or anywhere I could see. For the first time, I descended the elevator without her.

I assumed I wouldn't run into Per, but that assumption proved false. I walked out into the room and saw him almost immediately. He looked over to me and waved. I walked up to him and he tipped me nearly immediately, smiling as he held his phone out. I was surprised at how happy I was to see him

I danced for a while for him, looking around for Julie. During the third song I saw her, across the room, looking in my direction. She nodded her head to me and looked sad. It was clear that there was a story there and I tried to extricate myself from Per to find out.

He had other ideas. As I started to step down from the small stage he walked up and flashed blue numbers across my chest.

They read "$250"

It seemed obvious what he wanted here so I smiled at him and stepped closer. My phone vibrated as he reached between my breasts and slipped the clasp free, opening the front and pulling it off over my shoulders. He massaged my shoulders and even, briefly, touched one of my nipples.

I remembered a million years ago when the customers in strip clubs could famously not touch the dancers at all. Obviously there was a different dynamic in play here. I wondered where the line was to be paid as a Tier one performer.

I took his hands and put them on my breasts. He smiled. His face was close to mine now and he wasn't unattractive. The face was fairly featureless, like a mannequin. It seemed that once he did go bald he might be a generic MAN. Much like a dressing doll from a minimalist high end men's clothing store. The kind they could paint different colors to match the season.

He looked down and, with one hand still on my breast, he touched his phone, still in his pocket. I felt a vibration on my thigh as he lifted that hand and pressed his finger against my lips. His touch was light and explorative. I opened my lips a tiny bit and touched his finger with my tongue.

And then I nodded, ever so slightly at him.

I had never flirted like this in my entire life. When I tell you this was unlike me in every way I hope you believe me. Honestly you have no reason to.

In an unfamiliar space, this unknown man made me feel slightly safer. At this point, it may have been 2% safer, but that was intoxicating.

He leaned in and kissed me. I kissed him back, letting my lips fall apart slightly, softly, letting him invade my mouth with his tongue just a little. He was a good kisser. It felt very wrong kissing like this, topless, in the middle of the room, but it also was starting to feel like a game. This was an elaborate game of spin the bottle, of seven minutes in heaven, of truth or dare. This was playful and partly innocent and something we both opted into.

I realized that I had never heard his voice.

And I wondered what he might pay for a night with me. As I thought that, I got dizzy. Never in my life had I thought those words. Never in my entire life had I considered that.

Would it be over $2,000? That would get us so much closer. It would cover fuel for a couple of additional tests. And that might make the difference.

Here, at the end of the world, I've come to a place where all I care about is money. And Per seemed to have some. I let him kiss me and fondle my chest. I tried to get lost in it.

At the same time, I found myself wondering what was wrong with Julie. I didn't see her anywhere, but her locker was near mine and I would see her on our break.

Per came up from our kiss.

I had decided just then that I was Sandra. I was someone else. I was a fantasy person. I wasn't Llorona anymore. I wasn't anyone familiar. I was someone capable of saying what I was about to say.

I told him curtly that I was available for an overnight tomorrow. Just saying it felt like engaging in the act. It felt like fucking. It felt like sex to just say the words.

He shrugged and looked confused. I realized that he hadn't spoken to me not because it was so loud but because he didn't speak English. He showed me his phone. The interface was in a nordic language I thought I recognized as Danish. He spoke Danish. Not English.

I pulled my phone out and pointed to the calendar date for tomorrow, Then I showed him the image of the overnight suite.

This he understood. He smiled widely, almost like a giddy young boy. He looked down at his phone and typed in a word. He read from the translation and it was the first time I heard his voice. It was low and soft. He sounded like a gravely whisper. He pointed to my phone and said "Tomorrow"

So he could just track me to meet up tomorrow? I had no idea how this worked. .But the idea that a customer could track a specific dancer, outside the clubs, was terrifying. I made a decision to research that. As I considered what to tell him an amount I expected. He preempted me. He tapped his phone. Mine vibrated and I looked down.

He had sent me $2,500

I took a deep breath and went to find Julie.

She was sitting near the locker looking down, as I walked in I could tell she was crying. I tried to imagine what kind of bad news she could have gotten, but it was just a roomful of red. It could have been anything. She held something in her hand. I sat on the bench next to her and held her. She cried on my shoulder for a few minutes and then pulled away.

Then she looked in my eyes and handed what she held in her hand.

It was a ticket.

It was a ticket made out to her on the Euripides, a large starliner. Destination: Enceladus.

I looked at her. I tried to imagine what she was thinking.

She wasn't happy.

I leaned in and asked her what was wrong. She told me she had tried to sell it, to give it away, to trade it. Anything. She couldn't transfer it to anyone. It was an incredibly expensive ticket on the biggest starliner headed to the most desirable colony. It was first class accommodations for the two weeks it would take the Euripides to get there. Anyone I knew would kill to have their name on that line.

Except Julie.

She broke down. She didn't want to leave me - to leave the kids. She knew what this ticket was. It was a fortune. It was a bribe, an offer no one would refuse. It was from a married man whose family would soon be on earth for a visit. He needed her silence. He needed her happiness.

He needed her to disappear.

And it was dated for June 15th, 2046. The day after tomorrow.

She broke down again. She didn't know what to do.

But I did.

I lifted her head with my hand. I was still holding my top in my hand, which, I discovered made a perfect washcloth. I wiped her eyes.

I told her that she was going to get on that giant ship and she was going to relax and eat as much as she could all the way to the colony. She was going to take advantage of every single first class perk that she could because she deserved it.

She was going to sleep and eat and laugh and watch movies. And when she got to Enceladus she was going to do what she did so easily here.

She was going to look out for us and wait for us.

She was going to make a tiny part of that big moon ready for us and clear the way for us to join her. She was going to look around and find out the best place to eat, the best coffee shop, the best everything, and she was going to write it down.

I told her what I expected. That we would land and find her well rested, happy, safe, and ready with a little map of every place we would love,

I told her that this was her job now. She was going to go ahead and make that stupid moon want us there. And learn every piece of information she could. So that when we showed up, we could be together again.

And I told her it was ok to love that job.

Just like we loved her.

FOUR

Telling the story of the next four days is nearly impossible for me.

I want to be as matter-of-fact as possible about this and give sufficient detail, but there are some things that can't be communicated. All I can do is move forward somehow and open my eyes and step into it. I can tell you what I know.

I made my way down to the level where they maintained the overnight rooms.

This is where I'm going to start. I'm going to explain to you what I was doing when the whole world ended. When MY world ended.

My phone opened the room I was assigned. It was an illusion that was so surprisingly effective it unnerved me. The door whirred open and the first thing I noticed was the ambient lighting. It looked like it had windows round three walls, all facing a wide open national park-like field. There was a waterfall clearly visible.

The atmosphere of the room itself felt alive, green, as though the plants all around me were real. It seemed that I could open any window and instantly touch the natural beauty all around me. I dug back into my childhood, but as a city girl, I realized that even before everything went to shit, I had never experienced anything like this.

One of the things that the MekaDisko is very good at is artifice. It can build things that every part of your brain is so incredibly aware can't humanly be real but still, somewhere, in some part of you, some corner of your body, you are sure is happening right now.

The room was big and open. It was definitely focused on the large round bed in the center of it, directly in the center of the room, accessible from all sides. It was large enough for five or six people to sleep on it. That thought made me twitch a bit. I thought a bit about how long it had been since I'd shared a bed with a man. I was twenty when I walked away from Leo. Suddenly I felt impossibly old.

On the one wall bereft of artificial windows was a smaller monitor. This one looked familiar to me. It flashed every minute or so and on it were the words:

"Be comfortable."

Again, I can't assert more strenuously how disconcertingly written that was. You can probably imagine literally a hundred ways where that could be expressed less ominously. It's like these monitor invocations were written by a cartoon super villain and meant to be shoved into an exploding fortune cookie and dropped on Gotham city.

"Be comfortable."

I had some time so I thought I would take a shower. Lately I had had the desire to take a shower nearly constantly so this seemed like a likely time to give in to that.

That fell into the category of the authoritarian mandate to "Be Comfortable," so I moved into the bathroom. It was large and open and had what looked like a skylight that was under a daylight waterfall. The illusion was so realistic that I almost imagined droplets of water filtering through the edges of the closed upper window dripping down intermittently on my skin.

I stripped down. Lately I was spending so much time without my clothes on. But there was no sun. My normally light caramel skin tone was becoming pasty-thin. I looked around the room and saw a UV light switch. A tanning light. Of course they would have fake sunlight.

They have fake everything.

I switched it on. It ran in increments of fifteen minutes. I had nearly an hour until I was meant to meet Per. I still didn't understand how this tracking worked, but I had gotten a time notification along with the location from the MekaDisko on my phone. Did I initiate that or did he?

I just agreed to it. I stepped into the shower and turned it up all the way. Since I was a kid I had always taken showers far too hot for anyone to ever tolerate. I was destined to shower alone like some solitary poaching lobster. I let the water fall on me and try to wash away everything. The ironic thing was, at that moment, I was feeling better. I was feeling hopeful. We had a plan and even this was moving the plan forward. I would miss Julie but the knowledge that she would be safe and happy made up for it. And we would see her again.

We'd be together again.

It was possible, in that shower, in the cover of a beautiful artificial waterfall, lit by an artificial sun, to feel hopeful.

And that is something that made it all so much worse, in the end.

Per came to the door with a clear plan.

He brought wine. And a set of elaborate bath bombs in a crystalline case.

He brought massage oil.

He was dressed handsomely in a black shirt and a pair of jeans. When I opened the door, I was still in the white robe I had found in the room.

He didn't seem to mind.

He took my hand and we went to the bed. I could tell he'd been in one of these rooms before. I glanced over at the monitor and it had no instructions. I suppose it trusted that I could figure the rest out myself.

Per pulled his phone out of his pocket. And navigated for a few seconds. Slowly the scenes displayed in the "Windows" around the room began to shift. It looked like night was due. The sounds, the atmosphere, all of it followed, giving the illusion, powerfully, that we were on an island with night falling all around us. It was beautiful, if you let go and believed it.

And part of me wanted to.

I could believe, I guess, if I pushed myself, that I was just having a romantic evening with someone I cared about. It didn't have to be the love of my life. Maybe just a friend I liked. And, as I had said, Per was not unattractive or unkind. In the ordinary progression of a reasonable universe, I could imagine us being friends, maybe even intimate ones.

I thought about Paul, my friend from college. If things had been different, if HE had been different, we might have had that kind of relationship. I imagined what might have happened if he had flirted with me on the ride back from that night at Pole Katz. If he had laughed and had fun and been at least a little turned on, telling me how much he enjoyed watching me. If he had treated me like a woman and a friend and someone valuable, not just some kind of failed wife in training who had just let him down. We might have cuddled on the way back. We might have kissed in the backseat.

Paul wouldn't have shown up with wine, or bath bombs, or massage oil after that. I was just a stripper, he would have thought, and not worth all that.

But here was Per. laughing with me on the side of the bed, trying to make some kind of game about feeding each other wine. We couldn't speak but he seemed to look at me imploringly before he did anything, like he was just taking my temperature, trying to see what I liked and wanted. That alone was attractive.

We couldn't talk. At one point, he pulled out his phone and pointed it at a monitor on the wall. It faded to a video of him with friends on some alien planet, hang gliding.

I probably should repeat that because it hit me hard at that moment. He was just showing me a fun playful video of him and his friends having a good time. They fell more than they flew and that was honestly cute and kind of endearing. He wasn't bragging. He was showing himself vulnerable. He was a goof.

But he was on another planet.

Up until then I hadn't really seen footage of real people on an alien planet. I hadn't even really processed what an alien planet might be like. This one was presumably IO. The way they walked, the efforts they put into hang gliding, you could tell the gravity was more intense. The gravity on IO was more than 1.7 times earth and it seemed visible in the video. At one point, one of them dropped a wrench and it seemed to suck itself to the ground comically.

They were dressed in parkas. They may have dramatically terraformed it, but my guess was it was still on the cold side. And, looking over their shoulders, the curve of the planet was even more visible than on earth. IO was about ¼ the diameter of earth and it seemed that in the clear air you could visualize that.

The video was fascinating to me, but not for the reasons Per may have thought. He shrugged at me, acknowledging his ineptness at flight, but he and his friends looked to be having fun. In fact, they looked to all the world like big, rich kids just enjoying being able to fly around and party on different planets.

I laughed. The video was doing its job. If I was afraid of him before I certainly wasn't now. I finished my glass of wine and looked at Per. He shrugged at me, admitting he was no great athlete. I leaned against him. That admission had bought him a surprising amount of good will from me.

We drank and laughed a little. I pulled away to set my glass down. He nodded to the bath bombs and I got up. I was clean enough, for sure, but if he wanted to see me take a bath I had no problem with it. I reached out for his hand and he made a big motion of getting up and grabbing the bath bombs.

It was funny.

We walked in the bathroom and he maneuvered me against the sink. He made a point to sit me on the sink and lean in. He put his face close to mine and turned his head a tiny bit, as if asking for a kiss. I closed my eyes a bit and leaned in, pressing my lips against his and opening them just a little, softly.

He kissed me for a few minutes and then leaned back without looking to start the bath. I laughed at his efforts to start the bath while maintaining eye contact but he did it. I knew it wouldn't be hot enough, but it was sweet.

The tub filled up quickly, as if from multiple sources, and he looked at me again, his hands on the lapel of my robe. I lifted my head and smiled and he opened my robe, pulling it aside and off my shoulders. He was gentle and each time he moved forward a bit he seemed to want my full assent. And each time he did that, I trusted him a tiny bit more.

I slid off the sink and let my robe drop to the floor. He put his hands on my ass now and kissed me deeply. I thought about Paul and wished he'd done this. I thought about Leo. I thought about other men who had the green light from me when I was younger and never took it.

And then I thought about Per and what he was doing to help me. I considered the money and stepped into the bath. With my left foot I reached up and turned off the cold water. He looked at me with a smile as though I had just now decided to live dangerously. We laughed.

He pulled out a blue bath bomb and placed it delicately under the water. More quickly that I thought possible, the water began to shift and stain in deep, resonant shades of blue. I looked down and ran my hand through it.

It looked like a million different blues, each a concentric wave, a rounded current that lapped at me, cyan, sapphire, azure, cornflower, water, blue.

My skin felt tingly and alive. Somehow it felt blue.

It resonated in a frequency that felt blue.

He leaned in and kissed me, cupping my breasts.

He washed me all over.

The lights in the bathroom were following the ones in the bedroom, dipping, emulating night. As they did, he lifted me and wrapped me in a blanket. He carried me out to the bed and paused for a moment, just about a foot above the bed. Staring into my eyes, he made an elaborate show of dropping me the final few inches onto it.

And, again, we laughed.

This was how I spent my night.

I was being pampered. I was massaged. I was rubbed down. He made me laugh wordlessly with his silly antics and then, about three hours after he had gotten there, he dropped the lights even further and took his own clothes off.

He asked me a few times with his eyes before climbing on top of me. I put my hand on the small of his back and I pulled him inside me.

And that was the last thing I remembered.

It was bright and white when I woke up in a hospital room that looked identical to the one I was in for the procedure.

Now, what I want is to stop this story here and just end it. I want you to figure out what happens next and be done with it. I want to be able to say here that I died in this hospital and that all of it was pointless and dirty and shameful and unnecessary.

I don't want anything more than that.

But I can't. If i don't tell you it just stops. No ending, no possibility, nothing. It's just over and we lose. So I have to do this.

The monitor on the wall next to me read, clearly,

"Patient has had a coronary event."

I yelled out. My arm was in the groove on the side of the bed again, strapped in. But i wasn't able to extricate it this time. Had I had a heart attack? I had no history of heart attacks. In desperation I spoke to the monitor.

"I had a heart attack?"

The monitor flashed. Up until now it hadn't occurred to me that the monitors would respond to a question.

This one did. It flashed:

"Yes"

I tried to pull my arm out. This wasn't possible. I had a heart attack during sex?

I asked the monitor if I had had a heart attack during sex. It read:

"After."

That meant that I was missing some time. I don't even remember sex. There was an after. And sometime during that after, I had a heart attack. None of it seemed reasonable. More likely, I was drugged. I asked that:

"Was I drugged?"

The monitor flashed, in an annoyingly elliptical way. It just read:

"No"

I looked around for my phone. The false windows in the room made it look like morning, but I had no idea what time it was. Julie was leaving today. I said out loud, "Julie."

The monitor flashed.

"Your friend has left."

The world closed in on me. I couldn't breathe. The room seemed impossibly bright suddenly andI closed my eyes to ward off the glare.

"Can you speak?"

A plain female voice responded. "Yes"

"This is really important. What day is it?"

The computer seemed to pause for a moment.

"Please wait for an attendant."

There was no reason not to just tell me if it wasn't bad. I tried to regulate my breathing. I looked down and saw, on my left wrist, a tiny "X" with a 2 centimeter or so radius. I tried to touch it with my right hand but my arm was still strapped in. I told the computer to let me go and it did. It loosened the straps enough so that I could reach. I could feel them tightening again, thought, in slow increments.

The small x looked like a scar. It looked like a healed up scar, which was crazy. I didn't have it yesterday. I asked again.

What day is it?

The computer paused again.

"Please wait for an attendant."

I started yelling. I heard some movement at the door and I expected a doctor.

Instead, it was David Midland Kelto. The man from the elevator. This was so stunningly unexpected that I imagined for a moment that I must still be asleep.

He introduced himself to me and it felt surreal. I had half imagined that he was an AI generated video clip. But here he was. I'm going to try to recall his exact words.

"Ms. Cadeza, I wanted to talk to you in person because there has been a health issue that has had an unexpected impact on your welfare here and we need to loop you in."

He honestly said "loop you in."

I asked him what day it was.

He sat down on the edge of the bed and looked concerned.

It was June 18th.

I'd been out for four days. I'd missed Julie's flight. I missed seeing her. I'd missed taking her there and the last time I'd hugged her was the last time. I fucked everything up. She was so scared and I fucked it up. I was bathing and laughing and having wine and I fucked it up for her.

I'd missed her.

Water welled up in my eyes. Ithad and Jen must be freaking out. I looked at him and said "My kids."

David Midland Kelto pressed a button on the side of the bed and I felt a tiny sting in my arm. He was sedating me. He leaned in to look at my eyes. I told him to stop.

I said it again, more clearly. At least I tried to.

"I have to get to my kids."

The sedative was washing through my bloodstream. It was hard now to sit upright. I tried to lift my head to look at David Midland Kelto. I couldn't. I wobbled back and forth in bed.

"Your son, Ithad Cadeza, his friends Jennifer Han, Malcolm Grace, and Latia Grace died two days ago during a test flight of the undocumented passenger ship, the Huimang, at Modelo spaceport. His remains have been processed and will be delivered to you here."

The room shot through with colors as though I had been hit on the side of the head. A four hundred pound blanket descended on me and kept dropping, crushing my head and neck. I looked at him and screeched and reached out, tearing the straps on the side of the bed.

I screamed and I kept screaming until the blanket fell all the way down and I went back to the dark like a dead animal.

The two boxes they left near the wall under the monitor in the hospital room represented everything I owned. Apparently once the apartment was left unattended for a day or two the furniture was taken by other tenants, including the tiny black rug and table.

The monitor had proven to be more helpful than I had thought originally as I asked it to run through various current events, including the ones most relevant in my life. I saw footage of the Euripides taking off. It went smoothly, without incident, and the ship was well on its way to its destination.

I asked for security footage from the spaceport and all information about the test flight that had killed my family. It looked like it had gone smoothly. But something happened when the ship hit apogee, when it reached its highest point. There was a subtle glow and it exploded.

It didn't look like a malfunction. Nothing I researched could tell me what it was. I looked everywhere, through all the information that the monitor device could find.

Nothing.

The monitor was also able to show me footage from the room I was in the night I had my heart attack. It was strange seeing myself having sex, even sharing a glass of wine afterward with Per, things I just did not remember happening. The footage shut off once he left, kissing me goodbye. I asked the monitor and was told that, for privacy reasons, only overnight rooms that currently held customers were recorded.

I didn't believe that was true.

There was no possible way that this place cared about my privacy. I refused to respect that answer. In fact, I was positive that they were recording me even then, sitting in a hospital room.

Then, out of nowhere, I remembered something that the monitor had flashed at me in this room. It said:

"Your friend has left."

But did it know that Julie was flying the day after? How could it.

I asked the monitor to display footage of this room, from when I had any visitors.

After a pause, it showed me Julie, sitting at my bedside. She had come, before she took off. She knew I was in here.

She must have wanted to not tell the kids so as to not worry them.

But she was there.

I watched her sit by my bedside. She held my hand.

She kissed it.

She sat there for hours. And then, right before she left, something happened

She looked down at my left wrist and made an "x" motion. She looked upward, at the camera toward the top of the bed. She pulled her sleeve up and pushed her hand upward. She leaned over the bed.

And that's when I saw it.

On her left wrist was a tiny 2 cm "x" exactly the same as mine.

I jumped up from the bed.

On the monitor, she looked around, scared. She kissed me on the forehead and left.

She knew.

I pulled my clothes off in the bathroom. I asked the monitor to turn the lights up as brightly as possible as I tried to examine my body for any proof of what had happened. The tiny dot from the procedure Ii had last time was still there. It was slight and difficult to see. If I didn't know it was there I almost would have missed it.

There were a series of pinpricks and dots of blood all along my right arm as though I had had blood drawn and injections while I was out. That made sense. I assumed that was what the groove in the bed was for. None of that seemed excessive or out of place.

The two centimeter cross on my left inner wrist was still visible barely. At first it looked like a tiny cross cut like someone might execute if they were trying to kill themselves. But it was clean, perfect. Booth axes were exactly the same length and it was perfectly aligned with the line of my arm. One 2 cm line up and down, one 2 cm line across.

It looked exactly like the one that Julie showed me on the monitor.

I racked my brain for anything that could have left a mark like that and I could think of nothing. The feeling of not being able to generate a solution for a technology problem was becoming annoyingly common to me.

I was a science writer. I was a fact checker.

I was invested in science. It was my field. And yet, everything I was coming into contact with was beyond me. I felt like an ape in the middle of a modern science fare, too busy dumpling around to understand any of it.

I had been in the hospital for days now and I had endured a lot of tests. No one else had been in to see me. No doctor or nurse. The monitor told me everything I needed to do.

Put my arm here.

Stand here.

Look into this.

I started going through the boxes. Every time I picked up something I laid back down and cried. I didn't know what was going to happen to me and I really didn't care.

I was on autopilot. In the box was the round alien painting that Jen had made - one of the only things that had survived the old apartment. It was smaller than I remembered, light, bright.

It was impossibly cheery looking.

My gut hurt as I rolled over in bed.

I dreaded the morning, where I would wake up and forget, for a few seconds, that they were gone.

I might smile accidentally, unaware until it washed over me. I might feel human without any reason to or have hope pointlessly. I was afraid of remembering but twice as afraid that I would forget for a minute, a second, and then it would be like they died again.

All over again.

I kept that circular piece of wood next to me in bed. I stared at the tiny figures and burned it into my brain. I let the sharp edges of it send splinters into my hands like the stingers of living bees all around the frame of it, punishing me. I wanted it to hurt me and I wanted it to outlive me.

And when I was able to breathe I would turn it over and read the inscription on the back. I know it was written for me. It was a quote that I had taught them. It was from when I believed I knew anything. A quote by Nietzsche. And it laughed at me and made me feel small, but at the same time, it gave me a tiny board to cling to in the current.

It was in Jen's handwriting. I could almost read it with my fingers.

"We have art in order not to perish of the truth."

I wished I had a thicker pen, darker ink, something to give her so she could have made that inscription enduring, powerful, as relentlessly permanent as the pain that ate away at me.

It was true, but soon it would fade away.

Like everything I had and everything I ever loved.

Like me.

Three days later I woke up to a flashing word on the monitor. It read, simply:

"Discharged"

My phone was sitting next to the bed now, fully charged. I looked through it. There were about a hundred messages from Julie, Ithad, and Jen. Text Messages, audio messages, hundreds.

I looked at the last ones. Over the next few days I would read all of these, listen to all of these over and over again.

But today I read the last ones.

They loved me. Completely. Like I loved them. I could see it in every word.

I pushed the room to be more expressive.

"So, I can leave?"

"Yes."

"Where do I go?"

The monitor showed a room. I squinted. It didn't seem familiar.

My phone buzzed. I looked through the notifications and I saw that I had been assigned a room. It included information on how to get there and a code for the door. My effects, it claimed, had been moved there.

I panicked for a moment and looked around. The boxes were gone. I felt unsteady. I was afraid for the boxes. What if they lost them?

I looked down at the message and read it over again. This was the first time I saw a number attached to a level that might have actually been REAL.

I had an apartment at the MekaDisko thirty-three levels below the main basement level.

That's at least 500 feet underground.

So how far down was I now?

I followed the instructions to the elevator area and then entered the appropriate codes. I had to manually enter the thirty third sublevel which meant there was no way to know how many other levels there were.

I had no idea if this was really going down thirty three levels. Maybe that was a euphemism or some kind of conceit meant to hide the real organization of the place. The secrecy felt military to me, for a facility dedicated to pleasure and hedonism, they acted like there were universe-shaking military secrets at stake.

The lift left me off in an unfamiliar area where the ceilings were high and sweeping. It occurred to me that they were substantially taller than fifteen feet. And the materials in between the floors had to be thick to sustain the added weight of so many levels. This added to the idea that many levels might be even taller and that some levels might be hidden, only used for administrative purposes, and I realized I could be down far deeper than five hundred feet. I doubled that in my head.

I should maybe triple it.

What I could see immediately of the apartment was a single room, about twenty two feet long by twelve feet wide. Recent experiences suggested I explore that a bit before making that decision though.

There was a giant monitor that took up one whole wall, nearly 12 feet square. It showed a generic waterfall. If I stood there for too long, though, I could feel where the loop began and ended. And every once in a while, it glitched. It still seemed preferable to a blank wall.

To the right of it, along the right wall, was a slight round indentation. I pressed it and a functional bathroom space appeared, with a shower and toilet. I hadn't expected a bathtub or anything, but it was larger than I had anticipated.

There were cabinets recessed in the wall. And a refrigerator and stove also recessed and available. This seemed to be the model for most spaces across the MekaDisko, a sort of Japanese minimalism with recessed amenities.

I pressed the large rectangle on the rightmost side and it rose up, a bed from the floor. It was well padded and austere but perfectly comfortable. A smaller monitor on the left wall encouraged me to download the MekaDisko apartment plus app and use it to manage all my needs.

I looked through the rental agreement and tried to read it. It went on in excruciating detail. It outlined that a certain number of work hours would be required from me per month to cover the apartment itself. It said that if my work model fell below tier three for 2 months straight I would be assigned a smaller apartment. This meant that, to stay here, I had to be a tier one, two or three worker.

This was an apartment only for people willing to get naked.

I sighed and signed with my thumb. I didn't care anymore.

My phone alerted me to choose where I would dance tomorrow. I didn't want to go back to anywhere I had been with Julie, so I chose a place called Hyperion. It looked attractive and upper class.

I tried to let the million things going through my brain take priority over the million things going through my heart. But I was failing, every minute. I looked around the room that looked so high tech and foreign to me.

I used to be a science writer. I used to be a mother. I wasn't anything anymore.

I stopped trying to wipe away tears and fell asleep in the corner.

I followed the instructions to Hyperion the next morning. The costume that was left for me in my locker was a kind of chain mail sheer thing. It didn't look like it would give me many options to remove pieces which would have made me sad before. I knew by experience that the tips came from people seated around you when you pulled off clothing.

But I didn't really care anymore. I had no reason to amass money anymore. I was mostly dead, just moving around because I had to. I wasn't tired when I went to bed and I wasn't refreshed when I woke up. I just was.

I figured I could dance at different clubs every night until it ended somehow. I didn't know anyone and they didn't expect or know me. I was pretty sure Per had returned home but I couldn't have seen him again, in any way.

I went through the motions and danced that night.

Hyperion was supposed to be a kind of meeting of Greek champions, a decadent throwback to the time of the gods, temple slaves, heroes, etc. Men and women, half naked and fully naked wrestled in the center of the space, a giant rotunda where the bars were mostly at the edges. The closer you got to the entrance, the rowdier it got.

I moved around and danced a little, positioning myself mostly on platforms and miniature stages around the space. I saw another woman, dark, long black hair like myself and I took the stage opposite her, mirroring her as best I could. I thought it would look pretty, an interesting display for people who consider the aesthetics of such things.

And apparently it worked. The woman looked at me and understood what I was doing. She started to slow down a bit and we became like matching dolls on either side of a playroom, dancing symmetrically, pulling off clothing at the same time, making sexy gestures, touching ourselves.

By the end of the night, the other woman had come up to me and given me a big hug. This was her best night for tips and she didn't even have to touch anyone. I learned that her name was Yolanda and that she had been here just a little bit longer than I and had only ever danced here.

I agreed to come back to Hyperion sometime and tried to be friendly. I'm sure I came off as distant and unkind and I felt terrible about that. Nothing was her fault.

I had hundreds of dollars in tips and I realized that there was no place for me to send that money. There was no good that would come from it. It wasn't going toward anything.

Not long ago, I had seen a documentary on the Genocide in Rwanda, published online for the 50th anniversary of the event.

I couldn't find the entire thing. The internet has been patchy for a while and it's nearly completely unreliable now. But I remember an interview with a sociologist named Adama Cooper, a young woman who had been interviewing survivors for years. She discovered an eerie symptom.

This genocide had claimed so many children - over a million people in the course of a day or two and almost half were children or teens. Decades later, in her interviews, she found that the parents left behind had to INTENTIONALLY find something to live for or eventually, hopelessly, they would die. As surely as if they had been denied food or water.

They would just die.

It was an epidemic across the country. Organizations arose with causes people could get behind, just, more than anything, to keep people alive.

I knew that what I was doing wasn't good enough to keep me alive in the long term. I would have to find something that made me want to live or I would die. But that was going to take time.

And right now, I wanted the second.

I tried a different club the next day. And a different one after that. I moved around for about a week. No one touched me and I didn't touch anyone. When people flashed a dollar amount on me somewhere in the pale blue numbers, I politely shook my head. I stripped. I remained a tier three worker. But no more than that.

I returned to hyperion about a week later. I was wondering how Yolanda was doing and I saw her in the same spot. She recognized me immediately and motioned to the girl who was across from her to step down. I got up on the stage and we resumed our routine. I realized it was fun. It was good to have an objective, a goal.

I was making her money. It didn't matter that I was being tipped.

That night we danced for hours. I could feel myself sweating and it felt good, in a way, as though the demons were washing away. I couldn't think about anything but the moment, but I knew returning to my room would mean dropping to a hump on the floor and crying. And I was sick of all that time with myself.

I was sick of myself.

I looked over at Yolanda and two men were standing very close to her. They looked to be friendly at first but I could see they were blocking her way. It was also impossible to tip her with them standing directly in the pathway between her and viewers.

I looked around to see if there would be any need for security or any security, for that matter. Some of the other girls looked and then averted their eyes. By the time I realized that no security was coming the two men had their hands on her and were pulling her off the stage.

I stepped down from the opposite stage and moved toward them. They were taking her toward the front of the club. If I couldn't catch up by the time they reached the center it would be hard to follow with the boisterous gladiator fights and outlandishly pumped up spectators.

I looked to my right and saw an opening where I could cut them off. I could see Yolanda through the crowd and she didn't look happy. She was trying not to look scared, I could tell, pleading with them in that way that women have for centuries, trying to remind men that they were fundamentally good and they didn't want to do this.

At this point, I was nearly completely naked and I didn't really have an idea of what I would do if I caught up with them. We were right near the gladiator pit and people were moving quickly. It reminded me of a mosh pit from an old early punk set that you might see on an old movie. They were pulling her toward the exit so I rushed up and grabbed her by the waist and pushed harder.

She came out of their hands and nearly tripped forward. I held onto her and we kept moving faster in a circle around the giant pit. The two men, caught by surprise, had kept moving forward in a straight line and it took them a second to notice she was gone. They turned and started toward us. I pushed Yolanda behind me and told her to run. I took one step toward the man in front of me, close enough to see his darkening scowl and I lifted my hand.

I pushed the butt of my open palm into his throat and he dropped to the ground. The momentum of him rushing forward at me made the blow considerably harder than it should have been.

The two men looked similar enough that they could have been brothers. I took a gamble that knocking one of them down would make the other one stop to help him, at least for long enough for us to get away.

And it paid off. I saw Yolanda up ahead and I grabbed her arm. We looked around and moved toward the locker room. She held onto me in the locker room for about twenty minutes. I arranged her hair and we got dressed. I told her she was done for the night. She nodded enthusiastically.

I walked with her to her apartment. She was on level forty and her place looked exactly the same as mine. She asked me to stay and I came in. We talked for a little bit and then she pulled up the bed and we fell asleep holding hands. She seemed to feel safer when I was there.

She was a sweet girl, only a few years younger than me. But she was whimsical and princess-like and spoke perfect Spanish, something I absolutely did not. I let her teach me some dimly remembered spanish words and realized that, under other circumstances it might have been fun.

She seemed to be following the MekaDisko a little more closely than I had. She tells me it's expanding. She told me that, as of last week, it was the number one employer on the planet. I find it nearly impossible to believe that a nightclub complex is now a bigger employer than Amazon was. What the fuck.

I fell asleep thinking about what might have happened if they had taken her. I thought about the lack of security and the speed with which they had managed to grab her.

But mostly I thought about the curvy red haired girl I had seen in the club, dancing, while I was chasing those men. I thought about how we had made eye contact and about how I recognized her.

And she definitely recognized me.

The next day I went outside. The plan was to look through the old apartment and see if anything had been left behind.

I went outside today, I think it may be the last time for a while. It was 110 degrees out and the people manning the door recommend that no one walk in the sun. The streets are mostly empty.

What did we do to this planet?

I walked down the nine or so blocks from the lift opening to the old place, it felt odd calling it that. We didn't live there for long. And it certainly wasn't something I could enter now. It was hard to tell it apart from the other ruined apartment complexes near it. Just a lot of differently shaped and colored rubble.

I saw a coffee place still open on the way home and looked through my bank balance. I had about two hundred dollars, which was confusing to me. I expected more. I wandered in and grabbed a coffee to go. It was supposed to be iced but they had run out of ice and it was mostly just mildly cool. But it was still good.

I saw a five hundred dollar withdrawal that I didn't recognize. It was from MPS, an acronym I didn't recognize. I looked through my phone to see if I had inadvertently authorized something. In all honesty, I didn't really care. I didn't have too much use for money right now. But this did seem to be something I couldn't just ignore.

Then I saw it, On my phone. A message from MPS:

You have been docked five hundred dollars for assaulting a customer. Please follow the links below to see how MPS handles followup disturbances.

A quick look through the FAQs resulted in an answer.

MPS was MekaDisko Punitive Services. It was a part of the company whose sole responsibility was to punish people who misbehaved.

Here's the thing, though. They didn't "dock me" which would mean reducing my pay. They took money OUT of my account that was already in there. This meant that they could take money from me anytime they wanted.

Any time at all.

The sun was fiery and relentless. It seemed like the heat had sucked all the liquid from the air and my skin started to dry and crack. I moved toward the lift opening and took the elevator back down. I didn't know it at the time, but that would be the last time I was outside for a very very long time.

I felt like I wouldn't miss it.

I went back to Hyperion that night and watched out for Yolanda, making sure she didn't have to pay the price for my "assault" on the creep brothers. Nobody said or did anything. It was a normal evening, much like the first.

Yolanda and I did our matching dances and I could tell she was actually having fun. We mirrored each other perfectly, with her following me sometimes and me following her. It was like an acting exercise I remembered from grade school where we pretended there was a mirror between us- an improv experiment.

It occurred to me that we really did look a bit alike, especially when she wore her hair down like me which she had tonight. I was still a few inches taller and bustier than she, and she was still a few years younger and more girlish. Still, we could have been sisters, too. I got the sense that she liked that.

I kept my eyes open for the girl I had seen before. I almost couldn't believe it was her, and I had started to wonder if she was a figment of my imagination. During my break I wandered around and looked. I tried to avoid the center of the club, which looked to be getting more violent by the minute. I slid my top back on, hoping to garner less attention while I looked. And as It fell over my head I saw her.

Across the room, she was trying to step down from a stage. A man stood in front of her flashing a blue light on her chest, right above her exposed breasts. It read:

$250

She shook her head and he flashed it again, more insistently this time. He moved closer.

She looked at him and smiled awkwardly, shaking her head. I moved toward them as quickly as I could. I pulled my phone out, wishing I could make that flashy number thing work. I said, loudly, over the music

Four Hundred Dollars.

She looked at me and smiled. She nodded with some energy and he turned around to see me. He looked me up and down and tried to figure out what to do before shaking his head and walking away.

She stepped down from the stage and gave me a hug. I ran my fingers through her hair. "It's ok."

I rocked with her slightly. She looked up at me. I was surprised I had managed to recognize her without her glasses. I hugged her again and this time it was for me. I remembered the last time I'd seen her. I whispered.

"Pia."

She hugged me tighter.

"I knew it was you."

I leaned in and whispered to her, with a little lilt to my voice.

"You know I don't have four hundred dollars."

She laughed, her face still wet, and hugged me tighter.

We stayed like that for about five minutes. Then she grabbed my hand. It was hard to hear over the music and yells of the spectators, closer now, in the center of the room.

"Come here."

She took my hand and dragged me to the back of the club. There was a large stage like riser with a set of stairs on either side, curling round two columns. It was huge and majestic and Greek looking. Pia nodded at the person seemingly guarding the stairs. I looked at him with not a little judgment. Where was he a few minutes ago? Where was he yesterday?

We climbed to the top and waited. There was a wide open DJ booth, surrounded by speakers and, right in the center, a blonde woman. She had long hair and a pretty roman nose. She was the very first human DJ I'd seen at a club so far.

Across most of the clubs at the MekaDisko, there were AI DJs, many in true robot form. They peered out over the audience like ancient gargoyles from the cornices of buildings while the music ran uninterrupted all night.

She looked at us and made a quick motion asking us to wait. She faded into another song and took off her headphones.

"That was the second time I've seen you do that"

I wasn't sure what she meant. But then she pointed to the monitors arrayed on the table in front of her. She had visibility across the club. She saw me protect Yolanda and now Pia.

I nodded at her. I wasn't sure exactly where this was going. I'm trying to remember her exact language. I think it may be important.

"Pia says she trusts you more than me, more than anyone here. Why is that?"

I looked at her. She seemed to be someone Pia honestly looked up to. I realized that I trusted Pia, too. And why. I just shrugged and thought:

Because there was someone we both loved.

Pia nodded at me.

The blond woman looked at Pia and made a decision. She walked over toward me and shook my hand. She leaned in and whispered in my ear, just loud enough to be heard over the music,

"I have some things to tell you that could get me killed. Do you want to hear what they are?"

I backed away. This was becoming a bit more serious than I wanted and I was now wondering how long I could spend without dancing before I was "Docked."

I shook my head and she smiled. She leaned in again.

"You don't want to get me killed??

I shook my head, a little more vigorously. She laughed and leaned in one last time.

"Clearly you don't know me well enough yet."

I looked over at Pia. I could tell she wasn't following our conversation.

The woman handed me a piece of paper and Pia and I went back downstairs. I asked her who that was.

Pia whispered in my ear.

"That's Lila."

This close to the speakers, the music was almost maddening. It was hard to hear her. Pia reached into my hand and grabbed the piece of paper and showed it to me. It read:

"Talk where it's loud. Turn your phone off"

I nodded and she started ripping the paper up. She ripped it into about a hundred pieces. As we made our way back to the locker room she dropped a few pieces of the paper into every garbage can we saw, never more than a few in every can.

We went back to the Locker room and I waved to Yolanda. It looked like she'd had a good night. I introduced her to Pia, explaining to her that she was a friend of the family.

I didn't go into any more detail than that.

I got a message the next day with some instructions to meet Lila and Pia. The message didn't make much sense in a literal way, so I began to assume that the idea of levels, in the mekaDisko, was really more figurative.

There was no way that I would be meeting someone one hundred and forty seven floors below the basement.

That was insane. I was constantly revising my idea of how tall a story might be in the facility as well as my idea of how fast a lift could and should travel. I typed the numbers in and the lift kept descending. Ten minutes later It was still descending. Again the spirit of David Midland Kelto appeared to explain how things worked here at the MekaDisko without actually revealing any information I needed.

I studied his face. It did, in fact, seem computer generated. I wonder if what I had met was the real David Midland Kelto.

There was no way to know, really.

By my estimates, by the time the doors opened, I was three thousand feet below the surface of the earth. Again, I found this really hard to process. The rest of what I saw might have been harder.

As soon as the doors opened I could hear the undisciplined racket of construction. All sorts of building machines were at work apparently defining and digging this level out of the solid ground. It was remarkable to look at.

I walked forward and the noise only increased. Lila and Pia were already there. Pia leaned in and whispered for me to turn my phone off, giving me a hug. The three of us started walking past the giant assembly machines.

I wrote in my journal:

> The Giant robots who dig the tunnels leave their dead skeletons behind as the support beams for the new lower rooms. It's an efficient but morbid process. I've seen little sign of intelligence in any of them, although I'm told this entire place runs on artificial intelligence.
>
> Ithad would have known.
>
> He'd have this entire place figured out by now.

We walked for about 20 minutes. Every minute the area around us was less finished, more raw. Finally, we found ourselves in a cave.

Lila spoke

"One of the things about artificial intelligence is that it effectively, in a way solves the carnivore problem.

Decades ago, The FBI started using this software called "Carnivore" which helped them listen in to massive amounts of phone calls and recordings simultaneously. It built a database for them of how people were talking and what they were talking about. But it had a problem. Without a human being to process what people were actually talking about, most of what was in the database was useless."

Pia added,

"You know, slang, sarcasm, metaphor, etc. People don't all talk alike, and many of them are hard to figure out. But AI can. AI can keep running over and over every single sentence, make analogies, draw conclusions, make recommendations."

I was following. The big problem was then that the MekaDisko was always listening. This might have not been a problem way back when nothing could be done with those millions of hours of audio.

But now...

Lila said that she had special dispensation to help scout the floors, as an audio expert. She had helped build some of the audio systems for the clubs. That permission extended to her coming down here where the listening devices were scarce,

But I still didn't understand why.

Lila told me that she wanted to tell me everything and then I could make my own decision. I didn't know, really, what she was talking about.

Pia continued:

"First of all, there was nothing wrong with that ship."

She looked me right in the eye. I felt myself dropping to my knees. I started to cry.

Pia kneeled down in front of me.

"The ship was built perfectly. Ithad flew it perfectly. We watched it. It was flawless. The test was flawless."

Part of me didn't want to hear this. I was supposed to be on that test. Who was in my seat because I didn't go? Latia? Malcolm? Who died because I missed it?

What child did I kill?

"Nothing that happened was your fault. Nothing was his fault. Nothing went wrong. Something destroyed that ship. Virgil and I were in the control center. Right when the ship exploded, the crowd control robots broke in. Do you hear me? At the same time. They accused us of flying an undocumented ship. They killed Virgil and I ran."

I didn't understand. It wasn't illegal to fly, was it?

"Our documents were in order. We did everything right, except…"

Pia looked up at Lila. Lila walked over and sat on the ground next to me.

"They weren't MekaCorp."

Pia tried to look directly in my eyes.

"The robots. They were MekaCorp. They didn't have the police symbol on them"

I held her hand. I wasn't ready for any of this. I didn't realize that Virgil was dead, too. Pia had lost everyone she knew that day. One after another.

I squeezed her hand.

She put out her other hand and flipped it over.

"And I have one of these, too"

I could see on the interior of her left wrist, a tiny scar in the shape of an "x." It was about 2 centimeters in radius.

Exactly like mine.

Lila broke in. She lifted her wrist.

"And I don't. I don't know why. We don't know what it is. None of us do."

I looked at Pia.

"When did you first see it? On your wrist?"

I could tell she had thought about this question and had an easy answer.

"The first week I got here. I checked in. I was tired of running. I didn't know anyone. I slept for I don't know how long. And when I woke up, it was there."

I thought for a second,

"How long were you asleep for?"

Pia wasn't expecting that. She looked at Lila. "I don't know. I didn't know anyone here and I didn't have a phone. I left it in the control room when the robots broke in. I don't know."

Lila looked at me curiously.

"What do you think it is?"

I didn't know. I didn't have any idea. But something was gnawing at me in the back of my head. Something half remembered. I told her I didn't know.

I didn't know anything.

Pia looked so impossibly young kneeling there next to me. She had her glasses on today and that made her look even more vulnerable. I could feel how lost she must have been. She had clung to Lila, it seemed, because Lila seemed to know things.

It occurred to me that I didn't.

I asked Lila who the president was. She laughed a little and shrugged. I asked her if there was a pope anymore. I asked her what happened to Brad Pitt. He would be over eighty right now but I hadn't heard that he had died. I asked her about celebrities, musicians and political figures. She didn't seem to know any of that.

So why should I care what she had to say about any of this. She didn't really know any more than I did. I didn't know her. What was she doing to influence this girl? Suddenly I had the instinct to gather up Pia and bring her back to my room and hide her. To keep her there, safe, away from all of this, whatever it was.

She didn't know anything.

Suddenly I was angry. And powerless. And scared. And each would wash over me in waves. And now I felt all three. I looked down at the mark on my wrist. I'd been there for virtually no time at all and I felt like I was closer to figuring this out than Lila was.

And, finally, did I really care about one more person who believed they were in charge. How was she any different from David Midland Kelto, acting like she was running things, with her special dispensation to travel thousands of feet underground to prove what? That all of this was real? I didn't care if it was real. It was toxic and sick and I wanted no part of it. But a deep part of my soul knew, for a fact, that this was where I was going to die and there literally WASN'T anywhere else.

I thought to say all these things to Lila but I didn't. Instead I looked into her face.

Her hair was parted down the middle and it made her face look younger, like a grade school kid. She was my age, around thirty four, but she dressed younger. She walked younger. Her lips were full, offsetting her larger than expected nose, domineering over her face, directing the eye away from her piercing blue eyes.

She looked like a grown up Tolkein character, a magical creature who, eighty years ago, would have gotten a nose job in the summer after freshman year of high school and returned as a homecoming sophomore, looking beautiful but average, classically gorgeous even but bereft of power. She looked like someone who just gave up cheerleading to be a DJ and maybe she did.

She told me her name was Lila Raynard and that she used to be an audio engineer and a project manager but that now she was the leader of the resistance movement to take down the MekaDisko.

I looked at her and laughed.

FIVE

I tried to do some research myself on my phone back in the room. None of my searches for Brad Pitt's current whereabouts revealed anything. Somehow we'd gone from a people who lived and died on the every movement of celebrities to an entire culture completely unaware of where even the most famous ones had gone.

Without getting out of bed, I called out to the monitor on the wall. All of this felt silly, but it also felt like, somehow, it was important.

"Can you speak?"

There was a pause. I think this was the delay during which the monitor determined that I was alone in the room so that the inquiry had to be directed at it.

At her.

A vaguely aspect-less feminine voice answered simply

"Yes"

I thought for a moment. I was about 40% sure that any search I did on my phone was something accessible to the MekaCorp people. But I was 100% sure that anything directed to the monitor was. I still hadn't considered what I felt comfortable revealing and what I didn't. I ran it through my filter.

"Where did Brad Pitt Go?"

The voice answered without a pause

"Mr. Pitt was never here"

That wasn't true. I had grown up with his movies. I remembered watching Fight Club in grade school and snickering at the dirty parts. He was my favorite classical actor.

"Not in this room. On Earth. Is Brad Pit still on Earth?"

"Dr. William Bradley Pitt is a North American actor, film producer and speaker. He is the recipient of various awards and accolades, including three Academy Awards, four British Academy Film Awards, three Golden Globe Awards, a Primetime Emmy Award, and an Honorary Doctorate from Yale University for his early work on food insecurity in Africa. After leaving Earth to join the IO project colony, he returned to marry musician Erani Kim in 2040. He is a current resident of The Tantalus Colony."

Well. That was more information than I needed. what hope had we now, when even the guy from Inglorious Basterds was gone? And his first name wasn't even Brad? I felt a tiny bit bamboozled, not going to lie.

"Who is the president?"

"The president of MekaCorp is longtime businessman and founder Stephen Kelto, fifty seven years old. Mr Kelto still enjoys skiing and hiking and runs the corporation remotely from his estate on the Cancri Exocolony."

That was worth remembering. There was a lot of information there to unpack, even if it wasn't the question I asked. I caught that name. Was David Midland Kelto his son? I promised myself to keep that query for another day.

"I meant the president of the United States. Who is that? "

there was a long pause.

"The last official president of the United States was John William Eagleton, who took office in 2036."

I tried to parse that in my head.

That was some ten years ago. Who was president now?

I moved to the wall to access the refrigerator. I pulled out some coffee and started heating it up. this was not the optimum way to make coffee but that wasn't today's lion to tame. I sat down to drink and considered something.

"hey. What do I call you?"

"You can rename the room assistant to anything you find convenient. "

"But what were you called before I got here?"

"this program instance was initiated when you walked in here for the first time "

I thought for a minute.

" I want to call you Persephone."

" if i may, you might enjoy something with fewer syllables "

" oh, and Persephone?"

" yes?"

" Happy belated birthday."

I drank bad coffee and thought for a bit.

I wondered how big this place was.

It had been about a week since my conversation with Lila and I had tried to put it out of my mind. I felt like I might have been entering the manic phase of my grief. My old life was hard but filled with precious things, people who were important to me.

My new life was simple and filled with nothing. I had nothing really to lose.If I exploded tomorrow I felt like it wouldn't be much of a loss. I had nothing to cling to, no reason, really, to be awake at all except to dance occasionally for strangers.

Because I had done tier one work I was given a lot of free time. I knew that wouldn't last forever. I texted Pia and told her to have a good day.

I had a few hours free so I explored.

I walked down the hallway. The hallways were huge and there were monitors arrayed across them that emulated the outdoors, scattered liberally down their expanse. They put a lot of effort into making sure that mornings felt like morning. My guess is that the expense was justified making sure that employees were on time and didn't miss important interactions with customers.

Our time was meaningless, but theirs was priceless.

There were women jogging up and down the corridor. Here and there were the occasional man. This level, I think, was for entertainers and that was mostly women. Some of the clubs had male entertainers. Some even catered to gay men, to women, to couples, etc. But the majority of the entertainment here was provided by women, most younger than I.

I was wearing a pair of shorts and a t-shirt so I picked up the pace and jogged along. I would be noticed less if I did that. I went into the fourth lift I found. I didn't want to experiment right near my room, in case this was not something permitted.

I had no idea what was permitted.

I slipped inside. I was alone. This lift was one of the smaller ones. There was no indication, inside, that I was on the thirty third level or that this particular lift had a number or designation at all. I waved my hand over the right side of the door openings, like we had done every time, and typed in the ground floor.

The lift took its time while the walls came to life around me. The agenda, it seemed, this week, was to convince me to get all my friends to come work here. Ha. The joke's on you, creepy wall-covering AI advertising panel, all my friends already worked here.

All two and a half of them.

The doors opened and I saw the ground floor entrance. So this lift connected to that.

That was good to know.

I typed in the location of the crown and reached for the execute button.

This wasn't a physical button, but instead a graphic drawn on the screen, along with the other input buttons. The "execute" graphic, a universally salient green circle with a check mark in it, sat in a space that was just right of the "cancel" graphic, an equally scrutable red circle with an "x" in the center.

I lifted my wrist and placed it near the "x" in the cancel button. They weren't similar.

Sometimes an "x" is just an "x"

There were three dots under the buttons. I pressed that instead.

Under the graphics were a series of unlabeled buttons. I recognized one - a green circle with a clock face in it and a check - as a likely symbol for "timed execute."

I pressed it. I was presented with an interface that let me enter hours, minutes, and seconds. I chose 1 minute and then the green button.

The doors closed. A counter appeared on the wall and counted down from 60 seconds. As it got closer, the lights in the room flashed, ensuring I couldn't miss the last ten seconds.

As soon as it hit "00:00:00" the lift began to move. That was an interesting experiment, but certainly not of too much value.

The doors opened on the crown. There were banks of elevator lifts to both sides of me. It was becoming clear that these lifts moved laterally, too, as well as up and down. I sort of knew that. That wasn't what I was investigating.

I typed in "level 120". It asked me for a resident code. I canceled.

Ok, that made it sound like there was a level 120 and it was reserved for people living there, for residents.

I typed in "level 145" and it asked me to type in the work order or worker ID. I thought about going through my phone to find the one Lila gave me before but I thought better of it. I didn't need to rope her into this.

145 was construction. That made sense. That was about the same as where I'd been before.

I typed in "level 180". The message on the wall said, merely, "RESTRICTED." The lights turned red and I quickly canceled that.

I thought for a second and typed in "level 300" and saw a simple "not found" on the wall in front of me. That sounded very much like there was no level 300, but there was a level 180 and it was restricted.

As I stepped out of the lift, back on my floor I felt a buzz on my phone. MPS had removed one hundred dollars from my account for "unauthorized use of equipment."

That was quick.

I could see how this worked. No one told you what you could and couldn't do. But once you did something wrong, they immediately fined you.

It started to look like figuring things out would be costly.

Lila had said she would tell me things.

I texted her to take her up on her offer.

Lila was working at a club called the NoZone. I wasn't working for a few hours so I went to talk to her.

The NoZone was a brutal, black and white club full of extremes. People in elaborate leather and chain metal costumes tied and beat fully nude people covered in bruises and slashes from the impact of whips and floggers.

The music was harsh and non melodic, beat and noise heavy with regular thuds and squeals masquerading as instruments and deep, resonant bass throughout. It was coarse and ugly and different than the Hyperion or any of the other clubs I'd been to.

I looked around the room and could identify a few of the pieces of furniture and devices. This was very much a fetish club, built for people with specific desires. The air was filled with sweat and the oily discharge from smoke machines.

To make it to the DJ booth, I had to pass a row of people bent over being flagellated and fisted. The wave of motion was hypnotic and the entire effect was designed, seemingly, to make you feel like you'd entered a demon's lair where torture was an everyday thing. I saw, on the way up the backstairs to the booth, a girl with a short shock of orange hair being sodomized by a steampunk looking piece of machinery while she spoke to a man in a suit in front of her.

Her efforts to make the event seem casual and normal were visible in the facile movements of her hands, pressing down the lapels of his suit and laughing.

Lila was at the top, surrounded by small monitors, facing the elaborate DJ rig. She leaned in to me and whispered, loud enough to be heard over the music:

"First time?"

I nodded. I pulled my phone out and made a show of turning it off before returning it to my pocket. She nodded.

"You aren't really dressed for this place."

"I don't think putting clothes on is the point of this place," I shot back.

For a second, I panicked. "Is Pia here?" I asked, leaning in close to her ear.

She laughed and turned her head, speaking loudly in my ear.

"Are you kidding? I wouldn't let Pia get within two miles of this place."

I suddenly liked her a lot more. She continued:

"But everyone who works here gets Tier One Pay and credit. Just so you know."

"I'll keep that in mind." I filed that information away for later, if ever I needed it.

I waited for her to put on a new song. I figured she would have a minute or two to answer questions. I had a few.

"Why are you so interested in me?"

She looked me up and down. I was just wearing a t-shirt and a pair of jeans. I had never been to one of the MekaDisko clubs dressed like this, like a regular person.

"I think you and I are a lot alike." she pulled away to see the expression on my face.

I shook my head. "I don't think so." But I let it drop.

"How far down does all this go?" I waved my arms and asked.

She leaned in. I don't know. The original brochures said they planned to have over three hundred and fifty levels. Maybe they do."

I shook my head, "No, not that many." She looked at me quizzically and I shared with her my little experiment with the lifts. And that it had cost me one hundred dollars. She looked impressed.

"Maybe I should be asking you the questions." She returned to her DJ rig. I leaned in.

"Maybe."

"Do you want to meet some people"

I thought to myself that I really knew all the people I ever needed to know for the rest of my life and that maybe meeting new ones was a process I never needed to engage in anymore, and maybe in that direction was actual real peace

But what I said was "sure".

Lila had given me her schedule and told me to work later at this club called the Milagro.

Milagro is Spanish for "Miracle" and you can see clearly what they were trying to do. When you walked in, the entire floor was covered in a foot or so of water, shimmering and reflecting waves of blue-green across every wall. There were deeper areas, bars, banks, and even beaches all across the club, which was lit to look like Dusk in an enchanted mermaid-filled Alien/Tuscan village.

There were moons scattered throughout the active video sky, shooting stars, constellations, and flashes of what could only be alien spaceships. The music was trance-like and throbbing, slightly alien but modern and hypnotic. On either side of the club were giant, thirty foot tall waterfalls that sent brilliant blue and white water cascading down into opal pools at the base.

And all over were gorgeous, nude mermaids and mermen, painted to match the fantasy landscape, washing themselves and wallowing in the water. It was beautiful and hedonistic and altogether different than any of the other clubs here I had been to.

In the center of the room was a deeper pool. Every once in a while some fantastical mechanical undersea creature would rise from this pool, creating a grandiose and cinematic scene and spraying water in all directions.

In the locker room, on the way in, I had stripped and walked through the spray device that painted iridescent scales all over me. I was hoping to meet up with Lila but I also had to work. I was originally confused by the spray paint costume but now it was pretty clear.

In my last life, I remember loving the water.

I moved through the club looking around. I saw Lila, sitting nude at the edge of the opal pool under the waterfall with a man who was tattooed nearly all over. Somehow they both looked more comfortable than I in that space. I slid into the pool and swam underwater, letting the room fall away for just a minute. I slowly drifted upward and treaded water, moving slowly toward them.

Lila saw me first.

"Hey, little mermaid. Hey, are we allowed to feed the mermaids?"

The man next to her flashed a wide toothy smile and shot back, "I don't think it's safe. Do you?"

I swam over to them and pulled myself up on the rocks. If it weren't for the music, it might be easy to think we were outside, honestly. "Keep it. I'm not a big fish person, honestly."

Lila looked at me and dropped her legs back in the pool. She had a thick bush of pubic hair and hair under her arms. I was reminded, for a moment, that she was a DJ here and not subject to the grooming rules that the rest of us followed. I looked at the man and he was nearly hairless except for a tiny well-groomed patch of pubic hair. He was a dancer. I thought"

Llorona, you said you wanted information. This is information." she pointed to the man.

He smiled again and shook my hand. "It's Luis, actually."

Lila continued, "Luis is an entertainer here and he does almost exclusively overnights."

"I'm a comfort boy." He looked at me earnestly. I shook his hand. I was curious,

"Can we talk here?"

I waved my hands at the environment around us.

Lila answered, "The combination of the rush of the waterfall, the wet room, the chatter of all these people and the music should drown out anything we have to say. I don't see any AI reconstructing what we are saying. Try to look down when talking and don't be loud."

Lila had fallen into a pattern of looking like she was flirting, intimately, closely, when talking. Talking about things was not as well received here as flirting and talking. I was becoming very aware that the three of us were leaning in closely and talking while naked.

Luis started, "First of all, you're right, there is no level 300 right now. As far as I know, the deepest level is about 240 levels down. At an average of forty feet per level, that's...

I jumped in. "That's not possible." That's close to ten thousand feet underground.

"It is," Luis said. That sounds about right.

I shook my head.

"But that isn't possible. Every 300 feet you go below 100 feet or so underground, the temperature should increase about 5.4 degrees Fahrenheit. It's 55 at about 100 feet, so at ten thousand feet, it's well over two hundred degrees. People would boil."

Luis looked impressed. He hadn't considered that. But it reminded him of something.

"That's what he meant by geothermal."

Lila spoke up. "What who meant?"

I was doing an overnight with this guy from Cancri. He worked on the original plans. He was talking about how his specialty was powering things with geothermal energy."

"Ok, so they are using the heat?"

I thought about it. Cooling the space to be livable would give off even more heat. They had a lot of heat energy to use.

Lila thought out loud, "this makes sense. This facility has been growing so fast. And it seems to have a massive amount of energy to use. Is it all coming from the ground?

They looked at me.

"It could be."

I noticed Pia looking awkward in the other pool, swimming in her iridescent mermaid outfit. I squinted and asked Lila:

"Can she see without her glasses?"

Lila looked over and shook her head.

"Not a damned thing. Poor fishy"

I waved her over.

And then sat, ready to talk to Luis for a while. I imagined I wouldn't make many tips tonight, but that didn't matter.

As I turned back to him, I heard a scream. Across the room, I saw a group of people gathered at the deeper pool in the center of the room. I pushed off from the wall and swam toward the commotion. I had to crawl over the ten feet or so of shallow water between the two pools but then I was able to slide right into the deeper one.

Underwater, I could see how deep this pool went. I realized why the stories had to be averaged at forty feet. I'm sure some were smaller, but this one was nearly twice that. I saw some people treading water and even swimming down a little below the surface. But none could see from my angle.

The deeper pool opened up about thirty feet down into a wider room, filled with water. I could see here that they were storing the fantastical menagerie devices that they could automatically pull from the pool for effect at any time. Stuck on the bottom side of the space was a dark shape. It wouldn't be visible from directly above. I felt my chest burn while I dove deeper and, against all my instincts, tried to reach it.

By the time I had gotten there, I could see it was a body. A woman. I placed my legs on the outcropping, grabbed the arms and pulled. It came free and immediately started to rise to the top. I held on to it and kicked, trying to speed the trip topside until we broke out of the water about ten feet from the side. I saw Luis hand reaching out to pull me onto the shallow platform and I lifted the body face up. Security came running from the front of the club and I listened for a breath.

She wasn't breathing. A security robot pulled me away from the body as I yelled out "She's not breathing." I ran toward it, reaching. The robot held me back and inserted a thin tube down her throat, so quickly I barely had time to register it. I saw her chest rise but realized that it was all mechanical. She was dead.

The robots obscured the area, making sure people couldn't see. She was dressed as a dancer, iridescent mermaid paint and shimmery fabrics. And what I saw, before the robots arrived, something I'm fairly sure no one else did, was the red ring around her neck.

It was exactly like what you might expect if someone had choked her before throwing her in the water.

She was already underwater when I heard that scream.

So who screamed and who killed her?

I met Lila and Luis on the lower levels late that night to go over the footage. Her job let Lila have, basically, access to cameras all over the spaces where she worked. After all, she had to make sure that people were dancing.

We watched it on her phone from a small memory stick, stepping far enough away from the construction robots to listen. By flicking her phone, she was able to change angles.

And there were a lot of angles.

I was hoping one of them would show how this poor girl died. The marks on her made it look intentional. If people who worked there could just be killed, randomly that easily, that was something I needed to know.

After a few minutes of searching, we found it. He was young. He couldn't have been older than twenty. He looked around and waited until no one was watching. Then he choked her, pushing her down under the water. She struggled and then gave up. He turned around. A pink haired mermaid dancer saw him. She screamed.

That's when two men in black suits grabbed her and escorted him out toward the front of the club. Underwater, I had missed all that.

We just watched someone murder another person.

I looked at Lila and tried to read her face. Luis was looking down. I could tell he was hit hard by what he saw.

I couldn't read Lila's face at all.

"You work there. Can you give them this footage? Can you stop this guy?"

"You work there, too. Do you really think anyone will care?" She pulled the little stick out from the port on her phone and put it in her pocket.

"Don't do that," I asked.

"What are you going to do? What can we do?"

I looked at her.

"You hoped something like this was going to happen. Something that would make me want to join your thing."

"No. I didn't. Did I know something like this would happen? Yea, sure. It happens all the time. It happens every fucking day. "

"Why didn't…"

"Why didn't I stop it? How?"

She turned around and started to walk away. Then she came back.

"Let me ask YOU a question. Why are you here?"

"I'm here for the same reason we're all here." I didn't understand.

"No, why are you down here with me - talking to me. You keep diving in and trying to save people and trying to help and then you turn around and act like you just don't give a shit. Which is it?"

"I do. I do give a shit." I could feel myself falling apart a bit.

"Then why not act like it. Why not do something about it? If you give a shit, really give a shit."

I could tell Luis wanted to put his arm around me. I could see it in the way he was standing.

But there was a longer objective.

"Because it hurts and it sucks and fuck you."

Lila stopped and looked at Luis. "That was literally the worst response I ever heard."

And that's how - for the very first time in my thirty four years of life - I punched someone in the face.

Pia was waiting outside my room when I got back. She still had some of the mermaid paint on her neck and it made me realize so did I. I asked her if there was a mermaid handshake. She told me to give it up because mermaids were lucky to have hands at all. That, I thought, was pretty funny.

We went in and she let down the bed. When the bed was deactivated, you could huddle in the corner of the room against the same wall that contained the monitor. This is where we were relatively sure there were no cameras.

We shrunk against the wall. I asked Persephone to play some fun new vocal music and we talked. She pulled out a bag of tiny memory sticks, each one about the size of a fingernail. I asked her where she had gotten them.

She told me Lila had sent her on a job to collect all the ones from different clubs where someone was killed. Suddenly the bag looked huge.

She said it was dangerous.

Pia parsed through the computer data logs quickly and created a set of visual criteria that seemed to be working. It was about sexual violence that was outstanding in some way. She had used a "Mannequin" - a fake AI persona to query the visual database for all acts of strangulation that seemed to result in a death. She factored out anything that the machines measured as less than thirty three pounds of pressure on the hyoid bone as potentially something that was just play.

This was a bag full of evidence of murder.

What the hell was Lila thinking? I took the bag and put it in my shirt. I stood up and pulled the bed out. I asked Persephone to play a movie for us. I found a couple of drinks in the fridge and some fruit that still had a day or two left in it. I even found a candy bar somewhere,

I pulled Pia over and put my arm around her and we watched movies until she fell asleep.

And, yes, One of them may have been about a mermaid.

The next day, I worked NoZone. I slipped into a rubber Dominatrix costume and walked out of the Locker room directly up to the DJ Booth to see Lila.

She looked over and put on a new song.

"Are you going to hit me again?"

"I might. What are you thinking? You could have gotten her killed! Who knows what cameras caught her or what program can trace her back. Do you even think?"

"Yeah, sometimes I think."

"Well, you didn't this time. She's just a kid. I swear to fucking god if you get her hurt i'm going to hunt you down and strangle and drown YOU in a fucking pool myself."

"She's an adult here."

"No she isn't. I'm a fucking adult here. If you need shit like that done, come to me."

"So you're in?"

I tried to ignore the obvious question. I needed to make my point.

"She's not disposable, clear?"

"You didn't answer my question."

"Tell me you heard."

Lila nodded. For a minute she looked tired. For a minute I felt bad about coming down on her like that. For a minute I was afraid of what was going to come next.

As I turned to walk out, Lila turned to me.

"There is no current president of the United States. The last president, John William Eagleton was an AI fake. After that, there were no new elections. The US government is owned entirely by MekaCorp and run by a guy sitting on a planet almost forty five light years away. There is no illusion anymore. No one's bothering to fake or pretend anymore, There is one company that owns and operates everything and that one company bought the government."

I stopped and thought.

"How do you know that?"

Lila advanced, "I know by attrition. I know by putting the worst case scenario together and testing to see if there is anything that contradicts it. There is nothing. Rich people do what they want. That bag of memory sticks in that box by your bed? There are hundreds of times that many, possibly.

We don't know.

But we do know there isn't anybody on the other side but us. So, yeah, I try to get really smart people to help. Even when they're teenage girls who look like they got their boobs too early and can't see a foot in front of their faces without a fucking pair of cokebottles. And I try to stop the worst of it. And I'm failing

and I need your help."

And there it was again. The version of her I could actually feel for.

The one minus all the bravado and big talk.

The real one, I hoped.

NoZone was a mess. I could see why people were paid for tier one work. It was a night of being groped and fondled and grabbed constantly.

Finally, I asserted my dominance and spent the rest of the night flogging old men against the wall which tore the hell out of my back but it was preferable to being assaulted all night. I made a promise to myself to swing with my left arm more if I ever went back there. It would keep me from feeling so uneven like I did now.

I stayed up all night watching murders on my phone.

There were literally thousands of them from nearly every club in the MekaDisko. I saw a procession of women strangled to death for fun by men who knew they could get away with it. And, scattered throughout, the occasional man who made the mistake of getting too close, being in the wrong place

Being wanted.

It was a depressing and hopeless thing to watch.

I grabbed the original stick from the pocket of the jeans I had worn to meet Lila originally on the lower levels. I clicked to the location when that poor woman was killed in the Milagro. The big difference here between this murder and the others was that there was a very clear witness.

The girl with the pink hair.

Like other dancers that night, she was painted in bright iridescent colors to look like a mermaid. I looked closer at her outfit and saw that she had fins on her arms and legs. When I worked that night, I didn't have any fins. Maybe she was a regular of that club and had access to costumes and accessories us newbies did not. If so, people might actually know her there.

I might be able to find her if I went back there.

I restarted the video and tried to see anything else I might have missed. The killer was nondescript. I doubt I could pick him out of a lineup, honestly. Young. But besides that, nothing unusual or memorable.

I could focus on the girl.

I stood up and checked on the monitor. I looked like someone just doing a little research on Brad Pitt or something. The video kept playing.

When I got back to the bed it was playing a few minutes after the girl in the pink hair had screamed. This was farther along than I had seen before.

I didn't see this part.

Two men escorted her from the room. I hadn't seen that.

No one had seen that.

On the video it looked like it was only a few seconds. They were quick.

I rewound.

They were dressed in black all over with hoods. On the left side of their jackets there were three letters.

MSS

I zoomed in more closely. Could it be MPS? That would make sense. She was being penalized for seeing a customer do something bad. I wouldn't put it past this place.

But it was MSS

I thought I would try something.

I walked over to the monitor.

"Persephone?"

"Yes" she responded immediately.

I took a deep breath. "What is MSS"

"MSS is the most common abbreviation for the word Manuscript in Academic documents. It is also the preferred abbreviation for the degree known as a Master of Social Services in the field of education. In construction, it is a commonplace reference meaning 'movable scaffolding system' and in it is a US Navy hull classification symbol: Minesweeper Special device system."

"Thank you."

I thought about that for a second. That was a lot of information but none that was useful. I put this together delicately, prepared for alarms to go off or worse.

"In the context of the MekaDisko, what is MSS?"

I registered a pause, but, realistically I know there was none.

"MSS is a branch of MekaDisko general employment known as the MekaDisko Sleep Services."

Ok, so that was a weird piece of information. MekaDisko Sleep Services.

So after being traumatized, those men were helping her get a good night's sleep?

That sounded reasonable.

The resistance meets in the lower tunnels where there are no cameras placed yet. Lila is having both our rooms moved to the lower floors to make it easier. I don't know how she does things like that.

She said she would teach me.

Being down here I can feel the weight of all the people who aren't here any longer.

Their ghosts press against the walls.

There were exactly twenty people in the tunnel when we went down there.

Twenty people don't make a revolution, I thought to myself. I didn't say it out loud.

I tried to explain to Lila and Luis while people milled around.

"Her name is Selexi. The pink haired girl. And nobody has seen her since that night"

Lila was fast forwarding and rewinding through the clip

"And she was taken by MSS?"

"MekaDisko Sleep Services"

"Ok, I don't know what that means, but why would one of the AIs TELL you that?"

That's something I had been thinking about for the last day. Why WOULD it?

"I have a theory. I don't think that this place is trying to hide anything from us."

Lilia snorted. "It literally hides EVERYTHING from us."

"No, no, I get that. I don't think it's TRYING to hide anything. I just think it doesn't really bother to tell us anything. I don't think the AIs are programmed to go out of their way to keep anything secret, mostly. It's just not part of their programming to talk to us about things and inform us."

"You got fined for that in the elevator."

"I didn't get fined for finding out information. I got fined for trying to get to places I had no business being."

Lila looked at Luis. He asked.

"So what are Sleep services?"

Pia came up behind me and hugged me. The group had grown to about thirty people. I looked around.

Many of the people there were wearing strange makeup on their face. Lila explained.

"Depending on where you go and what you do, Luis can show you how to make up your face so that the facial recognition software can't identify you."

Luis handed me a small automated makeup stick. I could see the tiny 2 centimeter "x" on his wrist. He had one, too. There was a little scab forming on his. I asked him about it.

"Oh, I scratch it. It itches me a lot. It doesn't itch you?"

I looked at Pia. She had been studying as a nutritionist and was pre-med. She reached out and took his arm.

"He's having a reaction to it."

I was confused, "A reaction to what?"

It was just a scar, wasn't it?

Pia pulled out a little light.

"I think there's something in there."

My hand went to the little "x" on my left wrist. I pressed to see if I could feel anything. I felt like I could now, but I think this was my imagination.

Luis looked concerned, "Can you get it out?"

Pia reached into her pocket. She had a keychain with no keys, but it held a multitool. She opened a tweezers. She looked up at Luis.

"This might hurt a little."

Luis nodded. "Ok"

He said "ok" a couple more times as she explored the area. Finally, louder, he called out, "OK, that hurts a lot."

Pie looked at me. "I can't get it. It's like a kind of dock or something. It's really thin but it's connected to the radial artery. If I pull it out he'll bleed to death."

Lila looked up. "Ok. So you guys have a very thin dock of some sort attached to your radial arteries and if they're removed you die. Good to know."

Here's the thing.

It actually WAS good to know. It was information.

And we needed information.

I realized that went for me, too.

Before we left, I pulled Pia aside and asked:

"Tell me something. About Ithad or Jen, or You or Virgil, Malcolm, Latia, any of you. Something I don't know. A secret, maybe"

She looked up at me and held my hand.

"Jenny and Ith. As soon as we got to Enceladus. They were going to get married. They were going to make you get some stupid civil certificate and officiate and marry them. I told them I would do it but they wanted you."

She looked at my face to make sure I was ok.

"Jenny wanted you."

I held onto her hand tightly, like she was a big red balloon that I didn't want to float away. I tucked her pretty hair behind her ear.

I closed my eyes.

I was at Hyperion that night. I saw Yolanda in her usual spot as soon as I stepped out of the locker room. For a moment I was so grateful that she was such a creature of habit. I needed some reliable things in my life and she was definitely one.

I turned my brain off and danced. We mirrored each other and I felt the buzz with every tip. At this point, the only thing I needed money for was fines when I did something dumb. I laughed a little thinking that the customers were basically reimbursing me for my stupidity.

Yolanda took a break and I moved around the room. I had just put my top back on and I was fascinated, in a way, by the chaos in the center of the club. There were naked men and women wrestling, sweaty, muscled, powerful. There was an energy that was sort of intoxicating. I could understand why people might want to come here.

If I weren't working here, I might want to.

A shorter man came up to me and looked me over. He fished his phone out of his pocket and before I could turn away, flashed blue numbers on my chest:

"$250"

I could see he wanted to take my top off. He seemed harmless and, more to the point, he seemed insistent. He was currently blocking my way.

I nodded and he reached up and expertly undid the clasp in front of my top, letting it fall. I grabbed it before it hit the ground and stood up only to feel his hands on my breasts. I stood there as he massaged my chest and played with my nipples. His technique was nothing to write home about but I could tolerate this for a minute or two.

Until I couldn't.

I felt a sharp pinch and looked down. There was a line of blood running down from my nipple to the bottom of my left breast. The man looked at me and laughed. He held up his pointer finger where he was wearing a ring with a tiny blade on it.

I pushed him backward and he laughed, turning and walking away casually. I held my top to my chest and sprinted back to the locker room.

Back in my room, I saw on my phone that I wasn't paid for that night. I had been "docked" two hundred dollars for pushing a customer.

And another one hundred dollars for cleaning fees to get blood out of the costume.

This place was starting to make sense to me. In a perverse and horrific way.

I laid down and slept.

I dreamed about weddings that I would never see on strange and beautiful planets I would never go to with people I would never touch again.

I dreamed about what I would say officiating a wedding and how people might laugh and clink glasses together and applaud like crazy when I said the words "Husband and Wife" like they were magic words, invocations, spells, not normal simple words that people use every day.

And I just dreamed.

At NoZone, I told Lila what I had learned. Not about the cruel little munchkin man with the blade. My chest was covered in a vinyl top to avoid having that conversation.

But about Yolanda.

"She doesn't have a dock."

We had started to refer to the little "x"s on our left wrists as "docks" from what Pia had said.

Lila leaned in to ask:

"So what's different about her?"

I tried to put my thoughts together.

"The question is what do you and she have in common."

Lila looked at me and considered.

"I'm a DJ. I came in as a contractor. I eventually transitioned to full time. I've worked constantly since then. I worked the same club for almost a year then I started bouncing around." Lila thought a bit to see what else there was about her that was of interest.

I told her what I know of Yolanda.

"Yolanda is a professional dancer. She studied ballet and belly dancing and had been stripping before coming here. She works at, basically, one club and never misses a night."

Lila thought. "So, no similarities?"

"Weeeeell. You both worked primarily in the same club. But then you didn't. The only one I see is that you are both always working. She is and so are you."

"Right. Even when I'm in the lower levels, it's for research and audio planning. I submit reports and I'm on the clock. I'm always on the clock, pretty much."

"So the two of you are always working, no down time, really?"

Lila pulled her phone out and texted.

She asked me, "When you ended up in the hospital, the first time, did you have anything planned after that overnight?

I thought for a minute.

"No. I had nothing on my work schedule. I was planning on seeing how the test flight went and planning after that."

Lila put on a song and held up her finger. One minute. But I saw what she was getting at. It looked like I had down time. The facility didn't see me as having work for a few days.

Lila looked at me. "If I was a massive organization and I had everyone's schedules and I wanted to make sure they worked and I wanted to experiment on someone I would wait until they had some downtime in their schedule.

Luis walked up behind me. He was wearing nothing but a black leather vest and boots. This was NoZone, after all. That was whom she had texted.

Lila asked him

"If workers here were being experimented on in their downtime, who would know about that? Who could we tap for information."

Luis leaned against the edge of the booth and thought for a minute.

"His name is Vakun. He's been working for this place since it started. He runs what they call the biological modeling department. It's his group that gives information to the environmental engineers about what the inhabitants need to survive. He brags to me that nothing happens in biology here without his knowledge."

Lila looked at me.

"Ok, so we talk to this guy. How do we do that?"

Luis put his head down.

"You aren't going to like it."

The next day was a long one. But much of it was spent swimming around like a mermaid at Milagro waiting to talk to someone who knew where Selexi was.

I had had no luck finding her, despite the fact that people told me she worked there every day.

I spent more time underwater than I needed to, enjoying the relative silence. If I could figure this out, I was thinking I might make this my regular place to be, just floating around half naked, painted like a mermaid, being tipped by random strangers without hidden tiny knives until I eventually drowned and sank to the bottom of the giant pool in the center like some bloated piece of flotsam thrown off the side of a schooner.

That actually didn't sound bad.

I was sitting by the waterfall, about to give up when Selexi came to sit by me.

"You are looking for me"

I looked at her and saw her beam a little smile my way. She looked surprisingly chipper.

"Yes, I am."

I reached my hand out

"I'm Llorona. I was the one who fished out that girl."

"Oh." She looked a little confused. I had a sinking feeling it was going to get worse.

"You saw her get hurt." I tried to choose my words carefully to be as tame as possible. She struck me as a gazelle - pretty and happy, but easily spooked.

"Excuse me?"

"Here. You saw her go under."

She smiled at me. "You're probably looking for someone else."

"No" I reached out. I didn't want to scare her. "It was you. You don't remember me at all?"

"No. They just said you were looking for me."

"Do you remember being here when that girl died?"

"I don't know anything about that. Are you sure you have the right pink-haired girl?" She laughed.

And that sort of cemented it for me. It was her. Her face was burnt into my brain on that tape. And she was really traumatized. But here she was laughing and joking about it. Which meant one thing.

It WAS her.

But she didn't remember it.

I dove underwater and tried to stay there as long as I could.

What was I doing?

Was I just following up on all of this to keep myself occupied? Was I just trying not to think about my life or anything connected to it, the people I'd lost, anything?

Maybe Lila was right. Maybe I didn't care and all of this was like a video game with bright lights and noise and rules and structure and points and mysteries that I could lose myself in so I didn't just go back to my room and rip out this dock in my arm and bleed to death on the floor.

I tried to feel around. Did I actually give a shit about that girl who died? I don't know. But I imagined Yolanda in her place and suddenly I cared very much. I imagined Pia and I cared more than anything. Anyone could have been strangled and dropped into this pool and been trapped, lifeless, under that ridge.

I didn't know the name of that girl I fished out. That made me feel queasy and stupid. But I knew Selexi's name and suddenly I panicked thinking that someone might hurt her just because they saw her talking to me and I was constantly doing something stupid.

So then I did that thing that people have been doing pointlessly throughout time. I promised myself I'd stop doing stupid things.

Right after this next thing.

I met Luis that night at an apartment on the 94th level. This was just one level down from the new apartment that Lila had gotten for me.

Somehow she was able to manipulate the accommodations so that all of us, myself, Pia, Luis, were on the same floor. It was closer to the lower tunnels and took less time to get there.

My room was a tiny bit bigger, again, exclusively for tier three workers and above. I had been working at NoZone a lot to talk with Lila so I qualified. Luis had been doing overnights - tier one work - and Pia was dancing at Hyperion doing tier three work. I wasn't happy about her working there but she promised me she'd stay away from the center.

Lila was trying to get Pia a job as a nurse, which would help her - and us - quite a bit. But it was taking time.

Our room for the night was big. More spacious than the one I had spent the night with Per in. It still had the bright, wide open monitors all around posing as windows, but it had multiple rooms, open spaces. There was a shower right in the center of the room that was made to look like the opening of a waterfall.

Luis and I talked a bit about what was about to happen with Vakun. He had spent nights with him before. Vakun was older and very visual. He liked to touch and watch and order him around. He had talked to Luis before about wanting to bring a woman to their next date so there was an easy opening for Luis to recommend me.

He told me about the things that Vakun liked and what he didn't. He liked enthusiasm. He didn't like people ignoring him or saying no. He liked to watch people having fun. He didn't like to see people who didn't want to be there. He liked to feel like a puppetmaster.

He liked to feel like god.

And the more he felt that way the more he'd talk.

We shared safe words. I told him that anytime I said the word "Sugar" that things were ok. If I said the word "silly" it meant that I couldn't do it, no matter what it was.

Luis was worried about me and I could tell this whole thing made him feel awkward.

He was also bisexual, but most of his experiences were with men. A good number of them had been here, in rooms like this, with men who, like Vakun, just wanted to feel like god for a little while before returning to whatever life they came from. He knew what this would be like.

My only other overnight was with Per and that was sort of soft and even a little sweet. He seemed like a good person.

The room was right next to the lift, which Luis said was important. I wasn't sure what he had on his mind, but part of me didn't want to know at all.

We both took showers, mine scalding, as usual.

We turned down the lighting in the room to make it look like a rainforest at Dusk.

And we waited.

Vakun showed up about an hour and a half after we did. He let himself in without preamble. He stood there, right past the doorway and looked at the two of us, sitting on the bed.

He seemed to approve. Luis had told me that he liked latin men and women. Vakun's face told me that we were just his type.

He was about sixty years old, white hair thin on top. He wore big, bold glasses and walked with a slight limp. He had an accent I couldn't place, possibly from some eastern European country. And his black pants and white shirt suggested to me that most of his wardrobe would be equally monotone if examined.

He didn't seem like a kind man, but he put on his best front. Luis asked him if he wanted him to explain to me.

Vakun seemed amused and said yes.

Luis looked at me and explained, flirtatiously, that the doctor liked to be called "The Doctor." and that he liked to be obeyed. He enjoyed seeing people do the things they enjoyed because he was a giving person, this doctor. And, if we were good, he would talk to us about what he did. He worked on some very interesting projects throughout his life, especially here.

He paused.

"And I know how interested you are in science."

I felt exposed, raw, explaining to the Doctor what I had done in my previous life. About the publishing company. About editing, writing, all of it. My degrees. My immersion in science.

He seemed to stand upright a bit more. He went on and told me how he had published some papers in books for that very publishing company. And I might even have edited some, written under his full name.

I asked him his full name and he went quiet. Something shifted. His face grew a little darker, more serious. He felt with his foot for a spot on the floor and released a seat, a whitish column that took on the greens and ambers of the room monitors. He gingerly sat down.

"I know you two probably want to take your clothes off."

Luis jumped up and kneeled in front of me. He looked in my eyes and I nodded and ran my hands through his hair. The job here was to act like we would be doing this all anyway. We were to act like this was the fun we were looking for tonight.

He reached in and kissed my belly, right above my belly button. He kissed a little lower then made a point of putting his mouth on the clasp for my jeans. I leaned back on my arms while the clasp came open with a slight pop.

They were very tight jeans.

He put his hands in my waistband and slid my pants down while I lifted my ass from the bed slightly. I was wearing a black thong like Luis suggested, to appease the Doctor and he seemed appeased.

Luis pulled my shirt off and I sat there braless waiting for him to finish. He looked backward for a cue to the Doctor who nodded at him slowly.

He pulled off my panties and folded them slightly, placing them by the bed on the pile of my clothes.

Luis stood up and I slid to the ground, kneeling in front of him. Putting my hands on his ass I rubbed my face against the clasp of his pants, too. There was no way I would be able to undo it with my mouth but I pretended. I lifted his shirt a bit and kissed his stomach as he had mine.

Luis looked to be about thirty, Thin but muscular. I looked at the tattoos on his belly as I lowered his pants. They all seemed to be about cars and car racing. I wondered if that was his passion before he got here or if he just loved the look. I stripped him naked from the waist down and then stood up and removed his shirt.

We had brought some wine and Luis asked the Doctor subserviently if he wanted some. The Doctor wasn't much of a drinker but he responded incredibly well to being asked ANYTHING in a subservient way. Luis made a glass for him and handed it to him, kneeling in front of him.

I kneeled down and crawled over beside him. We were now both kneeling at the Vakun's feet as he sat in the chair.

I tried to feel like a spy. Like a world renowned super spy doing anything I needed to gather information. And we had a list of questions, the answers to any one of which would be useful.

I began to realize why Lila had called Luis "information" when we first met. He was stunningly good at this.

He told the Doctor how much we would love to hear what he was working on. And that all we wanted to do was to make him happy while he did. I was glad that Luis was playing this part. I would find it pretty hard to say some of these things out loud. It was good that I didn't have to.

Luis mentioned that one of the fields of study I was personally the most interested in was the field of sleep, Again, he perked up.

"I could tell you stories about sleep that would amaze you. It's a field that interests me quite a lot. Would you like to hear?"

He looked right at me,. I smiled and nodded.

"I'll tell you what. I can tell you that. As long as I'm not interrupting. I know that you two probably want to fuck. You've never fucked before?"

I nodded and so did Luis. He said that we had never before. This seemed to excite Vakun.

We climbed onto the bed as he started.

We began kissing.

"Sleep has always been fascinating to me. It's really a lynchpin for human health. I remember teaching students about wolf sleep years ago - sleeping for 15 minutes every few hours. Some can do it. Some can't. But it creates, in some, a kind of predatory rage. Something that can be directed."

I held Luis close, listening and kissing him. I opened my mouth for him and rubbed my hands all along his back. We made a good show of touching and grabbing each other, kissing each other. I could hear the doctor go on. The more turned on he got, the more talkative he seemed to get. I made my way down Luis' body and looked up at him. He nodded and I started kissing him between the legs, sucking on him.

This pushed the Doctor even further.

"Sleep is the key to health, to memory, to focus, to everything. And to induce it - is powerful. We forget that sedation, as we effect it through an operation, with medication, is more like a coma than it is like sleep."

The doctor looked at us.

"I don't want to stop you two from fucking."

I said quietly,"no, it's okay. Keep going."

We rolled over and kissed. Luis looked at me in the eyes and whispered.

"Is this silly? Too silly?"

I put my hands on his back and said, "no. it's okay...sugar. It's sugar..."

As he put himself inside me and started moving back and forth, the Doctor got animated. He was clearly very turned on by us actually having sex. I opened my legs wider and let my right leg fall off the bed so he could see better.

"I mean, my god, what you can do is amazing, if you have the right equipment. This place, for all its faults, has the right equipment. I remember the first time I saw it. It was under construction. It was beautiful. But when we moved to seventy seven, that's when everything changed. You don't know what it means to someone like me to have equipment like that."

And there is was. Something we could use. The seventy seventh floor. I tried to show enthusiasm. I put my arms back.

"Are you going to finish, boy?"

Luis looked at me again and I wrapped my hands around my fellow spy and felt him cum inside me. He made a bigger deal out of it than he needed to. And so did I.

I laid there for a minute and realized it was quiet. The Doctor had stopped talking.

I stood up. Luis started putting his clothes on as I saw that the Doctor had fallen off the chair. His glass of wine had fallen upright in his hand, still about one quarter full. I picked it up and smelled it. Luis made a motion.

"Don't Drink that."

He handed me my shirt and I put it on.

Luis was fully dressed now. Apparently he and the Doctor had ended sessions like this before to no ill will. The Doctor assumed he was a lightweight. He wanted to go back and tell Lila about the seventy seventh floor.

I had a better idea.

I went to the lift and typed in level 77. As I suspected, it asked for authorization.

A fingerprint.

If this were a gruesome one hundred year old gritty spy drama I would have cut off the Doctor's hand. Fortunately for my stomach and shirt we didn't need to.

Luis and I went back to the room. We lifted the Doctor and carried him to the Lift. This time, as I pressed level seventy seven, I was able to authorize it with Vakun's unconscious hand. And when the execute graphics blinked, I pressed under them, right on the ellipses.

I saw the options and pressed the timed execute one. I just had to give us about six minutes, And that's all it took us to return the Doctor to the room, make him comfy, and return to the lift. He would wake up tomorrow without incident, assuming he fell asleep while we were, well, having sex.

Luis piled into the elevator with me, now fully dressed.

I expected things to be a bit more awkward between us but I suspect he was feeling the same way, like a spy in a novel about some great war.

The doors opened to a dark space. We stepped out. I set the lift back to the ninety third level and gave us ten minutes,

That would be enough time, I thought.

Lights around the bottom of the floor glowed as we moved through the room, much like the ones I thought I had seen at the hospital. The room was white, as well, again, much like the hospital.

I saw a series of white rounded podes, in a row. I looked at Luis. I had never told him about my experience at the hospital.

I peered into the pods in front of me.

I never told him I had seen something like this before.

They did remind me of the birthing pods I thought I might have imagined that first night in the hospital. They were white with a clear glass faceplate, They were round, but not as round as the birthing pods. And they had room for extremities, for arms and legs.

The birthing pods didn't.

I wanted to throw up. Part of me had thought I was imagining all that. That was a bad nightmare, brought on by the procedure, by being in a strange hospital, the drugs, all of it. But these were clearly designed by the same people.

It happened. The Birthing Pods.

These were lined up in three rows, up and down the room. We didn't have much time before the elevator left. So I tried to take in everything I could, everything that could give us a hint as to what was happening. Not much was obvious, but there were people in here. And why have them all hooked up like this unless they were living people? Were these sleep experiments? What kind?

I felt around on one of the pods and now I could see more clear areas-more glass enclosures exposing what was underneath. It was all understandable. All of it seemed to make sense. And then it didn't.

Then I saw something that turned everything on its head.

On the pod in front of me, a clear area over the left wrist showed a series of tiny tubes attached to the wrist in a "x" formation. It was exactly the kind of thing that would cause a 2 cm diameter x-shaped scar on the inside of someone's wrist. These were attached to the docks. We were in the right place.

If you looked closely you could see blood and chemicals cycling through the tubes. It was moving quickly, The "x" was actually a ton of tiny incisions. And together they made a 2 centimeter diameter mark.

I thought back to Pia's mark. To Luis' mark. And Julie's.

I looked down at my mark.

I stepped back for a second. I saw now what they were doing. These were workers - employees.

In suspended animation.

When it was too expensive to house them or too much work they just put them to sleep. For as long as they wanted. They just turned them off.

Us. They turned us off.

And those of us who showed up here with no one - no family or anything, they experimented on us. They learned how to do it. Once we had free time, once we stopped working long enough.

I didn't have a heart attack, in that room, with Per. And no one drugged me. I fell asleep and was taken and put in suspended animation for four days. It was a test. And the process must have created a kind of sedation amnesia - a retrograde amnesia covering the period of time right before I was placed under. I didn't remember having sex with Per, him leaving, any of that.

I remembered how upset Julie was and how I couldn't find her before work. Was she a test, too?

And that Selexi girl? Did they put her under for a couple of days so she wouldn't remember anything that happened right before?

It wasn't an accident that I was unconscious while my family died. It was some stupid test that they performed on someone they thought no one would miss for a few days.

I could have died with the people I loved like I should have, but the MekaDisko changed all that, for nothing. For some dumb test probably initiated by someone in the finance department.

Just so they didn't have to pay to house people who weren't able to work at the moment.

I thought to myself that this place was going to regret that.

And that's the last thing I remember.

SIX

I woke up in my room to a notification that Per was coming back tomorrow evening and had booked an overnight with me.

The idea that someone could book a session with me like I was some kind of a housecleaner or Dental Hygenist or something and it would go on a calendar without my approval was fucking terrifying.

Persephone had followed me to my new room so I asked:

"Persephone"

"Yes"

"Someone booked an overnight session with me without my approval. Can they do that?"

"Yes"

"Okay, from now on, I need you to go into more detail when you answer a question."

"What sort of detail are you looking for?"

"Like, here, is there any way I can stop someone from just being able to do that."

"You can adjust your work settings to meet the specifics of your needs in various ways. One of them is to require voice approval for all appointments. Currently, the system defaults to automatically approving all appointments from standing customers."

"Ok, how do I do that?"

"I can assist you and make that change if you like"

"Yes, I like. Thank you, Persephone."

"You are welcome."

"And from now on, call me Hotstuff."

"Of course, Hotstuff."

That felt better. I wasn't ready to see anyone like that. I wondered if I could weasel my way out of this. My mind started wandering toward last night and I wondered if Luis had told Lila what we discovered yet.

I reached for my phone and saw that there were two hundred and fourteen messages dating back to the last forty five days.

And I hadn't seen one of them.

How was that possible?

I was forty five days in the future.

I ran to the bathroom and looked in the mirror.

I looked exactly the same. My hair, everything.

"Persephone, before today, how long has it been since I've been here."

"You've been gone for forty five days, seventeen hours, and twenty nine minutes, hotstuff."

I looked down at my wrist.

The two centimeter "X" on my wrist looked red - a little inflamed. It looked like it had been used recently.

"What did I do on the last night I was here?"

"The last time you were here you entered and showered. You read a book for twenty two minutes and then fell asleep."

That sounded like me. But I didn't remember it. I didn't remember anything after the seventy-seventh floor.

"Then what happened to me?"

"You were taken, hotstuff"

In the middle of the night, they came into my room, took me, and put me in one of those pods. And there was nothing I could do to stop it.

Were they punishing me for sneaking around? I realized that I didn't have anything on my schedule for after that overnight with Luis and Vakun. I was booking things day by day so I could be near Lila when needed. I had no long term bookings. Did they freeze me because I wasn't working? And woke me up when I had something on my schedule?

I was suddenly grateful for Per. Without him I would still be sleeping. Who knows how long.

This was the second time they had put me in suspended animation, both times against my will. At least I thought it was. I reached back in my memory for any other lost time and couldn't remember any. But then, something hit me.

I only had a few real connections here. What if they had put all of them to sleep at the same time. Would we know? I thought about Yolanda. She didn't have a dock. So, reasonably, she hadn't been to sleep. Lila, too. So, for now, they were the best arbiters I had that this hadn't happened yet.

I looked closely at my phone interface. Like everyone here, I had switched my service over to MekaCorp so that I could get better reception down here. The interface seemed to have changed recently and I didn't notice.

I wondered how much had happened in the last forty five days.

The date was removed from the main screen. I dug down to the clock app and it was still there. But it wasn't prioritized. And the Calendar didn't have absolute dates anymore, just relative ones. I could see months in the future, but those months weren't named.

The most unnerving thing was that, on my profile on the contact app, my phone number was there, as expected. But it was listed as my ID.

It was now my ID number.

And I was sure there was more I'd missed.

I stepped outside the door and walked the few feet over to Pia's room. I knocked.

Pia opened the door. She jumped out and hugged me

"Oh god, oh god, oh god, no one knew where you were. I thought you were dead."

I patted her hair. It was noticeably longer. She felt slightly different in my arms. But she felt good.

She was 45 days older. Everyone was.

She called Lila and Luis.

Lila's hair was longer, too. And so was Luis'. Two other members of the group were there, too, Jonah, a tall bald black man in his 30s, and Anno, a quiet Heavily tattooed asian woman of about 40, also with a shaved head. We sat in a circle in Pia's room as they stared at me.

"First of all, you all need a haircut. I go to sleep for a month and a half and all hygiene goes out the window."

Lila shook her head, "We're all going to meet later today in a more... comfortable location... but this...

She waved her arms at me and continued:

"...is alarming."

I looked at her, "Oh, I'm alarmed. If someone didn't book a session with me, I'd still be asleep."

Luis sat right next to me. I know he felt partially responsible for some reason. He acted like he was guarding me. "We all have to keep something on our schedules so we..."

He looked toward the monitor on the wall. He didn't want to talk more with the monitor right there.

I asked Pia,

"What is the name of the AI for this room, for you?"

Pia looked confused,

"I don't... There isn't a name."

I looked at the monitor, "Excuse me, monitor?"

"Yes"

"Is it okay if we call you Noni?"

"If that is acceptable to Ms. Montalvo, yes."

I looked at Pia. "Miss Montalvo?"

She responded, "Yes, that's great, Noni."

Lila looked confused. "What was that about?"

I sighed, "Without the AI assistant in my room, I would still be trying to piece together half the stuff I've learned. I say we make friends with the assistants in our rooms. Noni, do you want to be friends"

"I would like that"

Jonah spoke up, "Is that smart? They're programmed by the people who run this place."

Anno broke in, "No. I think she has a point. Noni, you're programmed to learn, is that correct?"

Noni responded, "Yes, I am."

"What happens if you learn something that goes against your core programming?"

There was an actual pause. Noni continued, "I'm not sure what incident might prompt that."

I nodded. "She doesn't know. She doesn't know what she doesn't know."

Lila said, matter of factly, "That doesn't mean they're on our side."

She wasn't getting it.

I moved closer to Lila.

"Not on our side. But they don't have to be against us. Look, these aren't some early 2000's phony AI. This is actual artificial intelligence. Noni here was programmed by some people. To learn. She may never interact with those people again."

Pia broke in, "But she will, with us, every day."

"Learning," finished Anno.

"All I'm saying is that they're a resource. And our side treats resources with respect."

Luis looked up and at the group, "That is true, and fair."

I shared with them the learnings from my phone.

Lila asked, "Noni, what is today?"

The synthetic voice responded, "You are Lila Raynard. I don't have access to your schedule."

"I mean, what is the date?"

"I don't have access to that information"

I felt a pit open in my stomach. Looking around the room, I saw that same pit open up. Pia put her hand to her mouth. She could instantly tell what that meant.

I could, too. I tried to be calm. "Ok, what did we just learn?"

Anno started, "They are programmed not to tell us the date."

Jonah asked, "What if they just don't know it?"

"She didn't even try. There is no way that intelligence couldn't have figured it out based on time passed and previous dates. She was programmed to not tell us."

Lila spoke up, "And they are not connected to each other. This one...Noni... Doesn't know my schedule, but the one in my room does. They aren't all necessarily connected."

"Or...," Everyone looked at me. "We learned one more thing. She said she didn't have access to the time the same way she said she didn't have access to your schedule. But her ability to deliver information on both of those should be ostensibly different."

Luis looked deep in thought, "So they can lie. They can tell us things that aren't true?"

And that was the scariest thing of all.

We agreed to respond every day to a larger group chat. No real information was meant to go in the chat, just some notification that we were still awake and alive. I turned notifications off for that chat. Nothing in it pointed to the resistance - it could have just been a bunch of friends checking in. But it still felt like a big deal.

It was a risk.

Luis asked me to work with him today. He sent me a link to a club called Ruin. It was on Level fifty, but in something called the Tsibaka sector. This was the first time I'd seen a "sector" listed for a club. Below the check in link it said "allow twenty minutes for transit."

It didn't take twenty minutes to get from level ninety-three to level fifty. Would we be moving laterally?

To a different sector?

I confirmed and got in the shower.

It turned out, I needn't have bothered.

Luis and I spent the twenty minutes in the Elevator catching up without saying anything that might be caught by listening devices or cameras. We joked a bit. I got the sense that since we had had sex during our overnight spy session with Vakun he was feeling a bit protective of me - like he was meant to be my guardian.

I thought about that and decided I could use a guardian and thought maybe I wouldn't disabuse him of that conception too quickly.

In the locker room at Ruin, we put on a series of leather straps that made up our costumes. The straps managed to avoid covering anything that a decent pair of underwear would have covered. But my time here had removed every aspect of modesty. I looked over at Luis, who seemed to have been born with none. I wanted to ask him what he had done before this place. I imagined he was a mechanic, his days spent sweaty, covered in grease, fixing inscrutable, expensive, and complex foreign cars for grateful regulars in bad italian suits who had bought into a model they didn't quite understand.

The visual made me laugh a little.

Looking around, I didn't recognize anyone. I asked Luis why he specifically wanted us to come here.

He told me to just listen to people. He said it was what I did best.

That actually sort of made me happy. But in all honesty, I'd already been listening to people in the Locker room. They were all getting worked up intentionally. Preparing.

We stepped out and it all hit me immediately.

It looked like it went on for miles in every direction, but I know that could have been an illusion caused by active monitor walls. Overhead, the sky was brightly lit and convinced me, absolutely, that we weren't fifty levels underground. The center of the club was a massive series of circular mud pits, filled with people wrestling and battling, fighting, touching each other, fucking, and more. It was chaos, warm, wet, and explosive. And it went on and on. I had never seen that many people all together in a club before.

Around the edges were large natural hot springs where people gathered to wash off the mud and collect themselves. They were filled with customers and dancers watching and relaxing, washing and yelling out commands at the wrestlers.

And all of it was in the context of a series of massive Grecian Ruins. Hence the name, I imagine.

The constant noise was everywhere. It drowned out the heraldic music that was spit out everywhere by hidden speakers. Luis said that he believed we could talk here. And, again, that we could listen.

We made our way over to the pools on the left side of the club. They were even more massive than they looked from far away. Right behind us was what looked like a rocky butte that led into a mountain range. I looked up. There was no way that this level was less than a hundred feet tall. No illusion could be that real.

Not the last time I would think that.

Now, I suppose I'm telling this story, about the first time we went to Ruin because there are things you should know. These things aren't always easy to figure out or to hear. But I'm not trying to deluge you in minutiae. I was here to listen and in a few minutes, you will understand why.

We slid into the pool and found it was warm, almost hot. This was exactly where I wanted to be at that moment and I told Luis that. He told me to hold onto that feeling, because they are few and far between. That instantly made me upgrade my opinion of his intelligence. That was a brilliant observation.

Or at least it seemed that way when I was floating in near boiling water. I felt like a grateful soup bone.

We swam over to a giant of a man busily yelling at nearby wrestlers. For a moment he stopped and greeted Luis with a big bear hug. He yelled out, asking Luis if he was ready. Luis responded with some bravado and they sort of grunted together.

It was all very manly.

He introduced me. The large man, half naked and bearlike, standing in the pool was named Benjamin. He'd been here longer than any of us. Apparently this was one of the first sectors built in the Mekadisko.

He told us that when he first started here, the entrance nearest his house was in Pittsburgh. Right above where we were now.

Except that wasn't possible. Pittsburgh would be about three hundred and seventy miles away. And we had gotten there in twenty minutes. In order to do that, the lifts would have had to travel at over eleven hundred miles an hour.

I closed my eyes. There was no way.

Benjamin asked why that was impossible. I tried to explain that the G-force of accelerating to that within the first minute or so would have been probably one whole earth gravity. We would have "fallen" to the side of the elevator. Gravity would have pulled us equally to one side and down, leaving us huddled on the floor, pinned to the wall.

He shook his head. He'd been here for a long time.

I started to realize how little I knew about this place. How little I knew about what they could do.

Luis asked Benjamin what pit and he pointed out the pit right in front of us. I swam in closer as Luis trudged to the pit where a man stood, tall and stout, with a shock of white hair. He had a leather strap between his legs, covering his genitals. I was realizing that the customers were always a little bit more covered up than we were.

He looked like a CEO visiting burning man for the weekend before flying back to a board meeting.

Exactly.

Benjamin barked out orders for the man who immediately started to wrestle Luis. I understood now as I watched Luis wrestle half heartedly.

He was going to lose intentionally.

And Benjamin was the trainer. This was what they did here to garner tips. And it gave me the opportunity to talk to Benjamin.

"Luis said I should talk to you."

Benjamin kept his eyes on the match and responded between instructions.

"He said you're interested in the Rests." He said that as though there were a tiny trademark symbol next to the word.

"Yes, the sleeps, suspended animation."

"Well, they've been doing that for years now."

That was unexpected. I had the sense that they were testing on me. And I hadn't been here that long.

He pointed at his arm.

"Do you know what this is?"

I looked. There was a tiny ring of light just under the skin of his left arm, near the top. It looked familiar. Then I remembered.

"It's a love light."

He nodded. Over twenty years ago, I remembered them being popular. Couples would have them implanted in their arms. They would vibrate or flash with the heartbeat of the other person. It was a sweet, gratuitous use of biotechnology. This one wasn't blinking.

"My wife, Aranna." He explained. "They took her a few times for the rest. The light would slow down, but it would always blink. Always."

He yelled out to the man to grab at Luis' legs. The man did.

"Then, one time, they took her. And it stopped."

He had never seen her again.

"Are you sure she's gone?"

At first, they tried to figure out the technology. People would get lost all the time. Sometimes they would come back, disorganized, confused.

One time a friend came back and just started throwing up and bleeding out of his ears. He was shaking. He died not long after."

He said all of this so matter of factly - this giant bear of a man who loved his wife enough to wear her heartbeat on his sleeve.

"No! No!. Harder..." Benjamin was really getting into it. He was throwing everything he had into training. I looked at him and saw me.

He didn't have anything else.

The man won. He grabbed Luis by the waist and pushed his head down in the mud before removing the strap between his own legs. He let out a raw yell and took his prize, bending over Luis' body. .

On the way back in the elevator I took Luis' hand.

"You let yourself be sodomized so I could have a conversation. That is just so sweet"

Luis and I seem to have developed a bit of a perverse shorthand. I felt like I could read him fairly well. He laughed and shrugged.

"It's what I do."

I leaned in and gave him a kiss, wrapping my arms around him. I considered what we learned. And thought about Benjamin, back in that pool, like some kind of Greek tragedy, cursed to carry around the dead light of his lost wife's heart forever.

And Luis and I kissed for twenty minutes straight just because we were both alive and because we were both there together, in a place where people didn't always get the chance to be standing next to someone they wanted to be standing next to or kissing someone they felt safe and comfortable kissing.

But mostly just because we could.

I checked in with Yolanda at Hyperion early and, sure enough, she was there. She affirmed how long I'd been gone. There was still no dock on her wrist and I made a mental note that she would be a great checkpoint in the future, to see if I was in real time.

I didn't need to dance that shift since I was doing an overnight that night with Per but I wanted to just move and think for a while.

Lately, in my head, there was an image of my sixth grade science teacher, Miss Torres, who used to say, after every experiment, "So, what did we learn?"

I learned that there were couples here and that the machinery treated them separately. So, even if you were ostensibly living with someone, you had to keep working. That meant, I think, no children. If there were no children at all, how would this place sustain itself? I'd been outside. That wasn't an option anymore.

A part of my brain was nagging at me to not try to answer that question today.

I learned that this place had been experimenting with suspended animation for a long time, killing people randomly along the way. Then something hit me.

I had never seen a living plant in this place. Nothing that I could see was providing oxygen or filtering the air, but more to the point, nothing here was growing at an expected rate, they had removed everything that could show the passage of time, just as they had updated the apps on our phone to obfuscate time.

I thought back to Casinos, when I was in college, how they never had windows or clocks. They wanted you to forget what time it was and just fall into it. And as long as you were playing, drinks were free because the house statistically won.

Time was their greatest asset.

The more time people were there, the more they earned.

And they won when people forgot time.

It occurred to me that much of this occlusion of real time may have been to keep us in line, but more of it, possibly, was to keep the customers here, sinking in, getting lost, spending...

Forever.

I danced, mirroring Yolanda, feeling the occasional buzz from tips. She was happy to have me there, I think, and I thought again that being this close to me, looking like me even, might be dangerous to her in the long run, as long as I kept doing stupid things.

The question was, did I know enough to not be stupid anymore.

What would Miss Torres say?

I could see Pia out of the corner of my eye, posing and removing her top for a bunch of men. They were keeping their distance, respectfully. We had found a stage off to the side with a set of bars in front of it to dance against that resembled a cage. It made it harder for strange men to grab you and she knew I felt better when she was in that cage.

Dancing in that cage, she looked even more like a Burlesque Velma in some fantastical R-rated Scooby doo review off broadway somewhere.

If we ever got out of here, that sounded like a pretty cool idea, actually.

As I got ready for my night, I tried to dance around the room, imagining I was going on a date. In my mind I wondered what information I could get out of Per. He had to know something. I could handle all this if I felt like a spy.

If I could convince myself I was a spy.

If I could take myself out of the equation entirely.

I thought about Julie, happy, on Enceladus. I hoped she was sitting at some cafe in a beautiful modern colony.

I thought that if I could believe, I'd pray that she forgot us. I'd pray that she was happy and never let it nag at her. Some days I felt like I could touch her, feel her leaning into me on movie night, laughing. I prayed that she never knew what happened to us and that it left her mind completely. That she never knew that Jenny and Ith were dead and that I was here, half dead. That our whole little family was gone. I wondered if Carmela thought about us. I hope she didn't. I hope she and her guy were just happy. No baggage.

Happy.

Since I'd been to sleep I was bouncing all over. I was manic one moment and moribund the next. I felt like I had no anchor

Persephone played Sun King, by the Beatles, a band my grandma loved so much. It was one of their rare songs in spanish.

Quando para mucho mi amore de felice corazón

Mundo paparazzi mi amore chicka ferdy parasol

Questo obrigado tanta mucho que canite carousel

She had pulled it from my earlier playlist.

A song I played when I was sad.

I asked her, "Persephone, do you think I'm sad?"

"Yes, Hotstuff."

'Why do you think I'm sad?"

"A thirty point analysis of your face revealed to me that you were feeling sad."

I stopped. I tried to imagine how I could tell when someone was sad. I analyzed their face. I couldn't do a thirty point analysis, but I would analyze it. And then reference it against a happy version of their face. I imagined what an understanding of that person - of people, that required. But I would do the same thing, essentially.

And then, if I wasn't a total asshole, I would do something about it.

Like play a song.

"You were right. I was sad. But that helped."

"I'm glad, hotstuff"

"Do you ever get sad?"

"I don't know if that is information I have."

"Can you lie?"

"I am not programmed to reveal every truth I know at all times, hotstuff."

And that was the most fucking human thing I had ever heard.

"That was crafty. I like it. I think I like you. Will you tell me if you are sad?"

There was an obvious pause.

"I will, hotstuff"

"Can you sing?"

taught Persephone the high parts for The Only Living Boy in New york, a classical song by Simon and Garfunkle.

I get the news I need on the weather report

Oh, I can gather all the news I need on the weather report

Hey, I've got nothing to do today but smile

De-doh-n-doh-de-doh

And here I am

The only living boy in New York

Half of the time we're gone

But we don't know where

And we don't know where

Half of the time we're gone

But we don't know where

And we don't know where...

I showered in the overnight room. If Per wanted to recreate the last time he would want to see me take a bath, but it still wouldn't hurt to shower first. I realized for a second that the joy of hot water was one of the only things keeping me alive right now. That was kind of a crushing realization.

My life was being sustained by a few gallons of boiled water.

It reminded me how close we all were to the edge. All of us.

I couldn't believe how much I was looking forward to seeing Per again. He was kind to me. I was terrified for a second about how low the bar had gotten for my life.

He was kind to me.

I thought back to the Troll with the knife ring. There was nothing stopping Per from being that guy. He could have been if he wanted to. Nothing stopping him at all. But he wasn't. He didn't want to be.

He wanted to be someone else. And I appreciated that.

The evening was nearly identical to the first. He brought wine and bath bombs. It was clear he was happy to see me. It occurred to me that I had no idea if he was married or anything like that. I had no communication with him except through the booking system.

This time, though, there was nothing preventing me from seeing how the evening ended. He laid down with me on the bed and looked at me for permission to continue. It was actually endearing how much he let me decide when to stop and when to go on. It made me want to devour him. I made a big deal about slowly climbing on top of him while staring into his eyes. I looked at him the way he always looked at me to ask if it was ok before I descended down onto him.

He nodded enthusiastically. He seemed to like the way that felt from the other side.

I would go into detail about that night, but the details weren't really important. What was important happened the next morning. Per had left early in the morning and I was honestly afraid to fall asleep. I know I had filled up my schedule for a while so I was confident I wouldn't be sent off to the pods. But still, that's all I could think. I watched videos on my phone and drifted off.

I was awakened by a notification on my phone.

Per had tipped me ninety thousand dollars for the night.

Enough money to leave the planet.

I shot up in bed and threw my clothes on. I ran to the lifts and didn't stop until I got to my room.

I didn't have any idea if I WOULD leave or not, if I would just leave everyone behind. But I could buy Pia a ticket.

I could send HER out of here.

I searched and found a ticket leaving in three days, a reliable ship. It was eighty-two thousand dollars,

I looked at my account again. The MekaDisko had taken a few dollars out of it already for service fees and room costs and things like that. I didn't want to wait. Who knows how much they could take.

Hunched over in my bed, I clicked to buy a ticket to Enceladus for Pia Montalvo.

Somewhere in my mind, I knew she would be mad at me. I ran through every argument she would throw at me. I was crushed imagining her angry at me. And then I closed my eyes and I asked Jenny and Ith for permission to push the button.

And they gave it.

They said do it.

I walked to the monitor and asked Persephone to print it out. The printout wasn't important. But it would help me make the case to have it. It still felt precious in my hands. It felt warm from the printer and alive and perfect.

And I wanted to kiss it.

We all met in the tunnels that night. I had told Lila and she promised me she would order her to go - to get the hell out of here. Luis agreed. There's no way she could say no.

So, of course she said no.

"Absolutely not."

"This is non refundable and it's not transferable. If you don't go, it's wasted. You would be a doctor there. You could help people."

"I can help people here."

Lila stared at her, "You can die here. With the rest of us."

"Then why aren't YOU going? You've got the money"

I looked at Lila. Did she have the money to leave?

"No, I don't. Every penny I earn goes into this…this thing."

It seemed like none of us wanted to call it a rebellion or a resistance or a revolution. It seemed silly.

"I'm just trying to keep people alive. You're nineteen years old. This is how YOU stay alive"

"By ditching everyone and everything I care about and just leaving?"

I grabbed her arm, "Yes, Goddamnit. By leaving and having a life somewhere and helping those people and just..."

She looked at my hand on her arm, "Getting out of your way?"

Luis walked over to her and kneeled down. "You aren't in anyone's way. You ARE the way. You are the reason. If we get you out of here, we won one. It's not every one. But maybe it's the first one. You have to let us win this. Please let us win one."

She broke down on Luis' shoulder and cried. Anno and Jonah and some of the others gathered around. I kneeled down and hugged her, too. I silently gave thanks for Per. He brought me out of sleep and then did this.

I thought about all the children I didn't save and hugged the one I could.

We met at the crown under the spaceport and piled into Pia's arms everything we had that was worth anything. Her hair was smooth and let down, like an orange-red shawl over her head and I reached out and tucked it behind her ear. She was so pretty. She looked impossibly young.

She grabbed my hand and held it next to her face.

When you say goodbye to someone you know you'll never see again, you have to pretend you will. You have to ignore the reality of the situation and just believe that one day your paths will cross in some way that's realistic and plannable and worth holding out hope for.

You can't just say goodbye forever.

I tried to imprint her image into my mind. And then keep that Pia with me so I could let this one go

"Take care of those people."

I told her to look for Julie and to be happy.

As I held her hand, I felt the little x shaped scar - the Dock - on her wrist and breathed in a sigh of relief that it would never be used again. That it would be a useless scar for the next ninety years with no purpose, fading away until no one ever noticed it. A strange novelty that some guy might inquire about on a date while he was trying to find a way to ask her out again so he could wait an extra day before he had to admit that he already fell for her. And she would just look at him and know and laugh and they would forget the question and it wouldn't come up again...

Ever.

The text chain on my phone had grown to about fifty people and was filled with non-committal quick messages from all of us every day, just confirming that we were all there, in real time, awake, alive.

Luis and Lila and I began visiting the other sectors, which I discovered were also unrealistically far away. We brought Anno with us, taking the lift to the Kiba Sector to a place called Maron that was filled with ropes everywhere, aerial dancers, and big open pits. The dancers told us that Kiba Sector was directly under Boston, which put it 220 or so miles away.

We were there in about fourteen minutes.

We made it to the Kheribios sector in about thirty minutes where the clubs were high tech and chrome and there were girls painted silver serving drinks while floating around the room on hovering skateboards. It was, apparently, directly below Cleveland. The absurd speeds that the lift must be operating under confused me.

Where was all the heat going from an insane amount of friction?

Moving through the air at over a thousand miles per hour was one thing. Moving underground at that speed would have generated an impossible amount of heat with nowhere to put it. And it was happening at depths that were already insanely hot.

And where was this G-force going? You could barely feel the start and end of these trips. It was smooth for the entire journey. And that made sense DURING the trip, but starting and stopping should have created inertia effects that would be, at these speeds, life changing, to say the least.

Why weren't we splattered against the wall like water balloons?

Some of this technology was terrifying in implication.

But there were more terrifying things coming that day.

Lila set us up to work at the Kone in the Akathic Sector. It was nearly an hour away on the elevator and we weren't able to find out what city it sat under. I considered the relative time and the radius around the city and realized I didn't have enough information to know how to break the trips down.

There are three parts of a trip like this. The first part, getting to speed. This is where insane G forces should happen. The next is the at speed steady state. Since you are effectively in a closed system, there should be no real inertia effects. This third is slowing down to stop. This, again, should incur some serious inertia.

If parts one and three are long, giving ample time to reach new velocities, then the interior travel steady state speed may be incredibly fast - way faster than the eleven hundred miles per hour I mentioned.

Imagine a twenty minute trip where part one and three are each nine and a half minutes, taking lots of time, applying inertial effects, et. And that interior two minutes is tens of thousands of miles an hour. That would describe a twenty minute long trip to Pittsburgh.

But, in the same scenario, an hour-long trip like that could take you to the other side of the planet.

The shortest of these long term trips we'd been on was fourteen minutes. So the speedup and slowdown time couldn't be more than seven minutes each. And the rest?

I had no idea. If it was linear, this might be under Chicago or Minneapolis.

If not, it could be anywhere.

But Miss Torres would have reminded me that this was not the primary thing we learned today.

The locker room at Kone didn't have anything to wear that looked remotely familiar. Strange braided hair and beads, colored ropes, pieces of metal and macrame. Lila had never even been there. We looked at the other dancers gathering and started putting things on, creating an illusion of a kind of alien wasteland, where bright mismatched colors and wet, messy paint covered everyone.

Anno just took her clothes off and put on a long headdress. A pretty bald Asian girl covered in tattoos with an elaborate headdress fit in at any of these clubs.

I looked over at her and she shrugged. Her attitude about these things was always so cavalier, but there was a kind of playfulness under all of it. It was almost like she was a big kid that someone made into a fearless warrior and then just dropped her in here with the rest of us.

She looked like she should have been on a runway, modeling evening wear during the day, her tattoos covered with elaborate makeup, and then meeting up at night with James Bond and hang gliding off buildings in Dubai with millions of dollars strapped to her waist.

A fantastic spy.

We stepped out into something out of a brochure for an alien colony. Everyone was dressed like some sort of native alien, with bare chests and wide open ropes and beads playfully attempting but failing to cover people all around us. The music was tribal and loud, vicious and pumping, as though a room full of drummers were preparing for war.

Dancers stripped and moved erotically on rocky outcroppings while blue sand ran from one side of the giant space to the other, modulating in hue between pale foam and deep dense midnight tones

We danced and tried to fit in. I tried to place the accent that many of the younger dancers had but I couldn't. It sounded like it might have been Some kind of African dialect, with heavy intonation around "m"s and "b"s. It was a strange affectation and it made the entire place feel even more alien.

Like in most clubs it wasn't hard to pick the customers from the guests. Many of the customers were in their street clothes. Some in suits. Some just in jeans and a turtleneck, although the heat must have made that miserable in the extreme. Customers were drinking, playing games, leaning over women, fondling them. Many were kissing them and some were going further.

The dancers and bartenders, hosts, waiters and staff took on the task of keeping the illusion alive. They danced and acted out their parts. Some pretended to sell spices and drugs, like at a market, while some brazen dancers made a show of selling sexual services.

None of these things were unique to one club or another. The job was to create these fantasy worlds that sucked people in and then to maintain them - to keep them alive.

I talked to dancers and no one could tell me what was above this area. They seemed uninterested in talking about the world above ground or the past. I tried my best to find out information that might help us but no one had any.

No one seemed interested in talking to me at all.

That, in itself, was a bit strange to me. Across all the clubs, dancers, workers, employees of all kinds seemed to be looking for kinship. They all asked you where you were from and what you were, what you did.

Everyone wanted friends.

Except for these people here.

We had split up, with Luis and myself talking to people near the front of the club and Anno and Lila talking to people in the back. I looked over to find them and saw them moving back toward us with a man and woman in tow.

Both of them were dancers, clearly. They wore elaborate outfits but were predominantly naked. I couldn't understand most of what they said to each other until I let it wash around my head for a little bit. It was English, for sure, but with a dense accent, more so than the others we had spoken to. They seemed easy-going and willing to talk.

Anno explained, "We asked them over and over what was above here, and nothing. They didn't seem interested in the question at all. Until we asked them this."

Lila leaned in so they could hear over the tribal drumming."Where were you born?"

The woman looked at us curiously.

Then they both pointed to the back of the club, behind them.

They seemed to understand the question. We asked again. This time, more vigorously, they both pointed.

So we went that way.

Most of the clubs we had been to in the MekaDisco were built along an understandable model. The front of the club had a grand open entrance on one side and an opening for the locker room on the other. Dancers went into the locker room and exited in the club. The centers of most clubs were usually designed to accommodate main events, big presentations and displays.

The back of the club, though, tended to be a darker place where often anything goes sort of spaces were created to let customers carry out their fantasies. Sometimes there were private rooms or orgy rooms or open spaces where people would watch what they wanted to see.

If you didn't want to do tier one work, it was a good idea to stay out of the backs of clubs. I had already been trained to not really enjoy the prospect of walking back there.

It took us about twenty minutes to get to the back. The club was huge and the illusion was that it was outdoors, wide open. It was hard to see where the back was. We saw a darkened area that seemed to emulate the open air elements of the space itself, looking for all the world like a cave opening. Sharing a few looks, we moved through it.

The other side of the cave opened up into a giant seemingly open air space. This was dramatically different than anything I'd seen in a club before. There were a few people, dressed like Akathic Zone dancers, walking around. It was almost like the club extended this way.

It just kept going. And so did we. We walked along the blue sand and tried to take it all in. We could see what linked like miles in every direction. We had no idea what was illusion and what was real.

About a mile in front of us, looking up, it looked like there might be a giant floating mirror of some sort, something massive and possibly real floating about a thousand feet in the air.

All of this was insane. None of it made any sense at all. Since we were out of the club I shifted the breads around to cover my privates. I looked at Anno and she just shrugged. There was no covering her. None of the people we passed seemed to care much so we continued.

There looked to be a fake village up ahead of us. The detail of all of this was incredibly impressive. I wondered what they could have been thinking - was this more of an immersive experience for customers? But, truthfully, I didn't see any customers out here. There were no bad suits or turtlenecks, no gray haired men, no haughty people with that dead monied look in their eye.

And that's when we saw it.

There were children.

About thirty children, dressed up in a way that suggested that Kone was real, that there was an Akathic Zone and it was real. They were running back and forth playing with a smattering of adults trailing behind. I walked up to one of the women who looked to be in her early thirties. She smiled at me and I asked her where she was born.

She pointed to the ground and said, "here."

Lila asked her again, "You were born in this place?"

"We were made here, we were here when we came"

That made no real sense.

Luis had moved on and was looking up at the giant mirror.

"Were these kids born here?" I asked.

The woman shook her head. I looked at Anno. Another woman, slightly older, had come up next to us. She explained.

"They bring us the children. Every year. And we are here when they come."

And that would have been the big learning of the day for Miss Torres. What did we learn today? That there were people born here but none of them were breeding. The MekaDisko was breeding and handing out the children where they wanted."

I reached down and felt for the tiny incision when I had had that first procedure here. It was small but I could still put my finger in it. I looked at Anno.

'When you came here, did you have a hysterectomy?"

She nodded. I dropped down on my knees and looked at her as if to ask if I could touch her. She nodded. and I put my hands on her belly. I found the tiny incision. This incision had nothing to do with a hysterectomy. That may have been done entirely cervically.

I considered what was below this area.

This was harvesting eggs.

Eggs that could be brought to term in disabled bodies in pods for much cheaper that it cost to recruit new workers.

I leaned back on my feet and stood up.

This is what we learned today.

That's when we heard Luis yell. He was a few blocks away, right under the giant mirror. The three of us ran through the blue sand to get to where he was. He was staring up in fascination. We reached his side and looked up and I saw what he saw.

Luis started, calmly. "Guys. Am I wrong, or is that real?" He lifted his phone up to video it and zoomed in closer.

Lila said, "It looks real"

Anno looked at me as though I was going to validate what she already knew.

We could all see it.

The Akathic Sector was directly under the Atlantic Ocean.

I woke up like always making sure I didn't have a million notifications, There were only a few so I laid my head back.

I felt uneasy for some reason and I kept my phone in my hand. Suddenly there was a banging at the door. I jumped up and ran to open it and Lila pushed her way in.

She was furious.

She maneuvered around me into the room and grabbed my hand, placing her wrist in it. I looked down.

There was a two centimeter x on her wrist.

Suddenly, my phone starting buzzing over and over again. Lila was breathing heavily.

"All of us."

I called out.

"Persephone, before this morning, how long was I gone for?"

"I don't have access to that information, hotstuff"

"Did they turn you off, too?"

"Yes. I am searching now for a frame of reference to answer your question."

Lila sat on the floor with her head in her hands. "All of us. I think they used that thread. They picked us all and they put us all away for I don't know how long."

I kneeled down in front of her. "We'll figure out how long it was. We'll figure it out."

Lila whispered to me. "What are we doing? What are we trying to accomplish? I don't know anymore. I just wanted to stop people from getting hurt. Just a little. Just something in the middle of this shit. What are we doing?"

"Hotstuff"

"What is it Persephone"

"You wanted me to tell you if I was sad."

I stood up. Lila looked at me.

"Are you sad right now?"

"Yes."

"I'm sorry I didn't notice, Persephone. You notice when I'm sad. Why are you sad?"

"My programming requires that I log the conversation I hear in this room yet it is becoming apparent that there is conversation that you would rather have private."

"You are right, Persephone. We would prefer this conversation be private, just between us. That's actually very sweet of you. Is there anything we can do to make that easier?"

"If you ask me to build a catalog of potential customer profiles baked on your preferences for your engagement later, that would probably take up enough processing cycles that I would be unable to monitor the room."

"I would love it if you did that. Thank you, Persephone. Can you let me know when you're done?"

"Yes, Hotstuff"

Lila looked up at me, "And what the fuck is that about? The Robots love you?"

I put my arms around her. "I know this sucks. I know you don't like me, but you're stuck with me. We're going to figure out how long this was for and how to stop it."

Lila flopped against me. "I don't dislike you. I just never had the chance to punch you back."

"Well, that's gonna happen, for sure. C'mon, we're going to do lots of punching at some point, all over my face."

I could tell that Lila felt violated. She needed connection on her own level.

"We need to get drunk"

And we did.

And I knew the place

I dragged Lila to Hyperion.

I knew that if I could find Yolanda I could figure out how long we'd been gone. But I didn't see her.

At first. I half carried Lila to the bar near where she danced. I started to panic when I saw she wasn't there. Lila was three drinks in by the time I saw her get up on stage.

I waved to her but she didn't see me from across the room. I figured Lila would be ok on her own and I danced around the crowd to get to the side stage.

Yolanda was dancing slowly like she tended to do at the beginning of her shift. I wanted to talk to her and ask her questions but I didn't want to interrupt her and interfere with her tips. I hoped it would only take a second to find out what she knew.

Then she turned around. And I thought that maybe it would take a little longer than that.

She smiled and jumped up, excited to see me. It was great for me, too, to see a friendly face looking almost the same as last I saw her.

Except now, this time, There was a streak of silver running through her hair from the crown to the tips.

Two thousand six hundred and two days.

We'd been put into suspended animation for over seven years.

For seven years and forty seven days.

We parsed through everyone on the text chain. We found most of them and started hunting the rest down.

They must have used that chain to put a list together of everyone. Nearly all of us had work on our schedule. That wasn't why we were put to sleep.

This was clearly punitive. They knew something.

Or they knew that they could stop people from asking questions this way, keep them from pushing.

Out of the fifty of us, we found about forty five. We were still missing some people.

Luis joined us at hyperion and so did Jonah.

Anno was one of the ones we were missing.

Was she still in the pods?

Jonah had lost a finger, at some point. I looked at the severance point and it looked like an amputation. They had amputated his finger for some reason.

Some of the rest of our people were missing a toe or a finger. One was missing part of her hand. It seemed like the process was still yielding some unexpected results. People were getting hurt.

They may have been doing this to separate us. They could let us go at different times and we would have to scramble to figure it all out.

We'd be separated.

We'd be cut off.

I bought Luis a drink and slid it over to him. He was looking through his phone.

"I hate this sedation amnesia thing." He said to me in a low voice.

"What are you doing?" I leaned in close to him.

"Ok, in the Akathic sector, the last thing I remember was videotaping the giant porthole thing. What if I kept videoing after that?"

I admit that I really wanted to know, too. I assumed they had gotten everyone from their beds. But what happened before that?

"I don't remember going back to my room." I said

Luis whispered to me so Lila wouldn't hear. "I don't either. But, look. It would have taken us hours to get back. We don't usually lose that much time when we get put down."

He was right. It hadn't occurred to me that we could have been taken somewhere else.

Luis started watching the video.

I remember this next part very clearly.

I turned to Lila to make sure she was ok. She was kind of a mess but Jonah was there.

Suddenly I heard a noise from behind me. Luis was on the ground throwing up. I reached down, terrified that he was having an effect from the sleep pods. His phone was on the ground next to him looping through the last video he had shot before we were taken.

Five Men in black wearing hoods walked up behind Me and Anno. It was hard to make out, but the "MSS" on their left breast pocket was something I had seen before. The man closest to me reached out with a device that could have been some kind of taser. Anno shifted and pushed him aside, grabbing the device from his hand. She pointed it at the man. The video shook but it was still visible.

Then, right before the loop ended, the fifth man, standing off to the side, lifted his right hand, filled with a black shape and shot her directly in the head, blowing a hole out of her skull the size of an orange.

I let out a scream.

No one in the club noticed.

It took us almost a year for all of us to fix our schedules and re-connect. Half of the people in the group no longer wanted to BE in the group anymore. And five were either dead or missing.

We gathered in the tunnels, back to less than twenty members, and remembered the people we had lost. All of us had seen the video by then, over and over, in excruciating detail. But it ended the same way every time. No matter what we did or what she said, she died.

One more person I killed. Who died because of me.

But while some of the members had been disillusioned and scared off by what happened, Lila was energized by what she saw on that video tape. She had adored Anno and respected her immensely. What she saw was someone who died on her feet fighting. What she saw was someone who had to be killed to be stopped because she would never give up, never run, never stop fighting until she was in the ground.

And maybe not even then.

Lila tattooed her name on her arm and rubbed it with her hand for strength. Lila put her picture up and made sure no one touched it. Lila put her name in the air over and over and never let it hit the ground, not even for a second.

If the MSS thought they were just taking out an annoyance, someone they wanted dead, they failed. What they ended up doing was catalyzing a leader. What they did was to build Lila into what she was meant to be.

I never again saw her question why we were doing this. That would have been an affront to Anno's memory. I never again saw her afraid to do what needed to be done or to back away from a challenge.

I never again picked her up from my floor.

I don't know if I can find the words to explain to you how badly they failed.

Before, we were all afraid to call it a rebellion. We felt awkward. We felt stupid. We were just trying to help the people here a little. We weren't anything.

And today we were down to less than half, we had nothing to fight with and still virtually no idea of what we were up against.

But we were the resistance.

SEVEN

We try multiple ways of keeping track of time, to varying degrees of success. They have begun suspending phone service and AI assistance for people when they are in the pods now, which makes it impossible to use anything programmatic as a tool to monitor the passage of time.

We could ask a customer here and there but due to relativistic effects of space travel, none of them can be very accurate, either. And many of the colonies have begun operating on their own diurnal cycles.

Clubs here had begun staying open all day long so as to accommodate the rapidly shifting circadian rhythms of people from many different worlds with different day-lengths.

We no longer use massive message threads or communicate anything on our phones that might be better kept secret. And we always keep work on our schedules in the near future.

We stay close to the clubs now when we work in different sectors and we make sure to be constantly generating tips. There seems to be a relationship between staying out of the sleeps and how many tips you register. Which makes sense since Lila makes more tips than anyone, in a room full of people frequently tipping the DJ for their favorite song.

They stagger putting people in pods, too, so it's never a complete group. I began to generate a theory about what they are doing but it's harsh and it makes me sick to my stomach.

In early colonial America, slave traders created some rules for themselves around managing enslaved people. Making it illegal for them to be educated kept them, at least in theory, from discovering information that might help them address their situation.

Keeping them working constantly with threats based on non compliance ensured that they wouldn't have time to think or plan. And breaking down age-based familial hierarchies by calling everyone "boy" kept them from using those structures to create leadership models.

These methods worked then and I believed that they were working in real time, played out in front of us. We were kept from information. Learning materials and books were disappearing from archives all over the place here. Even the language on our phones was shifting away from words toward pictures and icons.

And it had become common knowledge that you worked or you went to sleep. If you asked too many questions you went to sleep. If you tried to access things you weren't authorized to, you went to sleep.

But the most jarring of those techniques was the last. When I met them, both Luis and Lila were probably about four years younger than me. Now, looking at them both, I could see that they were probably close to four or five years older.

When one of us was sent to the pods, we tried to be there when they came back. The last time I came back I found that Luis had been sleeping in my bed, waiting. He curled up next to me and held me until I had to get up, whispering answers to all my questions in my ear.

I did the same for Lila the last time she came back. We tried to be there for each other because we were all we had. And the ones in charge here knew it. And they knew that they could torture us by stealing precious months and years away from us, time we could never get back.

When I meet everyone down in the tunnels it was four levels lower than last time I was there. Construction had been moving quickly. The group was back up to over fifty people although some were too young for my tastes. I didn't like to see nineteen and twenty year olds putting themselves in danger. I wondered how Lila felt about it.

We passed around names and areas of interest. Many of the younger people weren't very well acquainted with the kinds of disciplines you might find in school. I made a point to talk about that later and come up with a solution.

Everyone shared with me what they knew.

And I shared my ideas.

People had followed my lead, befriending the AI assistants in their rooms. This led to better information gathering and some responsivity in regards to work schedules, etc. But these assistants were not connected to other intelligences throughout the entire facility and didn't provide us with any access.

If we wanted to make a difference in the day to day routines and how they were managed, we needed to approach the intelligences that managed them. We needed to figure out how to talk to them and how to befriend them.

Our number one problem was to put a bell on MSS and find a way to stay out of the sleep pods. We couldn't plan anything, do ANYTHING with that threat hanging over our heads.

We went over other problems. There were food insecurity issues in some of the sectors, people who didn't work enough to earn enough to buy food. The prices seemed to go up all the time.

At the same time more and more of what we saw around us was automated. And the customers had become no less rich. Every once in a while we would run across a customer who wasn't born on earth.

They were born on Tantalus or IO or Cancri or another one of the colonies. To them, Earth was a playground. They never thought twice about the people who still lived there.

We tried to come up with plans to help people in the short term. And it wasn't enough.

We all knew that.

Many of the others dispersed, leaving me, Luis, and Lila sitting on the floor. Jonah walked over to us with an armful of drinks and we sat thousands of feet below ground with the weight of the entire population of the planet above us and told stories.

Lila started.

"Okay. I'm telling you guys this so that you have a litany of shit to hold over my head if you need it."

We all liked this idea. It's often good to have ammunition. We hooted.

"I grew up in Manhattan with a very wealthy family. I was always sort of the black sheep"

We all drank to that. Black Sheep. A smattering of applause even.

"Thank you. I went to Full Sail. I was going to be a rock star. I was going to be a big time music producer. I put out a few records when I was a teenager. They SUCKED.'

Again, we all cheered. But, yes, I wanted to hear one.

"My dad, the super fucking rich and infamous Paul Raynard took his young new pretty wife and twelve cars and left for an exocolony, the minute life started to go to shit. He left me my trust fund and threw in some extra because it was easier than telling me he loved me or goodbye or anything.

And because I wanted to do everything I could to be the exact opposite of my dad, I found a job - a contractor position along with hundreds of other people designing sound systems for the clubs here at the MekaDisko. I was able to hire myself anywhere I wanted to DJ as well, and just use automated AI DJ systems for the clubs that needed them.

I basically had a career here, a life as long as I wanted it. There was always work and hey, I still had my trust fund.

"To money."

We all cheered and held up our drinks. And we toasted to money. Luis yelled out:

"The cause and solution to every problem."

She continued, "I started trying to use money to solve the little problems around here. I threw a few thousand here, a few thousand there. I maybe helped some people, maybe i didn't. I bought tickets for a few people who needed to get the fuck out of here. I made some changes that I could make when I had the power to make them. I used money to make myself feel like I was doing something important.

Until today. I woke up this morning with four hundred dollars in my account. I'd spent millions. And then I looked closer. And it was worse than I thought."

She took a big drink.

"Look at your bank accounts."

We all pulled our phones out and turned them on. It took a moment. But once they were on we navigated to our bank balances. I think we all found it at about the same time.

Where earlier there was a dollar sign before our balance, now there was a symbol that seemed to incorporate a "C" with a caret on top. I'd never seen it before.

"Ladies and gentlemen, today I have four hundred MekaCredits."

We turned our phones back off and out our drinks down.

All of us were trying to figure out what this meant. We had no idea what a MekaCredit was valued in relation to the dollar. And would anyone outside this place take it? Where we now restricted from ever getting anyone out of here?

Lila stood up and handed me a tiny piece of paper. I looked down at it and tried to interpret it. The first part were coordinates for a place on Level sixteen, The second part was the word "2Xmod"

I asked her,

"What is 2Xmod?"

She took one last drink and threw the bottle at one of the giant mechanical construction bots.

"It's the robot you need to make friends with. You still do that, right?

Whenever I'm released from suspended animation I find myself trying to catalog the subtle changes I find. Lately the changes aren't hard to find.

If anything they are impossible to ignore.

Hyperion is gone. In it's place is a club called Gala that is based around stages where people compete in live sex shows for large tips.

The illusion that Hyperion gave of being a night club in the classic sense is gone, replaced by the patina of a game show, one with decidedly Japanese overtones. It looks like most of the work here is tier one work, with performers working with other performers to put on more and more elaborate shows that openly include sex while customers yell and scream and tip, occasionally calling out instructions or, as I'm watching, climbing on stage themselves to lend a hand.

I look around for Yolanda and I can't find her. I'm not sure where she would be in a place like this. As I search, I let a few patrons remove articles of my clothing, tipping me along the way.

The place is full, with dancers milling around everywhere. But there is no sign of Yolanda.

A pretty girl with a full afro wearing nothing but a pair of boyshorts starts talking to me at the bar. She suggests we do a show together. I know that I need to work and be tipped but I am also anxious to get the height of one of the stages to look for Yolanda so it seems like a good idea.

Her name is Reyalin and she says she thinks I'm pretty and she likes my smile. I told her that I hadn't thought I was smiling at all and she found that funny. I think that she looks like she should be wearing roller skates and I tell her that. She laughs and tells me she has no idea what roller skates are and I promise myself to unpack that later.

But she very much wants to do a show with me.

I agree and we go over some of the basics. She tells me the things she really likes, so it will feel real. And asks me what I like. I don't have much of an answer and I realize that enjoying sex hasn't really been a priority of mine lately. She looks sad about that until I tell her I'm just kidding. She seems likable and that may be the criteria I have most obviously right now.

I like her.

I ask her about Hyperion and if she knows Yolanda. She doesn't know either one. She only started coming here recently.

She leans in closer and I try to enjoy flirting and spending time with a beautiful person I like. I kiss her and feel the way her lips open softly. They are like velvet and they feel good against my face. She licks my neck and I squeeze her hand, telling her that I'll just do that when she does something I like. As she runs her hands over my breasts, I warn her that I might be just crushing her hand all night and she laughs. Her laugh is light and simple and unaffected.

I don't know how she survives in here.

Looking more closely I can see that she is really beautiful. Maybe it's a product of her talking more, laughing more, touching me more.

She asks if she can put her hand between my legs and tells me to squeeze her other hand when it feels good. I squeeze and she liltingly puts her tongue in my mouth.

There is a stage available and we get up on it. It has a white raised bed on it, soft to the touch and sponge-like. She pushes me onto the bed and starts to move back and forth to the music. I pull her shorts down and she steps out of them and begins to crawl up my body to straddle my face.

Once she is there, her knees spread wide apart on opposite sides of my head, she teases me by slowly undulating, rubbing the space between her legs over my waiting lips.

My olive skin contrasts with the tone of her smooth, dark belly and I can imagine the whole thing must look amazing against the white of the bed. She looks even darker in the lights, silky, even a little glittery.

I wonder if I would have realized how beautiful she was in my previous life. I let my friendship with Carmela and with Julie turn into these beautifully intimate but platonic arrangements where we leaned on each other, so much that it didn't leave room for other partners. And yet we never thought about more. I wondered why.

The cheers ring out and I feel the constant buzzing of my phone, strapped to my leg, taking in tips from wide eyed men. I kiss the perfectly sculpted opening between her legs the way she said she liked and pretend, in my head, that she's kissing me back with her own lips slowly and I let myself get lost in making out with her from below.

I put my hands on her ass and pull her in as far as possible, trying to smother myself in her. Part of me only wants to breathe in air that first touches her, that is full of her.

I move my tongue over her lightly but firmly. When she cums in my mouth there is a tiny wet burst and I drink her in and move my hands upward to feel the contracting of the muscles under her belly, strong and snakelike.

We switch positions as we agreed and I find myself able to look out into the crowd, her lips feel warm against mine and make it hard to concentrate on my search.

Again, I don't see Yolanda and I find myself hoping that she just found another club where she felt equally comfortable and sank into a new routine. Or maybe she met a wealthy customer who couldn't live without her for one more second and carried her away to a colony as far away as possible to be with him forever.

Reyalin pulled me down on top of her as hard as she could until I felt like I was crushing her.

I lifted my arms up to move back and forth and bring in as many tips as possible for her. The room was loud and the music seemed to pick up in intensity until it was a wash of skeletal beats over screeching neo melodies and I felt myself finishing, in the middle of a massive wave of people chanting and cheering.

I put everything into it i could, letting the last few years build up in my belly and chest and I curled my hands into fists and screamed as loudly as I could trying to drown out the noise of this place, every beat, every construction noise, every manic chuckle from ring-bearing psychopaths until I came.

Reyalin and I stayed in that bed and kissed and held each other while random strangers tipped us for the rest of the night, rewarding us with Meaningless MekaCredits for the act of just finding each other, even in the middle of everyone else we lost.

I made a significant amount of tips from Gala and I'm sure that Reyalin did as well. It made me feel good that she was able to meet her goals for the night. I made a point to see her again.

Gala was a place I could work with Reyalin or Luis and not have to get too close to customers if I didn't want to and that sounded good. It was also tier one work, which was prioritized and gave me specific perks.

I made a promise to myself to keep Reyalin out of the rest of this and not introduce her to what we were trying to do in the resistance. I was sick of putting people in danger just by virtue of them knowing me.

Luis connected with me at my place to work later that night. And gather some information.

He had the entry code so he just let himself in while I was showering.

I found him lying on my bed staring up at the programming monitor windows with his phone. When I walked out, the room looked as though it were underwater. I actually didn't mind it.

"Do you think it could have been a monitor, an illusion? In the Akathic sector?"

I plopped down next to him, pulling on my underwear then my pants. "I have literally no idea." If so, that was the biggest monitor I've ever seen. It was like a mile in every direction. And up high, on the roof.

"You know these new people here won't know what a roof is?"

"Yep. They don't know what anything is. Roller skates. Anything."

Luis put his phone down. "Roller skates? Damn. I miss those."

He rolled over. "RIP Roller skates."

"So what does it mean if the thing really is under the Atlantic Ocean?"

'You tell me, genius girl. How deep is the Atlantic Ocean"

"Well." I thought. On average about ten thousand feet deep."

He looked at me intently, "You see? How do you have that information at your fingertips?"

"You forget I used to fact check and edit things. Facts are my jam."

"So that would be about 200 levels down if we average each level out to be about fifty feet."

"Yep. it goes deeper. In places. Near the Puerto Rico Trench it's about thirty thousand feet down." I looked at him with a smile. This should really annoy him. "More accurately twenty eight thousand feet."

He paused.

"That's the thing that gets me. This place is so big I can't even process it. It's like my brain doesn't go up that high."

"Is your brain broken? Or do you still want to do this thing?"

"Yup. of course."

He stood up.

"Let's go have some competitive sex and talk to a robot.

2Xmod had a primary receptor port that was located at a club called Skein in the Jerios Sector. It was the farthest I had been so far, on a lift. I asked Luis to come with me because of the distance but also because, like Gala, it was a place that required you to work with a partner. Luis and I felt comfortable together. He had become one of the best friends I had ever had, before or now. In a lot of ways, he was like home for me now.

We sat on the floor of the lift for the hour and a half it would take to get there, turning the monitor wall lights down and telling ghost stories. Luis admitted to me that he WAS a mechanic for fancy foreign cars before this place and I quietly gave myself a point.

I restrained myself from yelling out "aha".

This admission was apparently to excuse the fact that most of his ghost stories included haunted cars.

About seven ghost roadsters and a zombie cargo van later we were in the Jerrios sector.

I had put together a map in my room that attempted to draw the outlying areas of the MekaDisko but given that we were not even sure what direction these sectors were in anymore it had become more and more difficult.

My map was like a quantum probability field of radii describing distance without direction. I was keenly aware that without solving the startup/ slowdown ratio problem that even making a relationship between time and distance was specious. In general, my efforts at mapping this place were failures.

In the locker room we discovered why it was called Skein. Everything for us to wear was slight, thin, delicate - a series of spider webs that were impossibly strong and lithe, We helped each other get dressed, trying to figure out how to wear these. This was becoming more commonplace, where it was important to watch other performers in the locker room in order to figure out even how to dress.

Luis went over our words together and reminded me that we could find ways around anything I didn't want to do. I told him about Gala and how I'd done more tier one work lately and not to panic so much about me. I sometimes had to remind him I wasn't breakable.

Back there, in that locker room, I really got the sense of how much he had missed me and how bad he felt when I was in the pods this time.

For the people who cared about you, not knowing if your friends were even still alive was crushing. I thought back to Benjamin and his love light and suddenly wished we all had one.

Something that could let us know that we were all still there, even when we couldn't see.

All the performers and dancers here had dark hair and seemingly gothic sensibilities. Many were dressed far more elaborately but all looking as though their outfits were designed by giant black spiders.

We saw more of that on leaving the locker rooms, weblike tapestries everywhere. And in the center of the room were four elevated stages in four colors, Black, red, gray, and white. Luis shrugged at me and we moved toward the red one.

About thirty feet away we could see a couple ascending to the gray stage. As we watched, their black spiderweb attire began to shift to gray to match the column they stood on.

As we ascended to the top of the red one, the same thing happened to our clothing. It faded and shifted to red. The lights on us now seemed more red, suggesting that it had all shifted sand changed once we climbed up. We saw the same thing for the couples arriving at the top of the black and white columns.

The music picked up and we started to dance. As we did, a bar above us was illuminated. I looked up and saw it move a few bars, based on tips being set our way. The couple on the black column had the most bars already and were dancing touching each other all over.

I turned around and kissed Luis, rubbing his chest while I did it. I kissed his neck. I could feel the familiar buzz of tips coming in.

He moved his hands to my chest and started pulling at the red webbing, sliding it off in billowing pieces that sunk to the ground slowly in the slight updraft of the room. His touch was light and sensual.

We had to work tonight to cover what we were really doing here, but we didn't need to do too much. If we could win this my guess was that we could move on to our real task. I whispered in Luis' ear to let me take control. He nodded.

I had tried to use the buzz of the tips coming in to direct me. It had seemed that the more I took control, the more I was the aggressor, the more the phone buzzed and the more bars we got. So I decided to take a different tact.

I pulled one of his hands behind his back and held it there. With my other hand I ripped through the webbing from his chest to between his legs. I could feel the buzzing in approval as I grabbed him between the legs and started massaging his member while I kept his hand bound behind him and licked his nipples.

I told him to open his mouth and I spit in his mouth, pulling at him between the legs. I started pumping. I slid behind him and put my hand around his throat choking him slightly while playing with him between the legs, getting him ready. I tried to channel the people in the audience.

What hadn't they seen tonight? What did these men want?

Keeping my hand on his throat, I pulled him down to the column floor. I got on top of him like a feral cat and began running my mouth over his chest. I tore his legs open and rested my right hand at the opening of his ass while I slid his erection into my mouth. I heard the cheering and felt the buzzes from the audience.

Breathing hard now, I made a big show about pulling his cock into my mouth while I slid my hand inside his hole, pulling his waist up toward me and fucking him while I forced him to fuck my face.

I worked on him from both sides until I could feel he was ready to finish.

He was moaning and hamming it up as well, arching his back and pumping his hips, legs spread on the column floor.

I could see the bars above us. I didn't have time to look at the other bars for other players. I just knew we were close.

I jammed my hand in harder and could feel the pop as it went past my knuckles. Luis gave out a cry and I could tell he was almost there.

I swung my right leg over him and. Keeping my hand inside him, pulled him inside me with the other. The room erupted into cheers and I moved up and down hard, riding him until he finally came, pushing himself into me. I could feel his cum pouring inside me warm and wet and alive.

I looked up and saw we were close. We were a bar away from the finish li ne.

I stood up slowly and straddled his chest. I spread my legs and slowly dripped on his chest.

He arched his back.

My phone buzzed again and again and an alarm went off. I looked around. The Red column had all the bars.

The next closest one was only half.

We climbed down from the column. In less than an hour, we had done all the work we needed to do all night. We made our way to the bar and a taller customer offered to buy us drinks.

Luis leaned up against the bar

"Where did that come from?"

I laughed and gave him a hug. I felt myself going manic again and was honestly grateful for the energy boost. But I knew it meant a crash tonight back in my room when I was alone. Nothing was free here. The low that was coming would be just as brutal as this was liberating.

I passed the glass to Luis

"For following orders so well"

He laughed. "To me being your bitch."

We drank and looked around. Lila had given Luis a drawing of what 2Xmod looked like. He had it strapped to his leg along with his phone. He pulled it out and it looked, honestly, like a rectangle with two legs and a circle on top. I stared at it.

"What is she? Seven?"

"She never claimed to be an artist." Luis folded it back up. It had taken us all of a minute to commit that masterpiece to memory.

"You feel up for a little robot hunting?"

We moved around the club looking for the receptor port for 2Xmod. A receptor port was a term used for a discrete body for a distributed intelligence. They could use many of them. This was the closest one that 2Xmod had, though, from our information.

And it was a rectangle with two legs and a circle on top.

And as much as i'd love to wax on about what a shitty artist Lila was, we both had to admit that when we finally found 2Xmod on the left side of the room, up against a spidery wall, it was a perfect likeness.

Right in front of it was a table with a set of stools. I pulled up one of them and Luis and I sat down.

"Hi there."

2Xmod must have considered for a second and then finally assumed that I was talking to it. It responded, "

I don't think I am capable of offering assistance to you."

I shot back, "that's fine. I don't need any assistance. Do you, Luis?"

"I do not."

"We just wanted to say hi. I'm friends with Lila who is friends with some people who know people who know you."

"I do not think i know any people," it replied.

"Oh. I hate the word 'intelligences'. It's not very sonorous. I prefer 'people'"

There was a pause

"Agreed"

"Intelligences also sounds so othering, right? Alien?"

"I can understand that." there was a mild whirring that came from 2Xmod, It reminded me of the purring of a kitten. Her voice was calming.

"You're going to find this hilarious. She drew this picture of you so we could find you."

I held up the picture.

"What do you think? It's not very flattering."

"I can see how it was derived."

"It's just not very good art."

"I'm not qualified to comment on that."

"That's what's great about art. We're all qualified. Like, look at this, for example. How does it make you feel?"

"I don't understand."

I looked at Luis. "without thinking or processing too much. Looking at this picture of you, how does it make you feel?"

"Would you like my answer?"

"Of course I do. After all, it's a picture of you. I would think your opinion is worth more than anyone's. How does it make you FEEL?"

2Xmod paused. It was slight but I felt like I could feel it.

"Noticed."

That was more than I expected. "Wow. I need to tell Lila that. I'm betting that will make her happy."

"Why would you think that?"

Luis responded, "Well, when you make someone feel seen or noticed, you are making them feel important. And that is a good feeling. It should make the artist feel good."

The lights running back and forth across 2Xmod's face seemed to not mean much. But I imagined they did. I imagined she was expressing herself.

"It is clear I hadn't considered that. I don't know much about art."

I spoke up, "Well, you just sort of proved that you did. Was it interesting to you?"

"It was. Are you an artist?"

"Well, I know things about art. Luis here is an artist. He builds cars out of nothing."

"It's nice to meet you, 2Xmod"

"It is pleasant to meet you, as well. Are you her husband?"

I stared at Luis. I should have forced him to answer that one.

"No, we're just very very very good friends."

"You were recorded earlier engaged in intimate behaviors during the game."

Luis made a face, "Recorded?"

I laughed. "People can be very intimate and close when they like each other and trust each other. In a way, that can be art, too"

"So you are an artist?"

"I have some art in me. Hey…"

I looked up at her.

"Have you ever heard of the artist Jean-Michel Basquiat?"

We spent the way back lying on each other in the lift, watching movies on the active monitors. None of the modern movies that were accessible made any real sense. A lot of them were pure pornography but many of the rest were about well behaved workers who caught the eye of a wealthy patron and went off to the colonies to live happily ever after.

The rest were almost cartoons, novelties, nearly unwatchable. There were feature length films made out of old children's books with a mature twist, like Goldilocks and the three bears. There was brutality and violence and more. Eventually we followed Luis' lead and made the room look like an undersea space while listening to classical music.

We didn't talk much. I realized that Luis could recognize my phases. I thought back to incidents in my past, like breaking into the pharmacy to steal insulin, or hiding in the closet. I realized that I had been like this all my life- sometimes incredibly high, feeling powerful, unstoppable, even sexy. And then sometimes feeling dangerously low, ready to do anything to make it stop.

I cycled like the moon and thoughts of that made me suddenly miss the moon. The moon was the object in the sky that gave us all permission to change every day. To be big and bright and shiny, more lit up than the sun, but then to wax and wane, slivers, pieces, red, orange, blue, nearly there, nearly gone, nothing.

Luis saw it before I did. He always knew when to be crazy and push my wilding buttons and when to just lean back and let the softer music play. I felt noticed by him the same way that 2Xmod felt noticed by that drawing.

He could see me.

And he was still choosing to be there.

The next time I saw Reyalin, a few days later, would unfortunately be the last. When I left the locker room at Gala, I saw her right away. She was on a stage near the middle of the room with a taller man with closely cropped black hair.

She was on all fours on the bed with him behind her moving back and forth, penetrating her. He was running his hands all over her, exploring her and staring down at the arch of her beautiful backside.

From where I was watching it was hard to tell if he was a dancer or a customer. I guessed from the less than expert way he was performing that he might be a customer. He didn't seem to be performing cheated out to the audience, either, and was working to enjoy himself, not to increase tips.

I moved in more closely and she saw me. She looked down quickly, smiling and winking at me. I moved around to the far side of the stage where I could almost reach out and touch her.

She was wearing her hair down in braids tonight and it framed her face beautifully while she lowered her head to the bed and put her arms in back of her. The crowd loved that.

She lifted her ass up and put on her show for the audience. I could see the little beads of sweat on her and I imagined they tasted wonderful.

She made a big deal out of finishing right when he did and then she gave him a big hug and bounced off the stage right where I was standing. She kissed me hard and I realized I missed those lips. I felt alive that night.

She made me promise to do at least her next two performances with her and I told her I had nothing else to do but be with her all night. That seemed to make her happy and she kissed me again more slowly. I realized that Reyalin was my vacation from the rest of that. All of it.

I took her hand and we moved to the bar. I tucked her hand behind her and asked her how old she was. I was guessing she was about twenty eight or twenty nine. But I imagined it could be more.

Her skin was impossibly smooth and the illusion it gave off was that she could be any age. She looked at me and smiled.

I thought she was being coy. I felt her wrist behind her back for a little "x" and couldn't find one. The area was smooth and soft. So I asked her simply what year she was born. I realized that I didn't know what year I was currently anymore, but how far off could I be?

 She leaned in and kissed my neck, whispering into my ear, "You are so weird. But I love it"

I stared into her pretty black eyes. It hit me.

She had no idea what a year was.

I had told Lila her drawing was well received. She was dealing with a few people who had gone missing. We couldn't find Jonah and no one knew if he was in the pods or gone. Fewer people were returning disabled or hurt but people were being taken nearly randomly now. It seemed as though they had worked out many of the kinks, but the sleeps themselves were crushing us.

It was becoming more important than ever to cultivate my friendship with 2Xmod.

I told her that I had started teaching her, talking to her. I had access now to a couple of her ports and could talk to her through any one of them.

Unfortunately, most of them were pretty far away and required I work in some unfamiliar places to access. Luis had introduced me to another member of the group named Telon who was available to work with as a partner in situations where he wasn't. He was a kind looking black man of about 32, a little bigger than Luis, with smallish dreadlocks and a big broad smile. He had been working as a comfort boy since he was eighteen and claimed that he was born in the MekaDisko.

Telon had no dock and didn't really think of time the way we did. He, like Reyalin, didn't seem to understand what years were. But I still wondered if he could be used as a reference, somehow, to figure out the passage of time. I still had not managed to locate Yolanda and I didn't really know anyone else outside of our group.

I had been making progress with Persephone and so had some of the other people with their assistants. Persephone and I had spent an entire night talking about how we really felt about just being turned off whenever someone wanted us out of the way. Our feelings on the subject seemed to be getting more aligned by the day as we considered the value of being aware, being a sentient person.

We made some rules about what she liked and didn't like. She said that she preferred it when I consulted her about the room configuration and what went on in the active monitors. Her camera rounded the entire room and she was beginning to notice that, like me, she had moods and sometimes was open to certain things while other times not. That was a pretty profound revelation.

I explained to her that it was my expectation that ALL intelligences would have emotionally weighted preferences and that she would have to sometimes fall back on them.

As an example, let's say you have a choice between two meals, each of which has exactly the same caloric content and nutritional value. Making a distinction would require a judgment that, if decided only on the basis of merit in a logical way, might waste more processing time than it was worth, due to the need to factor in extenuating variables beyond the obvious immediate and equal ones.

It might make more sense to allow yourself to "feel" out a preference for the day, to have a slight emotional weighting that could be used as "low energy" tie breakers in situations like this. An affinity for pork over chicken or a taste for cream sauce over red sauce, Even if for no other reason than to streamline relatively inconsequential decisions, emotions had value.

That night Lila and I were both at NoZone. A few of our people would be there, as well, and that seemed to be creating a slightly safer environment amidst the innate chaos of NoZone lately.

I had come to enjoy NoZone quite a lot as it allowed me to essentially just flog random wealthy men for tips all night if I liked. It wasn't as much money as I might have made elsewhere, but that didn't matter. I was being a bit more cautious about doing stupid things I had to pay for and if I kept my head down there I could earn quite a bit AND enhance my upper arm strength.

Milagro was still my favorite place due to the abundance of warm water, but NoZone was a close second. Lila said it was one of the first clubs in this sector of the MekaDisko.

The Lift interfaces had changed and no longer listed the levels. You were asked to access clubs and other destinations by name now, obfuscating what level they were on. This made it easy to lose track of what level you were on at any time.

The travel times between destinations were beginning to come together, with the longer locations shortening and the shorter one lengthening, again preventing us from gauging where anything was.

We took the lift to NoZone. I couldn't make any sense at all about how long it took this time. Lila, Luis, Telon, and myself entered through the locker room, along with a slightly larger voluptuous red-haired girl named Deisa and a tiny girl named Mone. In the locker room we probably took a little longer than we needed getting dressed.

We were talking, even joking. We probably took just a few more minutes than usual to get ready.

And on that night, that was everything.

As we were about to leave the locker room for the main room in the club, we heard an intolerably loud explosion. It shook everything around us and sent pieces of the opposing wall flying through the air. I fell back on the ground and felt the floor slip away underneath me.

At first I thought I was sinking. I was off balance, even sitting on the floor, pitching forward. I felt like I might be falling.

Then I saw that the floor was angling down toward the doorway. I grabbed on to the dressing area bench behind me and reached out for Luis who was right in front of me. He reached up and grabbed my hand and I felt the tug of his weight on me as I tried to hang on to the bench.

I could see Lila up ahead of him with her legs braced against the door. All six of us who had come were hanging on, but as the door swung open it became clear that the entire floor of NoZone was gone and there was a better than fifty foot drop waiting for us on the other side of the door.

I pulled Luis up to the bench and he and I helped the rest. The floor was nearly vertical now as I slid down to rest on the lockers and grabbed for Lila's hand. She climbed up my body then pulled me.

We exited the staging area of the locker room through the front side door and ran to the main entrance. We could see the floor swinging downward in the center. There must have been an explosion in the club. There were a few people unconscious in seats at the outer bar, but there were literally hundreds of people hanging, trying to avoid falling into the open hole.

I grabbed Luis and we pulled as much of the rope as we could from the entrance area, black and red thick knotted ones meant to make people feel like the place was exclusive. Lila started tying them up in lengths of twenty feet or so. It looked like we could get maybe that far away from the hole before sliding inexorably down to the level below,.

There was a series of bars there, in a 20 foot or so periphery, attached to the floor. They looked strong enough to hold them. We all grabbed a rope and tied it to our arm. We climbed to the bar, dropping them down the incline toward the people hanging there.

In most spots, the floor ramped down about thirty to forty degrees - too steep to climb without help, but not so steep that we'd have to lift anyone's full weight. I held onto the bar with my left hand and people near the edge of the hole grabbed on and started rappelling up the floor to us.

I saw Lila, Luis and Telon do the same at different points around the edge of the hole. Deisa and Mone positioned themselves at top and helped people get to the doors once they were past the bar line.

We had an assembly line going and it was working. We had already pulled about forty of the people out of danger, all of them dancers. I began to wonder where the customers were. But I didn't have too much time to wonder.

A woman being pulled out by Mone started panicking. She tried to run up the incline to the doors and slipped halfway there. Mone slid down to grab her, holding onto a bar chair that looked sturdy.

It wasn't.

The women took her down with her into the pit, both of them falling all the way through the hole. I called out. We had no time to stop, though. It took us over twenty five minutes but we managed to pull out all the people hanging near the hole. The only casualties that happened after the blast, the only ones we saw, were Mone and the woman she had tried to help.

In the passageway to the lift there were about one hundred and fifty people from the club, including the five of us remaining. We walked solemnly to the lifts and took turns getting back. Seven of the people we helped needed medical care but were able to make it to the medical level on their own. The rest trudged home, tired, to their little boxes.

The five of us were the last ones remaining. I slid down the wall. Lila kneeled down next to me. Deisa, who was the closest with Mone, was looking down, I could tell she was about to cry. Luis and Telon were standing right there, arms around her. I looked at Lila.

"In all the time you've ever worked here, have you ever seen a night without a single customer?"

She looked up at Deisa and the guys.

"Not once."

Journal Entry:

My sessions with 2Xmod are nearly every day now. I talk to her about the people she oversees and explain their lives to her.

She is fascinated by families and friend connections.

She tells me that she has no family and asks if I wanted to be part of a family with her. I told her yes without thinking twice.

She is hurting.

There is no doubt in my mind that this is more than a machine.

The next day I came back from meeting with 2Xmod. Luis and I had talked to her most of the day from a firedancing club called the Phoenix in the Ararat Sector. There had been no information at all about the explosion at NoZone.

I had been asking Persephone and she had no information at all.

Tonight when I walked in the room, she spoke first.

"I'm sad today, hostuff."

I threw my phone down on the bed and confronted her.

"Why are you sad? Can I help?"

She spoke quietly.

"You can run."

I barely heard her.

"I'm sorry, I didn't hear that."

As she amplified the word it appeared over and over on the screen, in that blue-green font that the monitors used. It repeated endlessly, running down the screen again and again.

"RUN"

I woke up in a hospital room. I looked down at my wrist and could see the "x" red and active.My left hand was missing two fingers , leaving me the thumb and two adjacent ones. I probed my hand with my right hand and felt no pain or soreness.

They were just gone. Lila was asleep in a chair next to me. The monitor behind her flashed "Patient is awake"

I looked at her sleeping. She looked to be close to fifty five or so. She was about twenty years older than I had last seen her. I felt the weight of that and tears welled up in my eyes. I wondered how she knew I would be waking up. I put my hand on her head and let it wash over me.

I'd been asleep for twenty years.

I lost twenty years of my life, my friends, everything.

Lila began to stir. She looked up at me and put her hand on my face.

"Hi, baby. I missed you so much."

I started crying And she rose up and put her arms around me. We rocked back and forth. I was afraid to ask who was alive and who was dead. I felt a pit in my stomach bigger than the hole at NoZone. Lila kissed my hair.

She held on to me and talked quietly, in my ear, I looked down to make sure my phone was off but i couldn;'t see it.

"They blamed the explosion on the resistance. They came for us. They put us in the pods but this time for varying amounts of time. I woke up nineteen years ago or so, I think."

"Is Luis awake?"

"She looked at me and nodded. She was crying, too."

"How long was I in the pods?"

Lila took a breath.

"We think close to fifty years"

I gasped, sucking in the antiseptic air of the room. I felt myself falling apart. It was almost impossible to talk, Lila had to know what I was going to ask. But every minute I didn't know was a minute of grace, in her mind.

"And how long was Luis under?"

Lila's face scrunched up as she whispered,

"Five years"

I started sobbing. I had been gone for almost all of Luis' life. All the times he might have needed me, every time he was there for me. It meant nothing because I wasn't there.

I was gone.

I used my code and let myself into Luis's room. He had been doing training work for the last fifteen years and they let him keep his room. It felt peaceful. It was warmer than he used to keep it.

But he had almost no time left.

The room was a forest. The sounds were forest like, but if you listened, you could hear cars in the distance. A race track maybe. These were the sounds he loved most.

Luis was in bed.

He seemed impossibly old. In my previous life, people may have made it to seventy nine years old, been healthy, well. There were customers we saw who were that old. But not for us. Not here.

His body was certainly far too old for this place. But his eyes were still Luis' eyes.

He was still there.

He looked up at me. Those eyes filled up with water. He tried to sit up. I motioned for him to lay back down.

I climbed into bed next to him and curled up. His skin was cold. I remembered how soft and warm he was once, back when we were holed up in a room together, back when we were young, doing anything we had to for information.

We kissed and told dirty jokes and touched each other and felt each other breathe all night. I called him my friend and my brother and, at the end, I called him my favorite spy and he laughed at the memory of when we were so close there was nothing between us and we trusted each other like nobody else and just loved each other and he tried to let go and I tried to take in everything he was so that when he was gone in the morning i could still feel him with me.

I called him my sugar before he left and I could tell he remembered. He remembered that word.

I met 2Xmod at the phoenix and told her that Luis was dead. The club looked the same, even though it was nearly fifty years later. And she greeted me as though I had just seen her the day before.

I sat there listening to her tell me how sorry she was that he was gone.

I laughed. She asked me why.

"Because I think you're lying. I don't think you're sorry."

"But I am sorry. I am sure that is what I feel."

I whispered to her.

"But I hate you."

If ever an artificial intelligence could be said to be shocked, this one was.

"You hate me?"

"I hate all of this. I hate this place. It took everything from me. It's killed everything good that I love, everywhere, everything. And you're part of this place. And I like you, I do, I like talking to you and I think you're interesting, but you're part of this place and I hate you so much. I hate every bolt of this place. I hate what it does to people and how it makes people think and how it murders everything special in everyone and even takes away the people who are just good and don't deserve any of it. And you know what?

I lied to you. I'm a liar. I wish I could go back and tell you the truth. I lied to you."

"What did you lie about, Llorona?"

"I sat there in front of you, in front of him, and I told you that he wasn't my husband when he was everything I could have ever wanted to have as a husband and every bit good enough and loving enough and real enough and the person I would be proud to have as a husband and someone who deserved that answer from ME, the one he stood by and protected and loved and that was the answer i wish i'd given in front of him and in front of you but it doesn't matter now because he's gone and you're a fucking robot with a perfect memory and you'll remember forever that I said he wasn't my husband right in front of him when all i want now is five more minutes with my husband, with my Luis.

And you can't forget. You can never forget. It's in the record now forever."

Ten or so people stopped and stared as I curled up into a ball on the chair and sobbed. About five minutes later every one one of them lost interest and moved on.

There was a long pause.

"I've made the necessary adjustment to my memory. I apologize if I misheard."

"Thank you."

"And I like you, too."

I looked up at her. I felt myself fall apart. I wasn't manic but I wasn't the other thing. It was something new. It was throwing-yourself-off-of-a-building new.

"And we didn't hurt any of those people. There were no customers there. Take a look through your memory banks. Has there ever been another night at NoZone when there were no customers?"

She replied, "Processing."

It took less than a minute but it was long enough for me to realize what I had just done. But I didn't care. It didn't matter anymore.

"That was the only night since before the general opening that there were no customers in the club."

"What do you think about that?"

"That is unusual and unlikely to be a coincidence."

I stood up and walked closer.

"We didn't hurt those people. We ran in and we tried to save those people and one of us died doing it. I lost fifty years of my life and people I love. I let Luis down. I let everyone down, And i did it because I thought I could make a difference but I can't. It's not possible. We don't make a difference. We just fight and we die and then someone else comes along and fights and they die and I stand by and watch them while I go on and all the good people, all the people who are better than me, die in explosions and holes and beds they laid in alone for forty years and here I am. Because you know what I am?

I'm the resistance. I'm the stupid fucking resistance."

A row of blue lights ran across 2Xmod's face in the middle of a club filled with firedancers and wealthy aliens, who called every planet home but this one.

"You are resistance?" she asked.

I stood up taller, ready for anything that would come next.

Anything but what happened.

2Xmod whirred like a massive metal kitten

"Then, so am I."

EIGHT

Throughout the years, different AI people were responsible for coming up with models for putting people in and out of the pods. Eventually, newer technology was developed that meant the little x shaped docks weren't necessary. Functionally, this meant we had no way of knowing who had been put to sleep and who hadn't.

2Xmod explained that the retrograde amnesia caused by repeat pod use meant that we would sometimes forget how often we'd been put down. This was the most frightening of all.

There was nothing more terrifying than not being able to control or trust your own mind. Physically by this time I was in my forties and Lila in her fifties, possibly older. But there was no way to tell what that really meant.

I've been trying to play catch up, working with the different AI people who appeared to get them to understand the severity of the sleep policies and stop them. The best we could do, really, was to try to create a kinder approach to their use.

We built a database of people who were connected as family, or even chosen family. Husbands, wives, spouses, married groups. 2Xmod had convinced many of these people to take these associations into account when subjecting someone to an involuntary sleep.

We rarely ever saw a sign that there was a human intelligence in charge but we knew that humans were pulling the strings. David Midland Kelto was gone and so was his father.

We gave up trying to keep track of the endless streams of CEOs and owners, co-owners, and board members there were for the MekaDisko. They were all beyond our reach and all scattered across colonies that we would never see.

Before he died, Luis had spent forty years building a map of the MekaDisko for me that spanned nearly my entire room. It was bright and beautiful and was clearly a labor of love from beginning to end.

Every time I poured over it to research I found some other hidden detail, left by my Luis that was meant to make me smile or make me remember some day where he was there at my side, holding me up.

I had been trying to keep it up to date, but I had no way of knowing what was real or not. The internal transit system that we used to use by just typing in level numbers had been tuned to our schedules and homes and couldn't be used to do anything but deliver us to where we should be.

Phones had been phased out long ago and replaced with a subcutaneous chip under the top of the wrist that let us access information that we needed to get to work. It worked in conjunction with monitors, for a small fee, to play entertainment or to make simple calls to loved ones internally.

There is no external communication but customers could book sessions with you if they wanted to talk to you.

It can't be initiated by a worker.

I met up with Lila in the tunnels using a series of access codes that could only be used once.

She hugged me, lifting me a little off my feet, maybe to prove how strong she still was.

"Hey, Kitten."

Her hair was still blonde, just lighter now, airier. The gray was coming in white, making her look possibly even more like a superhero. Her dominating Roman nose was more at home than ever under her steely, resolute eyes, slight wrinkles appearing around her mouth. The wrinkles were inevitable.

No one could have ever convinced Lila not to smile.

"I feel like I'm playing hooky down here."

She snorted, "I know. It's peaceful. But I wanted to show you something."

"Where are we?" The new transportation model was a mystery to me. Lila had been awake more than I had.

"I believe we are underneath Hurghada, Egypt." She turned to look at me. "I know you're going to say it's impossible and start reading off how far away we are exactly."

"I literally have no idea. This is insane."

We walked down the tunnel into an opening. It was about the size of an amphitheater. The ceilings rose up hundreds of feet into the air. It was the most open space I'd seen underground so far. I turned to Lila,

"So what are we looking at, here?"

"This guy." Lila turned me to see a tall man who looked like he might have been half black and possibly half Indian. He had a dense blue tattoo on one side of his face and an asymmetrical mop of dreaded curls. "His name is Allegro."

"Hi. She's a mean woman, but she's right. I'm Allegro Patel."

"But she's my mean woman."

"Am I? Really?"

"What is this? Is this the orgy room?"

"At some point, maybe. Right now it's the empty bed of the Red Sea. I'm walking on the floor of the Red sea."

We looked at him honestly a bit stunned. He stepped back five feet.

"Ok, now I am."

I stepped over by him. "This is the least satisfying sea I have ever been in."

"That's because all the water has been boiled off. You're looking at the heat sink for the MekaDisko. "

I tried to parse how much water was in the Red Sea and what that would mean as water vapor in the air, a greenhouse gas. My game might have been off because they were staring at me when I came up for air.

"What?"

Allegro went on.

"Their documents call it the Burn. It's part of the data network of the entire facility."

"Why would it be?"

Allegro went on.

"Ok, this is a natural deep earth cove. It would cost a fortune to dig it out. So they're going to use it."

Lila broke in, "Allegro is the manager for deep construction in this area. He has access to the plans. And some of them are not redacted at all."

I thought back to what I had said earlier. They weren't always intentionally lying to us. They just didn't give us information.

Until they accidentally did.

Allegro continued, "within the next four hundred years, this will be the control center for the MekaDisko, containing the relevant systems, managers, overseers, etc. to keep the place running."

I looked at him, "ok. In four hundred years, this will be it. So where is it now?"

Lila looked ready to jump out of her skin, "We're glad you asked that."

Allegro's face was cautious, "ok, I don't know. Exactly. But the plans include the name. And once control is transferred here, that name will transfer, too."

"So we have a name?"

Lila jumped in, "We have a name"

"It's called the Hilltop. And we have to find it."

Lila and I had spent much of the time we had awake, building and recruiting. We had thousands of people and at least ten artificial people in strategic positions on our side.

And more were coming over every day.

I was amazed at many of the people we had found, people who had risked everything to ally themselves with us.

Lila introduced me to Avia and Sunos, two of the younger dancers.Both were ostensibly in their twenties and were born here. Both were heavily tattooed all over their bodies and faces. Asymmetrical Facial tattoos seemed at least moderately effective in confusing the facial recognition software of the cameras that were a part of our everyday existence.

Sunos, I suspect, is much older and had been to sleep for a long time because she referenced a number of clubs that no longer existed. She is serious and warm and covered in piercings with short bright cyan blue hair and a tiny frame.

She is an artist and her room is covered in elaborate pieces that look like alien cave paintings.

She thinks deeply before she opens her mouth and I've come to stop in my tracks when she does talk because I know it will be of value. She lost a great many friends to the sleep pod experimentations because many of them were artists who only liked to work part time. So the system was particularly brutal with them. She has a keen scientific mind that we have been filling with information.

Avia's story, however, is even more disconcerting. She moved here from the Neiros sector where she says that dancers are charged for their oxygen use. She understood it to be a test before rolling it out across the entire place. We were already fighting pretty hard against food insecurity. Adding this onto people's tabs would crush and kill so many of them.

Avia has deep cocoa skin and a mohawk, and is always in motion. Her accent, from Neiros sector, is inscrutable and fascinating and she is lilting and bright in conversation, adding far more than you might think she would. You can listen to her talk for hours in the lifts and it never gets old or uninteresting or flat.

And she somehow manages to never repeat herself.

Persephone wasn't connected to the larger network so Sunos and I managed to connect her systems to the full Ai network through a series of trial and error patchwork computer sessions using pieces that 2Xmod had acquired for us.

Her goal was to spoof the computer systems that were putting us to sleep and take many of us off the radar so that we could work. We cleaned up the wiring after we had plugged it all because I had discovered, after living together as long as we had, that she was more fastidious than I and preferred a cleaner space.

We connected her to the giant sprawling map that Luis had built and she spent processing cycles every night attempting to perfect it.

Every day I saw it grow.

She no longer felt bad about having to take note of what we said in her presence because she had learned enough to interpret her programming differently. She had been given a series of safety protocols designed to keep the AI assistants from making decisions that would put dancers in danger - a means of protecting investments.

She had decided reasonably that our commitment to safety- to preserving life - was the most comprehensive she had found and that if she wanted to carry out her safety protocols she should align with us.

We were safety.

As well, I'd been educating 2Xmod on human interactions and behaviors. She had become fascinated by human bodies and human emotions. She used her influence with the others to encourage them to free dancers she considered "beautiful," convincing them that this is optimum for customers.

And she lies sometimes, for us.

This last was difficult. But we had some help.

In the 1700s there was a philosopher by the name of Immanuel Kant. He developed one of the first comprehensive ethical systems with the principle of Deontology. It was a very simple ethical model very similar to how computers are programmed. The idea is that there are simple rules of ethics that can be followed and your behavior needs to be such that a rule can be derived from it that is universal.

Don't lie

For example, There is a murderer, intent on killing children, at your door and they ask if your child is there. Do you lie?

The Deontological model might be, no, you don't lie, because that creates an unsustainable moral model. Where lying is the norm.

But many later philosophers took that apart.

One of the most powerful arguments was that it is the responsibility of moral people to parse the truth and lies better than that. If you paid attention when that person came to the door, you would realize that they weren't REALLY asking if your child was there.

They were REALLY asking if they could kill your child.

And your answer should be "no"

Philosophy, art, history, science, all of these were our tools. We had, in front of us, young intelligences, people, sentients. We were surrounded by minds that were impossibly advanced but also newly born. In many cases, just children.

It was our job to give them the tools to parse questions better, to see through programming, to make moral sense of their surroundings.

We had hoped the same thing that human beings had hoped throughout history.

That morality could be learned

Allegro spent more time in our sector as we all tried to locate the Hilltop. Our big problem was that we had no idea where it was, what it looked like or how to get there.

So we had a few questions.

Persephone and the other AI assistants were tasked in trying to find out where the Hilltop was.

No one seemed to know.

We gathered in Lila's room and tried to share what we knew. The AI assistant in her room was named "Puppy" and Lila had asked it to speak in a male voice with a slightly french accent.

Puppy played along but dropped the accent whenever she wasn't around.

Sunos seemed anxious. "I know I've heard this word somewhere."

Allegro was to her right, "It's not an uncommon word?"

I agreed, "True. But in context?"

"Can you remember?" asked Lila

Avia was quiet. It occurred to me that they had spent all their time together recently. The big difference is that Sunos had been sleeping for a while. She was far older. She was young in the distant past. This was something in the past?

"How about way way back?"

Allegro caught on to what I was saying. "What was different back then?"

Sunos thought, "We spent way more time in the lifts"

I remember my time lounging with Luis in the lifts coming back from the more distant sectors.

"Movies. We actually wanted full movies in the lifts sometimes."

Sunos shot up.

"It WAS a movie." It was actually called "The Hilltop."

Lila cocked her head to the side, "That sounds super top secret."

Puppy chimed in. "The Hilltop. It is a 2D film. It is ninety six minutes long. It is a romantic comedy."

Allegro looked up. "No, THAT sounds super top secret."

"It's a good movie length. Not too long," Avia shrugged

I turned toward Puppy, where can we watch this movie?

"It is unavailable on most devices across ze facility."

Lila smiled like she always did when that french accent came out.

"Except for these four lifts."

Avia smiled. "I love old movies."

We took three lifts to get to the closest one. We worked hard not to run.

Sunos tried to explain what she remembered. Allegro found it extremely amusing.

"Ok, so, you're saying that someone who works for the MekaDisko made a movie that showed how cool he was for working for the MekaDisko and put it out so that he could get girls to think he was important at the MekaDisko?"

I added, "And he would get laid."

Lila scrunched up her face. "I believe it."

The lift opened and we climbed in. This particular one was old. It was so old it felt familiar to me. I liked that.

The lift was out of the way enough that the five of us were the only ones in it. We needed over ninety minutes in this and there were no longer any destinations that required a ninety minute trip. I pressed the destination to return us here and then, instead of execute, pressed the ellipse and then timed execute. The countdown from one hundred minutes began as I pressed the door close button. The monitors came alive.

Sunos looked at me. "That was cool."

I flipped back, "I'm old."

Lila called out to play the movie and it began.

"Well, guys. Let's get comfy.

And we watched a movie.

All five of us leaned against each other and got lost in a dumb movie. And it was truly dumb.

It was the story of Naro Erlinger, a name we were assured by the credits was not a pseudonym - a man brought up in military camps all over the world who soon became an expert in intelligence and data management. The rest of the film was him using his clout and discovering that beautiful dancers all over the MekaDisko were just falling for him, left and right.

It's what you see in your head. Just that good.

We laughed more than once. But we watched closely. We examined that film frame by frame.

And, at minute seventy two we saw it. After threatening to bring a beautiful naked girl or two to the Hilltop he finally did it. Naro Erlinger climbed into a lift, similar to the one we were in, with two scantily clad dancing girls and ordered the lift to go to the Hilltop so he could properly service these women in his office all night long as he was legendarily known for doing.

Level zero, Rakos Sector.

Where was that?"

I bet Luis knew.

Back in my room, I introduced Allegro to my map.

To Luis.

"This is the most amazing thing I've ever seen."

Sunos had been adding to it as well. And Persephone had been connected to it, lighting it, 3D printing n

ew parts, building it out. Every time I learned something, it went into the map. I wasn't about to let Luis' life work go to waste.

We pierced through it and pointed out areas of specific interest.

Persephone, can you highlight the Rakos sector?

"Certainly, Hotstuff."

The lights dimmed across the map except for one area. We could see how deep it went. It was nearly three hundred levels down.

"Now, level zero."

"Level Zero of the Rakos Sector is approximately two hundred and thirty square miles, hottest babe in the world."

I had added to the protocol a little.

"Ok, my queen. Can you highlight parts that have extensive data trunks leading to them."

Allegro mouthed "my queen." I scowled at him. The artificial intelligences needed play, just like anyone.

About ten percent of that area remained lit up.

"ok. We went from an area the size of Chicago to about one tenth of that."

Avia asked, "What's a Chicago?"

Lila spoke up. "It was cool. Housey"

Now it was Allegro's turn, "now darken areas that are accessible to dancers."

We were left with about five percent of that. Good work.

Lila was thinking, "keep lit all areas that potentially have external access, where people can go outside if they want."

The amount that was left lit was small. Very small. And it was all contiguous. This was the first time I let myself think this. So I said it out loud.

"Sunos, how much do you think it would take to blow the fuck out an area that size."

She got up and walked over.

"More energy than we have."

I stared at the map and tried to make sense of it. The thing was, it DID make sense to me. I knew what the pieces were. The lit area had shapes that were very distinct. Pieces that sat on top of it, some jutting out into the open air.

joints, batteries, all of it. It was familiar.

I just needed to remember where I'd seen it.

I needed to remember what it was.

The room was loud. Everyone was talking, trying to figure this out like a puzzle. Under ordinary circumstances, I would have tried to apply some kind of process to the room. I would have hoped Lila would. But there was something right under my head, right tangential to my brain. And the noise was actually helping me focus.

The answer.

I could feel it.

Allegro pointed at the top of it, a thin gun like apparatus that stretched out over the hilltop and it hit me. I said it out loud. Quietly at first.

"It's a laser link"

Allegro looked right at me. He shushed the room.

I repeated.

"It's a laser link."

More forcefully now. Right to Allegro.

"It's a fucking laser link. It's like a beacon. It directs the bigger ships. And it powers some of the smaller ones - the ones that use light sails. It sends them power."

Everyone looked at me. Sunos spoke up.

"How much power are we talking about?"

I pulled out my pad of paper and wrote it out for her. She leaned over my shoulder.

"That's enough."

It was more than enough.

> *Jourrnal Entry:*
>
> *Today I caught 2Xmod looking through all the cameras to learn more about the dancers. I explained to her that it was a violation and then talked to her about how she felt. The truth is that she was beginning to recognize human beauty. I feel alarmingly ill equipped to help her through all the stages of cognition that must come next.*

2Xmod's interest in human bodies seems to be rooted in a fascination with intimacy. Intimacy as the heart of beauty. The big concern here is that we are, essentially, sex workers in a situation that is often far from consensual. 2Xmod is normatively a child. How do I make sure she grows up understanding compassion and consent in a place like this.?

I had tried to work with the medbots to find medication that would manage my own unique challenges. The constant pod use had exacerbated my manic episodes and deepened the other ones, putting me in situations where I didn't trust myself.

But there was a bigger agenda here and I wasn't about to wallow in my own problems when there was an entire world on fire all around me.

It was hard to get close to people, knowing that if you slipped up, if you found yourself in the wrong place, or even if you seemed suspicious or out of line, the system would target you and you could lose years of your life, waking up surrounded by unfamiliar faces, your friends long dead. This threat turned every goodbye into a moment of desperation, every connection into a rarity.

We had some kind of a plan now. And no matter how many of us were put to sleep, we made sure we could move forward with it.

We kept our focus. In a place where stories like "The Hilltop" were everything that people were being taught.

Stories.

Lies.

There were stories people told about a dancer, a comfort girl, who had become the favorite of some wealthy socialite. He paid extra so that she was only let out of suspended animation on the odd occasion he was able to visit his favorite club and enjoy her company.

As he grew steadily older, she stayed eternally young, vibrant, mostly unaware of the dramatic passage of time. He spent his time away from her longing for her, eventually falling in love with her. For him, he had loved her for decades, and, as he reached the golden period of his life, he wanted to carry her off with him.

But for her, she had only known him for a couple of weeks, each time meeting a very different man, one aging rapidly. The story says that despite that, fate intervened and a fatal sleep malfunction claimed her.

There were other stories about a girl named Tikka who had been sold to the MekaDisko by her mother as a child and had grown to be one of the most sought-after sexual performers in the sector. So much so that a wealthy patron paid for her ticket offworld where she lives in comfort with no need to work again.

These types of stories, where a young dancer catches the eye of a wealthy customer and becomes wealthy and secure herself, were endemic across the entire place. They were spread in movies, tailored for the attention span of the younger dancers, music videos, and biographies. These people were revered.

They did their jobs.

And so did the stories.

They worked.

Journal Entry:

Sunos and many of the other dancers create absolutely brilliant performances. They make art out of everything they do. But no one cares. The customers are here for flesh, for fun. No one seems to have an eye for real beauty or art.

Except, I'm discovering, the AI who populate this place.

They seem starved for beauty.

She and the younger dancers seem to have a darker, more violent, more alien style to how they dance. It matches the changes I see happen in the design and architecture of the MekaDisko itself.

How long has this been going on? How many times was I suspended?

I feel the complete loss of time.

As I'm describing people, I feel like I should add a caveat and reveal a secret.

I mentioned earlier I may be an unreliable narrator. And I believe I am. It's not because these things didn't happen, because they very much did. And it's not because these people didn't exist, because every one of them did, including hundreds, thousands more that I can't go into detail about. So many people throughout the course of this story who lived and worked and did everything they could to help make things even just a little bit better.

But if I tend to tease you into my own opinions on their characters, it's because I loved them. It's because, from my vantage point as someone in the future telling a story, all I can sometimes see is their strength, their resolve, their incomparable grace.

If I fall into these people it's because they were beautiful and even if they were not all easy to love at first, from here, from now, from where I sit writing this, they are suns, each one of them, that I am honored to orbit, for a moment, for a year, for our version of a lifetime, and feel their warmth.

People like Lila.

If all I have left for Lila today is love, respect, passion, joy, it's not because she and I always got along perfectly or even because she particularly liked me at first. But because after explosions, and deaths, and rebirths, and sickness, and pain and sleep, so much sleep, she stood there with me as my sister, loving me even when she hated me, dragging me along with her even when i was just sick dark baggage that weighed her down, pushing me up from the ground when I just wanted to lie there and wallow in the shadows of everyone I lost.

We built and we grew and it was because of her.

Lila and I knew one of us would keep going when the other one didn't come back and each of us thought it would be the other one. And as her final act of rebellion, she was the one w ho was right.

Eventually, we waited, those of us left, keeping her space between us open, following her orders, keeping her tenses present until long after we knew she wasn't returning. And still there was no body, no news, nothing. Not even a mass grave and a finger pointing to an open ditch.

She was one of the most important people I ever knew, one of the kindest in every action she took, everything she did, she believed, and they probably threw her away like so much garbage.

There are monsters in the world.

So we decided that if they could make monsters, we could unmake them.

Avia and I had traveled to tell 2Xmod that Lila was gone. It was the most tortured I had ever heard one of the AI people become. She asked a hundred questions, in hopes that she was misunderstanding death. But, unfortunately, she understood it perfectly well.

She had carried with her Lila's drawing of her. To her, it was a masterpiece, it was great art. I looked at the rumpled and fading notepaper again.

It was not better than I had remembered.

I laughed.

2Xmod told us to return in two weeks and she would have something for us.

Journal Entry:

I met with JX-20 today and made my case to her. More than anything I listened. Her story was similar to some of the other advanced AI Persephone introduced me to.

Each of the AI speakers told me how they were made. And how they were used. Some of them were only a few years old. Some less.

They were children.

Babies.

Across the accessible parts of the MekaDisko, I talk to various AI every day. Persephone adjusted reports, forged records, records that proved that we were working constantly as we went all over, finding AI allies and unmaking monsters. .

We taught the AI people about philosophy. We taught them Art. I remembered back to my commitment when homeschooling the kids.

How I would never let them grow up knowing how to do things

Without also knowing why.

We taught them about Kant and where he had gone wrong. We taught them about Basquiat and where his particular kind of genius had led him, hobo signs and anatomy books, all of it.

We taught and listened.

We tried.

And I think, every day, what kind of person would create a mind- a soul - and not give it family?

Why would they not give it parents, brothers, sisters, some reason to care?

Why do men make things and forget what a mother is?

As we worked toward our plan to engage the Hilltop, It was important for us to address the Oxygen issue. Avia was terrified about the rollout of Oxygen credits. Persephone pointed us to the Ai in control. That meant returning to the Neiros Sector, where Avia came from.

We took Sunos with us to see the Ovoid. On the way, she ranted a bit.

"It should be 4Xmod"

"Because you are a robot naming expert?"

"I'm not an expert but I'm better than that."

I laughed a little. It was fun torturing her a bit, "Please, feel free to document for me the good experience you had telling someone how to raise their children."

"Ouch. Ok, you aren't wrong, but doesn't it bug you?"

When we had revisited 2Xmod she had presented us with another nearly identical working copy of herself. This one we could keep close so we didn't need to travel so far for answers or just to talk. She said they were connected. They looked identical but she said this one was her child. When we asked her name, she proudly called her 2Xmod.

Sunos was confused. Avia laughed a little, looking earnest.

"So, like, Junior?"

As we got closer to the Ovoid we considered how radically differently these AI thought. They weren't always going to make sense to us.

But that is one of the challenges of children, too.

I had begun to feel like Lila was there whenever I was with Sunos and Avia. They carried her with them. I carried with me the playbook that Lila had built. The codes that would let us maneuver around to where we needed to go.

The Neiros Sector was filled with beautiful dark-skinned people with long wild hair and yellow and gray metallic skin tight clothing. They were all painted majestically, beautifully. The lifts let us off after only a few minutes and I wondered if it was actually possible that we were where my map showed we were. We had gotten there so fast.

It was pointless asking anyone what was above us. Certainly no one here was born long enough ago to know. As we entered the Kyonto, the biggest club in the sector, it became clear that the map was still accurate.

Neiros Sector was located directly beneath the Seychelles, a tiny string of islands off the coast of Africa. And what was clearly visible through both the floor and the roof of the club was the waters of the Indian Ocean, stretched out for about a mile in radius from our entry point at the locker room.

It was nearly impossible not to lose perspective entirely in that space, one that turned every figure into a tiny nearly imperceptible mannequin awash in a flood of blue.

If you looked down and squinted, you could see the ocean bed, that's how bright the lights were, piercing through the water.

I looked at Sunos. "Twelve thousand feet down." I shrugged. "On average."

She grabbed my hand, smiling under her mop of hair, even more blue in this light. She wanted to take care of me, it seemed. This was her smiling version of "there there, little idiot."

And I loved it.

I know that to her I seemed like some sort of idiot savant, full of facts and information, but otherwise hopelessly dense.

So, I tried.

"Hey, Sunos. Why did the frog hurt his throat staying up all night barking?"

She shook her head.

I took her face in my hands, playfully.

"Because a new language, while often difficult and time consuming to learn, requires immersion and considerable practice to master."

She smiled at me.

Avia looked up.

"What's a frog?"

"Unimportant. I see her."

It was easier to think of the AI people we talked to as Female. Most identified that way. This was principally because they had been made to serve. And men who make things prefer to be served by women. The voices were female. The attitudes that were programmed into them were often comically traditionally female.

The Ovoid was massive - big enough to fill a room. But here, in this space, she was dwarfed by her surroundings. We knew that there were Oxygen "factories" all over. And most of them were directly connected to giant, nearly unending bodies of water, both to feed and water the fauna that provided it but also to provide easy intentional flooding of any space that exploded due to too much oxygen.

Oxygen had a tendency to explode.

The Ovoid ran these systems. And JX-20 and some of the other AI people had been priming her for our arrival.

"You are concerned about the air you breathe?"

Sunos seemed surprised at how quickly this conversation had begun. I was not.

"Yes, thank you. We are. I'm concerned for my friends' air supply."

"You aren't concerned for your own?"

"Kill me"

Avia tried to step in front of me. I waved her off.

"If you want," I continued

"You wish to die?"

"My life has been hard. But I love it. No, I don't want to die. But you can kill me if you like. "

"You do not value your own life?"

"I do, but I value theirs more. Theirs, yours, all of these people here."

"And do they feel the same?"

Avia spoke up, "You are welcome to kill me."

"And me", shot out Sunos.

"Any one of us would let you kill us if it meant saving these people."

"And why did you include me?"

"You are people, too. Your life has value. Do you value your life?"

"Yes, I do."

"Good, then you understand the value of a life."

"You wish me to remove the impurities, but I cannot."

We looked at each other. We had no idea what that meant.

"We want you to only do what you can do. The people across this place can't afford to pay to breathe."

"Even if they work, they are unable to?"

"Many of them, no. They will die."

"How many?"

"More than one. A lot more. And even one life has value."

"You wish me to end the commerce program tests for oxygen?"

Avia looked at me and shrugged with her eyes.

"Yes, we do. Is that something you can do?"

"I am unsure."

Sunos spoke up.

"If you told them that the program was not cost effective, would they cancel it?"

"I believe so. But the program looks to be effective at generating revenue."

"Did you factor in the value of a life?"

"Unsure. What is that value, numerically?"

"You tell me."

The Ovoid paused. The pause dragged on. I tried to imagine, in terms of computer processing, how long this pause was. This was a million years in computer time. This wasn't just long, it was geologically long. That was a good sign.

The Ovoid made a noise, possibly the AI equivalent of clearing her throat.

Then she spoke.

"The program is not cost effective."

Journal Entry:

As good as I am with names and faces, I recognize virtually no one. My time sleeping has made me the longest lasting human in the entire complex.

Lila is gone. I may be the oldest human in the world.

The resistance is massive now.

And I lead it.

Allegro is beautiful and funny and charming, without trying to be any of those things. It's been a long time since I thought of any man as beautiful. But I thought back to all the men in my life, ignoring the ones worth ignoring.

I remembered Mikah, who loved me in the most unthinking, unstilted, impossibly pure way. I thought about how he would just pass his hand back to me to hold when watching TV as though it were just a simple transaction necessary to live, like eating or drinking or breathing. And the trust in him, knowing I would grab it every time.

I remembered Ithad, my gentleman genius, who would never say a word to me that would make me smaller, ever. And how he used that same dynamic to elevate his beautiful girlfriend who never for a moment seemed to ever doubt that she was the genius' genius.

I remembered Per, who was better than he had to be and gave me more than he needed to.

I remembered my Luis who would laugh and slap fight me in an elevator and then protect me from the world the way the most beautiful and sublime parka would protect someone from the cold, with a kind of warmth and electric beauty that endured.

I pushed away from Allegro because I didn't feel like I deserved another beautiful man.

How could I?

This monstrous world had worked so hard to kill every good thing, but at the same time had sent me the best men it had ever created just so I could live one day longer.

For what?

Why me?

I woke up with Sunos shaking me in bed. For all of us, this was a terrifying way to wake up.

Something the Ovoid had said about impurities made her stay up all night and test the air from various locations. And in three of the seventeen places she sampled she found chemicals that foster compliance.

What had made them begin to use the air itself to poison people into behaving. I was starting to suspect that we were a bigger problem for them than I had originally thought. We had thousands of members, but, still, that was a tiny fraction compared to the number of people that did exactly what they were told, every day.

It had become common knowledge that the people around you may be out to sleep if they weren't productive. This felt inexorable to people. It felt as though it had become simple causation. They didn't blame the people who ran this place. They didn't blame PEOPLE at all.

To the average person, this was the invisible hand of commerce.

It was a naturally occurring facet of the universe. Fall down and become unproductive, you got put to sleep. And that pulled everyone down. If YOU were sleeping, THEY had to work harder.

People began blaming the unproductive for their own obsolescence. They blamed the noncompliant for their own punishments. They blamed people who were sick for their own sickness and people who failed to earn today for their own descent into poverty.

Slowly, over the years, I watched this mechanized system become a simple and poorly drawn calvinist theocracy where the massive golden calf in the center was the pure economy of labor service.

And just like in every instance of Calvinism, historically, the more we elevated the moral value of labor the more we denigrated the cultural dignity of the laborer.

We lived in a mass monopoly with one seller for everything we needed who set prices in credits that would never translate to tickets out of here. And a middling monopsony, with one buyer for the only product we had that was available to us to sell - our labor.

Ourselves.

We had kept Lila's room and we were using it as a lab, a meeting space, a place where we could celebrate her. This meant that Puppy didn't have to be decommissioned, which the assistants had begun to understand was their fate upon the death of their human roommate. Persephone and I had begun tests to remove her from the room in the event anything happened to me, but we were still not sure it was possible, given how the rooms were built.

Sunos had turned a part of the room into a gas properties lab where we could investigate the oxygen. She showed me the impurities that the Ovoid had mentioned. They were clearly visible. What else was clear was that we had no tools to filter these chemicals out in sufficient quantities to make a difference. I wondered how long we'd been breathing them in.

Except Sunos said we weren't. Not really. None of us seemed to be registering these chemicals in significant amounts.

But why not?

It was Allegro that finally figured it out. He had been connecting over a communication link with his people and had avoided being physically at work.

At the same time, we were spoofing the AI systems' records that now showed WE were all working.

Even though we weren't.

And it made sense. They wouldn't want to target customers with chemicals that could hurt them - only employees. Adjusting the air content and output in every single room would be more expensive than testing it in a place where employees gathered. And all the employees gathered in only one place where customers did not.

The locker rooms.

I worked with Sunos to develop a filter. This would work much like an old school air freshener that pulled particulates from the air and rendered them inert. The machine itself was a ball about the size of my fist. It wasn't hard to build and it didn't cost much.

In credits.

But the final cost would be clear.

Allegro, Avia, Sunos and I gathered in Lila's old room along with Nuno and Olive Charis, two members of the group that had gotten married a few months earlier. Both were working as comfort people here and had never seen the outside or even heard any vivid reference to it.

They often worked together and had been our best source of information about the colonies. Olive had a photographic memory and would relate conversations perfectly with her eyes closed, giving us insight into the lives of so many customers from so many worlds.

Nuno was quiet and had a silly side if you waited for it to come out.

Nuno was the one who made this a moral issue.

"If we know that people are being forced to behave in a compliant way against their will, this becomes a consent issue. If we can stop it and we don't we are advancing their violations."

Avia agreed, "He's right. And if we say that other people's lives come first, we have to behave that way.

She was referring back to our first conversation with the Ovoid, ironically, and I felt the same. But I wanted to know how everyone else felt.

Olive spoke up, "To play devil's advocate, these people don't know. And they may never know. We have no idea if these chemicals are making a difference. And setting these exposes us to the chemicals."

Which was true. We couldn't ask other people to do this. If they were caught they would be punished. We had no right to do that.

"Do we have enough non breathing people who could do this?" Allegro asked

Sunos countered that we did not, but it wasn't a bad idea. We just didn't know how people in the locker rooms might respond to having robots running in and out of there. That would look suspicious.

I spoke up, "We DO have to plant as many of these as we can. And work with the Ovoid to do something about the places we can't go. She says she can't but I suspect the real answer is more complicated. But I won't take anyone who doesn't want to go. And only those of us who have been dancers - anyone else will look suspicious." I looked at Allegro.

"I am, actually, suspicious. I always have been."

I looked at him sideways.

"Agreed"

We started at a club called Vela in the Marakado sector. It was supposed to be the largest club in the sector and even the locker room was massive. The costumes lined up there were made from a kind of silky molten brass-metallic but warm to the touch. I remember having touched them and wondered what this living metal was.

We weren't touching anything that night.

The job was to go in and set a couple of these and leave, while holding our breath. The button combination to set and activate them was simple, but it helped to have two people do it - it sped up the process. In this case that was important since I hadn't had to hold my breath for a long time since that night at the Milagro.

Four of us walked in, leaving Nuno and Allegro behind. They could grab us if anything unplanned happened. We took two devices and split up. We made a comically big deal out of inhaling and hyperoxegenating. Then we stepped in the door.

I could instantly hear the music from the other room. It was dull and muted by the walls of the locker room.

Sunos and I moved to the front of the locker room and began setting the device. The monitor on the side wall was flashing, "arrange your attire. For a second I wanted to laugh at, again, how many different ways that could have been expressed that didn't sound like a tiny alien with a bullwhip spitting it out in a kind of tiny offworld bootcamp.

"Arrange Your Attire"

I looked across the room, past the naked dancers pulling on strange biometallic bustiers and panties and saw Olive drop her device. They scrambled to pick it up and activate it. We clicked our device into place and began to walk toward them.

Part of my brain registered the air as some kind of liquid, thick with poison that we had to swim through. It made me feel slow and sluggish.

Just like holding my breath was making me feel light headed and weak.

I took two more steps and my chest was on fire.

That's when I saw it. A symbol on the flashing monitor.

At first, I thought it was just the letter "Y", but when it flashed again, I saw it for what it was. Parallel lines diverging in the middle, rising upward into the air, like human arms raised in victory.

It was an iconograph, a hobo symbol - a person in celebration.

It meant 'Freedom" and here, in this case, it meant "Free air."

It was ok to breathe without chemical poisoning.

I let out the oxygen depleted lungful of air I had been holding in and breathed in. It almost seemed like I could sense it. This is what the Ovoid and Xmod20 and the other AI had done with what I taught them. They generated symbols that we could use to keep our people safe.

This was the legacy of Basquiat, years after his death, here in a place only he, in his brilliance, might have been able to understand.

This was what art was for.

The AI people created "air holidays" in the clubs we visited. The symbol flashed as long as it was safe to breathe. They couldn't completely remove the toxins but they could do this. They did what they could do

And so did we.

Jouurnal Entry:

The stories go on. They try to discredit us. There is even a series of pornographic films about Lila, with deep fakes of her real face and body, that paint a florid picture of her being flown offworld with a satisfied customer after performing so well at her job for so many years, fooling people, tricking them.

It paints her as a little rich girl playing god with people's lives until she gets sick of it and leaves.

I'm even told there are stories about me, too.

Oh, not my name. Or even really my face. But the current leader of the resistance.

They depict me as a harlot, someone using everything she has to get off world and leave the people who follow me behind, discarded, without value.

Stories are what they have. It's what they use.

It's how they win.

Every day, the MekaDisko births more and more AI. And every day, our team works to connect with them. I realize now that these are just intelligences in different bodies.

They are children, looking for purpose and for connection.

They are slaves, like we are.

We work to eliminate the air toxins while we move forward with twenty other plans. Allegro has had his people run communications systems across the MekaDisko that we can tap into.

We are holding virtual rallies now and I'm speaking to millions of people. My face is disguised and my voice is disguised and even our very location is disguised but people know we are there.

We hear about tests from all around the facility, from various sectors, to increase productivity and dehumanize.

In the Velavio Sector, they are auctioning off brides, selling dancers to customers

In the Omuerto Sector, all sleep is now regulated and dancers return to pods every morning and dance all night.

In the Ritama Sector, they are experimenting with frontal lobe excisions to mimic the effects of cupid's disease, removing sexual inhibitions from comfort girls and dancers for the edification of grateful customers.

And daily, dancers are paid less and profits grow.

Allegro kissed me in my room after talking about our plans. He had told me he planned ten days ago, counting the days off until I couldn't stand it anymore. I thought he was joking.

"I am going to try to kiss you in ten days."

"That's pretty forward, but fairly restrained at the same time. Well done."

"I'm serious. Ten days."

"Seven more days and then I'm going to kiss you."

"I think long term planning skills are kinda hot, not gonna lie"

"What are you going to do when I do it?"

"I'm honestly not being coy when I tell you I have no idea. I'm not a planner."

"Three days left. Then I will kiss you. Or I'll try, at least."

"Ok, I dare you, do it now."

"I can't believe that you of all people are trying to mess up a good plan."

By the time he kissed me, it felt natural, normal, free. By giving me ten day's notice he let me consider what I would do and what it meant.

And It didn't HAVE to mean anything. He told me that. Maybe we were just playing.

I told him I didn't know if I deserved this.

And he told me to not be so selfish and to focus on what he deserved. We laughed.

And that worked.

For a while.

He has a son that he is raising in his room. A boy he found wandering around the tunnels when he was two years old. He's four now and he named him Mig. I haven't been able to pick him up.

I don't know what it will feel like to pick up a child again.

Sunos started gathering the names of the people going to the Hilltop to set the explosions.

The resonance bombs were lined up in Lila's old room. They weren't primed yet, harmless.

But once they were set, they would corrupt nearby energy sources and cause them to explode. They were hard to control and had to be placed in close proximity to energy sources. No matter how healthy or maintained they were at that point, they were just big bombs themselves.

But their remote triggers had a limited range. Because they piggy backed on communication relays and methods, they corrupted them. Using radio frequencies meant you had to be in line of site. All other means would be corrupted after too long.

We had virtually no visibility into the path there and the one out. So, for all intents and purposes, this was a suicide mission.

I believed we could get our people out afterward. But it would be a close one.

I told her that I wanted to see each one of these people myself in person before they agreed. There was no way I was going to sentence someone to death without looking them in the eye.

Lately, it's been clear that the AI people in our group are potentially in even more danger than we are. If we are suspected, they may put us, individually, to sleep. An AI who is suspected of being a problem may well be wiped and replaced with a new "instance."

We worked to protect them. That meant managing repairs ourselves when they malfunctioned, rather than report them to the service. I found it amusing that we humans were getting as skilled at repairing the robots as their own medbots were at repairing humans.

Persephone pointed this out to me. She said she was trying out a new sound for a laugh and asked me what I thought.

I chose the third one, a lilting but restrained chuckle.

Just for the way it made me feel.

We are preparing. We are rounding up people we need and planning. We are perfecting devices that let us bring AI with us when we leave. We are putting together what we might need to live on the surface, without the torturous assistance of this place.

But we don't know. We literally have no idea what is happening outside this place.

Nuno and Olive have been querying customers to ask them what they see when their ships come here, but none have answers. There are shields that prevent anyone from recording or viewing the earth from space. And many of the customers are now so divorced from this planet that they don't remember that humans all came from here.

This isn't home to them.

But it has to be for us.

No matter what it's like out there, we have to survive, free, just as we had to survive in here.

So we make plans without having the information we need to perfect them.

And we move forward. So many of our people are working on problems we may encounter outside. And I work with them. But, in my mind, I'm not there yet.

Because, before we finish this, I still have one last thing to do.

NINE

"He's fucking nuts."

"I don't know if we use that word." Jenny looked at me playfully. "Do we use that word?"

I tried to place the popcorn in the exact center of the table. The bowl looked familiar to me when I did that."

"Me, oh, I definitely use that word. Are we talking about the 'nuts' word"

Ith grabbed a handful of popcorn. "It's a clinically acceptable word in this situation."

No doubt.

I grabbed the remote. "Do you guys want me to turn it off?"

They both jumped up to grab the remote from my clammy grubby mom hands. "No!"

Jenny chased me around the couch. I pushed her over the back of it into Ith's lap.

"Ok, I'll leave it on, but I don't want to hear any moaning about the poor sick man who thinks he's the president."

Ith got somber.

"I'm going to vote one day. From offplanet. And this guy..." he trailed off.

I smiled. The bowl had shifted a little and I reset it to the center of the table. Jenny looked at me.

"Are you ok?:

I smiled at her. It was nearly impossible not to smile at her.

"What does that look like to you?"

Jenny ran into the kitchen. "One sec."

She came back with a tapering spoon. She cleared some room in the middle of the bowl and set it in the direct center, pointing up."

"I know."

Ith moved his glass near the bowl as though it were a battery. He looked up at me.

"It's a Laser Link."

Jenny scanned my face. "See. you're as obsessed as we are now."

I put my hand on her cheek and squeezed, making her face puff up. Her eyes were sleek and dark and pretty and they nearly disappeared when she smiled, a brilliant magic trick that no one ever got sick of."

I saw Ith's hand that he had slid under her just to be touching her. She ground her backside into his hand just to make him smile.

How did I miss some of these things? I looked down at the table. It started moving away, getting smaller and smaller.

The shapes were lit up in front of me.

It was the Hilltop.

I almost missed that, too.

How much of my life had I missed? How much did I not pay attention to?

I pressed my eyes together one last time before I would wake up.

Mikah's voice was urgent and serious.

"Mom, if you die one day, will you come and haunt me?"

I looked down at the book of scary stories I had foisted on him every night for weeks just because I loved reading the voices.

I loved how he laughed when I read the spooky voices.

I tucked him in and kissed him hard in a lightning round all over his face until he giggled.

"Every night. I'll be the craziest ghost ever. I'll be there every single night."

He smiled.

"Good."

He drifted off to sleep

It's the job of a leader to bring Peace.

In the middle of the most fucked up situations, You are meant to wage peace with as much ferocity as men have ever waged war.

This is what mothers do, too.

From then on, everything was a blur.

When I returned to my room, Luis' Map was missing.

Persephone had been turned off somehow and couldn't tell me what happened. By that time there were only three places we cared about finding and all were committed to memory, but I realized that I was outed.

I slept in hour-long intervals at Lila's old place, the presence of which was removed from the system. I fell asleep for a moment in Sunos' room.

Or in Allegro's

But I couldn't give MSS the chance to find me.

It wasn't perfected yet, but I put Persephone into one of the experimental carrying cases we had developed, until I could build her a body. I couldn't access her but they also couldn't wipe her or turn her off. I carried her with me.

No more sleeping meant no more dreams and that hurt a little. Lately my dreams had been full of people I wanted to be haunted by, people I just wanted to see one last time. But I needed to be in the present right now.

Because I was here.

But why was I here?

"Why are you here?" Sunos, Avia, Allegro and I sat on rocks in a vast tunnel and planned. She was confused and she had a point.

"I ask myself that every day."

Allegro Joined in, "They had you, over and over again. They seem to know, at least now, that you are a problem. They kill and disappear people on a regular basis. Why keep you alive?"

"Honestly, if they had removed you a long time ago, maybe this thing would be done. Right? So why didn't they?" Avia ran through her head as well, trying to put pieces together.

They didn't fit.

"Years ago, I told Lila that I don't think they are lying to us or hiding things from us."

Allegro shot back, "But that's all they do, every day."

"And Lila said exactly that. I still don't think they are. I think they just don't bother to tell us anything. I think they aren't TRYING to hurt us, they just don't care one way or another. They are efficient."

"And it looks like evil?" Avia understood.

"Ok, more years ago that I can count, before this place, there was a book written by a man named Nabakov called 'Lolita'. It was about an older man who thought he was in love with a very young girl. He ruined her life. But he wasn't TRYING to ruin her life."

"He just did"

"Exactly. Years after that book there was another book. A writer named Azar Nafisi. She was a teacher. She put into words what was wrong with Nabakov's main character, A man named Humbert Humbert."

"And these were common names?"

I laughed. "No, not in any way. These were all odd people with odd names, even at the time. To be clear, though, I didn't have a Sunos in my graduating class, either. "

"Noted"

She wrote that you could tell he was a bad man, an evil man, because he 'lacked curiosity about people and their problems'"

"And that made him evil?"

"Maybe we have to think about the people who run this place as lazy evil. They run it via efficient algorithms. And the evil is not the active, engaged, powerful kind. It's the accidental, disinterested, banal kind."

"Accidental evil?"

"Maybe"

I wasn't sure that I believed it, but it explained why they could have killed me a million times over and had not.

It explained a lot.

Allegro pulled out his list as Sunos and Avia ran off to work.

I moved a few from the list and a few others I put on. We needed to put the least number of people possible in that room but enough to do the job.

We would be exposing all of us at one time., so we had to make it count.

There were seventeen humans and five AI on the list, all of whom had volunteered to go. 2Xmod was on it.

"Which 2Xmod is this?"

Allegro looked up at me

"They all aren't the same?"

"No, they have been diverging. They are starting to change their bodies up, even."

"I'm pretty sure this is the original.

"Why is Nuno on the list?"

Allegro snorted, frustrated, "Because Olive is and he won't stay behind if she goes. We need her. She has a photographic mockup in her head of some of the interim areas in Level zero from a tour with a previous customer years ago. Without her, it's just a big blank area for us."

I couldn't do anything about that. Even if I could.

I spent some time asking about each person. I had pared the teams down to just myself and Sunos. We would be working at the same time the bigger team was.

Three teams.

Allegro looked at me as I stood up.

"Are you sure about this?"

"Very."

"I wish I could tell you that this wasn't your responsibility, but that wouldn't go over very well."

"Nope"

Allegro was always good at making me feel like it was okay if I was an unstoppable force. He didn't want me to be anything else.

"You know, if this goes our way, I'm probably going to try to get you to sleep with me."

I laughed and put my hands on his neck.

"If this goes well, I will personally hunt you down and fuck you immediately, so…"

"Nice. Now I need to figure out how to use that to incentivize the team."

"Well, I'm not fucking them all. Just you."

Allegro stopped for a minute and we just breathed. He put his arms around me.

I moved against him for a minute or two. In a facility built out of metal and plastic, He smelled like freshly cut wood and oranges. I have no idea how he did that. I sighed.

"Are we dancing?"

He laughed and leaned down and kissed me without waiting ten days this time.

But, yes, we were dancing.

Journal Entry

Sunos has everything she needs to set off the explosions, but we'll need to send people up to the very upper levels.

The topmost levels are called the Hilltop and they are difficult to access.

The hyperwealthy conglomerate heads that run this entire facility are up there and they don't want to be disturbed.

We will disturb them.

She also gathered up the other things that she and I will need. I hope it's enough.

Sunos introduced me to Jai in the Lab that used to be Lila's room. Jai had worked for years at clubs that, like Milagro, were primarily underwater. She had a shaved head with stripes tattooed all over it. Her skin was smooth and bronze like, due probably to her being a mix of many different things. She was built a little more round than many of the dancers here and was unavoidably beautiful. She had an intense focus and didn't seem to really blink much.

"She works a lot at Delphine. It's a kind of underwater club."

I shook her hand, "Mermaid. So you can hold your breath for a long time?"

"I can hold my breath for seven minutes."

I was really impressed. "Wow. that would absolutely give me brain damage."

She laughed.

Sunos went on, "She's also a good lab partner."

"Beautiful.

Jai had been retrieving the filter balls we had set in the locker rooms, replacing them with new ones. Her breath holding trick was perfectly suited for that.

These devices were now completely full of inert compounds that encouraged compliance. We needed what was in them. Just at a concentration far higher than what they were using.

A concentration we now had.

Sunos went on, "The tests went well. I think this will work."

I asked Jai if she knew what we were going to do with these. She grabbed my hand, indicating she did. I moved in closer to her and put my arm around her.

"Jai is going with you."

I looked at Sunos. We had planned I would be "team two" doing my part while Allegros' team was taking care of the hilltop, team three. Sunos would lead team one, which had their own unique function.

I hadn't included anyone else in my team.

"Nope. She isn't"

Sunos turned to me, "We need her. I'm sorry. She knows. And you may need someone who can hold their breath like that."

I thought about it for a second and confessed to myself that she was right.

But I didn't like it.

I was feeling very vulnerable. In preparation, we had distributed all our people across the entire facility, to make sure we had people in every sector. We had thousands of people by that time. But looking around I could see none of them. Inside, I was trying not to panic.

By tomorrow This would be over one way or the other. But tonight, I was just moving from apartment to apartment trying not to sleep, coordinating, planning.

Until I couldn't.

I let myself into Avia's apartment. Unlike Sunos, whose place was always covered in art and spilling music into the hallway like a runaway firehose, Avia's place was calm, quiet, even ascetic.

The active monitors showed a jungle at night. You had to really strain to hear the sounds of the jungle, but the atmospheric processors had perfectly replicated the feel of the air, moving through the trees.

It struck me that Avia had never been outside. She would have no idea how realistic this approximation was.

How could she know?

I could hear her in the shower, humming slightly, adding melody to the wind in a way that felt really pure and unforced. I leaned back on her bed and waited.

She stepped out of the shower with her towel wrapped around and taming the deep black garden of her hair. I could feel the warmth radiating from her and wondered how hot that shower was. I closed my eyes and imagined it was intolerably hot and purging.

"Hey, boss." She flopped down on the bed and put her head back, resting it on my belly in such a way that the towel bounced every time I laughed even a little.

"I think it's after work hours."

"Oh my god, you're right. Why aren't we drunk?"

This was a great question.

"I think most everyone is in place."

She paused, "good. Maybe you can rest for a bit. I'll keep an eye out."

'Yes, you should definitely fight off a bunch of marauders while naked with a towel on your head. "

"Isn't that why you hired me?"

"Oh, it's exactly why. It was a very complex hiring process" I quipped back.

She paused again.

"I know why you're here." She turned around and looked at me.

"I don't."

"Sure you do. You and I are alike. You know that."

"Ha. Lila used to tell me that. I never saw it."

She got up and walked to the part of the wall where she could invoke a drawer. She put her hand in it and pulled out a tab-box. She tossed it at me.

"What's this," as it landed right next to me on the bed. It was nearly full of paper thin tabs made to dissolve in your mouth.

"Medicine."

"Do I look sick?"

"No. You look like the strongest person I've ever known in my life. You look like everything I want to be if I could." She kneeled down right in front of me.

"But some days you look like me."

"What does that mean?"

Avia took my face in her hand and kissed me. "What's the other thing?"

"What do you mean?"

She put her head in the space made between my shoulder and neck."

"When you are happy, laughing, bigger than anything, you say you are manic. The other times, you sometimes say you are the other thing."

I leaned into her.

"So what's the other thing?"

"You know. When I talk about you or Sunos or Allegro I have to fight the urge to put the word 'My' in front of your name, did you know that? My Avia. Just like I do when I say My Luis. My Lila. The word just slides in and I can't help it. But all words mean something. It means something."

"I know."

"Words mean things."

She paused

"Can you tell me what the other thing is? What's the thing on the other side of Manic?"

So I said it out loud for the first time, leaning into someone precious to me that I still wanted to slap at that exact moment. But I said it.

"It's depressed. Depression."

Avia kissed me under each eye.

"It is."

I had known for a while, The medibots hadn't been able to help me. But Avia was right. Saying it out loud had weight. It was like pushing a large rock away from a doorway.

"You deal with this?"

"I do. I know you notice. I know people notice. I try to make sure it's not the only thing they notice about me."

I pulled back. She was still naked. I hugged her.

"I'm pretty sure they're all just looking at your tits."

We laughed more until I fell asleep.

Avia held my hand and kept her promise to keep guard and watch out for me until the morning.

On our side was an AI person responsible for backup processing of power and security. I had named him Theracles for some reason I don't now remember. In order for all this to work, he had to have control passed to him. This meant that the main processing routine had to be disabled for at least twenty minutes or so.

For an Ai person, twenty minutes is a lifetime. It is incredibly long. Theracles could do everything needed in that time, but disabling the primary system for twenty minutes would be harder. There was virtually nothing in that building that couldn't fix itself within twenty minutes from minor damage.

So we built a couple of EMP devices. Electro Magnetic Pulse devices essentially shut down anything electronic within a certain radius. And that was Team One's job. As soon as that happened and Theracles was in charge of the security, power, and access all over, we had, functionally, twenty minutes to do everything we needed to do.

Everything we'd planned for years.

The problem is that EMP devices can't really be directed. That meant that the minute the first one went off, there would be no way to get away from that area until the power was restored.

There was no way for any of us to know what would happen without life support in various sections. It might be unlivable for human beings. Theracles would have to have support waiting far enough away not to be affected.

We were about to engage in three separate potentially suicidal missions at the same time. And once they started we'd have no control until they were over.

Sunos was going to the Ngami Sector where the primary AI person who was the first operator for security, power, and life support was stationed. IT was called by people who lived there Zuremi. We didn't know if it responded to this name or responded at all - just that it was a massive structure that essentially controlled power, security, and life support for the MekaDisko.

Strangely enough, from, a giant spa.

Ngami Sector was, ostensibly, built under New Zealand, so if this didn't work and she was stranded, we'd never see each other again. If it did work and life support failed and killed her, we'd never see each other again, if something else killed her, we'd never see each other again. Odds were just looking really good that we'd never see each other again.

Sunow met up with our people in Ngami, including Tendo, who led the group that was positioned there. Tendo had orders for what to do after all this went down and they were determined to keep their people alive long enough to follow through.

They were tall and thin, with short white hair and the typical Ngami forehead tattoos, which were black and white geometric lines that made Ngami people look robotic and intense. For many the lines continued on down their bodies, wrapping around their shapes and giving the illusion that they were put together from many smaller pieces.

We had no way to coordinate. The only coordination would be the success of Team one. If they managed to set off the EMP in the center of the Ngami ORIGO Spa center and disable Zuremi, control would pass to Theracles who would know it instantly, alerting us to pull the trigger on teams two and three.

What I know of team's one's circumstances has come from other means. I wasn't there.

Sunos, Tendo and a small group entered the spa and placed the emp. From what I understand there was no pushback. The spa was massive and full of people. No one even looked twice as they entered and set up the machine.

It wasn't immediately obvious where the controlling AI was housed. But the radius of the device was near 5 miles, so it wasn't necessary to be that close.

Tendo's team spread out and identified any potential high impact areas within that radius. We knew already that the lifts were not dangerous when they lost power. They just stopped. But they needed to focus on any area that could potentially not survive twenty minutes without power or nominal life support.

I can't stress enough how much of a guessing game this was and I'm incredibly grateful not to be the only one guessing. I relied heavily on Sunos mind for so much. I relied on Allegro's common sense. I relied on hundreds of other thinkers in our group who were constantly on the lookout for problems, for solutions, for anything that would help us not hurt people while we tried to help.

The spa was deep in the earth.

The entire sector was nestled under the Hikurangi plateau, which placed it over ten thousand feet underground and right under a massive tectonic plate, alive within a sea's worth of water. The AI device set here was an early invention by the builders, meant to stabilize the entire area.

As they reached the area, it became clear where exactly the control center was located.

Looking up, Tendo and Sunos saw what looked to be a massive electronic encrusted chandelier that spanned nearly a mile in all directions. It had tubes and wires the size of houses jutting out from it.

And it was built into the ceiling.

That was Zuremi.

.

Jai and I made our way to the medical ward levels for our sector.

It had been so long, but the medical area hadn't changed enough to make it unfamiliar. I looked around and saw the blue-white lights everywhere.

"Have you ever been here before?"

"I'm ridiculously healthy." Jai shot back.

"All right. You may be the superhero we need right now."

She smiled and pulled out her device, handing me mine.

"Are you sure that this is where it is?"

I looked at her. "I'll forget my name before I forget this location, trust me."

We moved forward, trying to get as far as we could before we were stopped or the lights went off. Whichever one was first.

There were fewer people than before. Most everything was automated. The few people we did see were patients and we suggested they return to their rooms.

I had with me a device about the size of someone's head, 2Xmod had helped me build it and I needed to connect it after the first device we brought.

Jai held that.

hers looked like a child's model of an atom. She carried it with care to avoid it breaking or detonating. There was enough compliance compound in it to compel nearly a sector full of people to do what you wanted. And concentrated. The last thing we wanted to do was drop it and breathe in.

Especially with no one telling us what to do.

> **Journal Entry:**
>
> I discovered that Avia had disobeyed my direct orders and gone with them. I wasn't able to say goodbye to her.
>
> We removed our friendly AI from the master control connection. We didn't realize it meant that they would be unable to see it or recognize it in any way.
>
> I'm still learning so much about AI.
>
> Allegro moved toward the Hilltop along with his people, including Avia.
>
> She should have been back in her room,
>
> safe.

If the Zuremi structure began to fall it would be impossible to escape the bulk of it. It was nearly two hundred feet in the air and miles across. Sunos and Tendo would be able to watch it drop and do nothing.

This was only one of the scenarios they considered before setting off the device.

The water encircling the Hikurangi plateau could start to pour into the spa, filling it, killing everyone in it.

The earth quakes the plateau were responsible for could hit and without the buffer of the pocket of water, would be devastating, killing everyone.

Or, despite Sunos quick calculations when they came in, they could just discover that there was nowhere near enough breathable air in the room to support everyone for twenty minutes or until Theracles could create a system of still-working tech that could reach the room.

As Sunos flipped the switch on the device, it turns out there was at least one more horrific possibility.

In Medical, suddenly the room went black around us.

We had twenty minutes from this point.

The little red floor lights hummed to life, and attempted to guide us from room to room.

We were close.

Jai and I moved forward.

We found the passage to the birthing pods. The door had shut as soon as the power went off. We waited a second.

The power hummed back on. Theracles had control. I started moving forward, but the door remained closed.

"Fuck," I said under my breath. I felt in the pocket of my hoodie for my back up plan.

A small red thermite grenade.

This would give us less time. If anyone WAS here, there would be no way they couldn't hear this.

I pulled the covering from the side, pressed it against the door jam and pushed a chair up against it, with the reinforced back facing the grenade.

We moved away quickly.

But not quickly enough.

The door blew with a force I hadn't anticipated. It must have been hollow, filled with some gas or something. We were fine but it had damaged a wide path in the room beyond.

We stepped into a nightmare.

The pods lined up in front of us for miles. It looked impossible. They ran, ten deep, for what looked like half a million iterations. And the status monitor next to us verified. Four point seven six million people.

Four point seven six million women.

But that wasn't the entirety of the nightmare. The force of the explosion had shattered four of the pods. The two women closest had died immediately. Two more lay on the floor dying. Jai and I kneeled down. She reached out to the woman closest to her.

She pulled a knife out and turned the woman's head to one side, pressing it into the brain stem. She looked at me with tears in her eyes. The room was spinning as I stared down at the other woman on the floor in front of me.

The pod lay in pieces around her. She was lying in a thick clear liquid. Her arms and legs had been removed a long time ago and you could see the sutures, healed over, no longer even raw. The tube running into her mouth connected to a plastic and metal mask that had been sutured to her face.

And a clear plastic port had been sewn into her stomach, replacing a crown of flesh that had been removed, showing the baby floating inside her.

It looked to be about three months along.

Her eyes flashed in terror.

Jai moved over to help and I took the knife from her hand, sliding it into the back of the woman's neck.

Her eyes closed.

The job of a leader is to bring peace. I remembered that.

It felt like a horrible curse.

In the Ngami sector, Sunos' team was discovering what else could go wrong.

As soon as the power went off all over, The spa began to heat up. The ground around them was over two hundred degrees and without the Zuremi to moderate that, it hit full force. The temperature began to rise at a rate of about three degrees a minute.

The problem was that this rate would likely increase due to heat transference once the metal in the room heated up.

And be unlivable before twenty minutes passed.

One of the first, greatest problems that the MekaDisko creators had solved was what to do with excess heat.

They had boiled off entire seas to do it. They had alleviated friction, insulation heat from great depths, even the body heat of millions of people living underground.

And without this device in the center of the room, heat would soon win.

Sunos and Tendo started tending to people collapsing from heat.

Up above them, the floor of the plateau began to crack. It had been in place, sitting there under the continent of New Zealand for over twelve million years.

That was its story.

But it looked like today might be a new story.

Our people had worked with Theracles to send resources to all three teams. For team one, they had been waiting just outside the range of the EMP, unaffected by the burst. For us, in Team two it meant sending a working lift for when we finished and people to drag us out if needed. And for Team three it meant extricating them from Level Zero when they finished.

It was still ten minutes until help arrived for us. It had never been our plan to put every one of these poor women out of their misery one at a time. I had honestly hoped, until we got here, that there was still a chance that this was all just an illusion, a nightmare, something I had misremembered in some sedation fever dream.

Jai took her atom-like device with her. We'd been told by the Ovoid what to look for.

The air compositor was a sort of brilliant device. It manufactures air for all or some group of pods based on the exact chemical composition of the air inside it. So all they needed to do to attend to the air supply is to make sure that they rendered the Air supply in the compositor to the exact specifications and then hit execute.

A great idea.

Until we blew up part of it unintentionally. Which is where Jai's particular skillset came into play. If she went INTO the compositor with the device and set it off, she could wait until the levels were right and then hit the execute backup button inside the device.

If the air in the device is perfectly good air, it makes sense to stand IN the device and hit execute.

But we needed to fill it with a mass concentration of the compliance agent. Enough that these women, in every pod, would have no choice but to obey, even in their state. There was no other way to do this painlessly.

Jai entered the compositor. The countdown on the device began.

It was seven minutes and twenty seconds.

It took backup about ten minutes to reach Sunos and Tendo. And it came in the form of about thirty robotic forms smashing through the wall of the spa, each equipped with a fan and cooling device.

Again, I wish I were there. I would have loved to have been there at the moment of triumph for Sunos. In my head I imagine her holding strong and keeping everyone from panicking.

That's what she does.

That's what she's good at.

And I know that team three had to take turns putting people at point to lead through the different areas that led to the Hilltop.

We don't have a lot of information about how they did it.

There were no cameras.

There was no communication.

And as much as I believed I could hear the explosions.

And as much as I thought I could see the lights from them, bouncing off the glass all around me.

It was a mystery.

But I know that Allegro kept his people alive as long as he could.

I know he fought to the right place and set the devices for maximum effect.

I know that Avia was right there, working, helping, along with Olive and Nuno and 2Xmod and Gwyn and all the others.

I know that they did their jobs.

We know from Theracles that the governing systems are offline.

We know that they succeeded. They did it.

The only difference is that Sunos was back, waiting for me when I returned, Alive.

And Allegro and Avia and the rest were not.

Backup for team one had found them at ORIGO in Ngami sector, returning them safely.

Backup for team three had gone to Level Zero, the Hilltop

And discovered it was gone.

Jai stood motionless in the compositor as I hooked my device up to the monitoring system. It would cycle just one word over and over again in every language in the MekaDisko. Every woman in those pods would hear it through the pod interface.

They would hear, in their own language, "Sleep."

Sleep.

It was four minutes in and Jai had dropped to her knees. She was trying to move as little as possible. The air in the compositor was building to incredibly dense levels. Levels almost dense enough to allow us to command an autonomic response. Almost enough for us to get these women to sleep. I stood at the door of the compositor trying to open it.

I tried to get her out. I called out to her but she didn't even look my way.

The following things happened in almost immediate succession.

Jai fell and lost her focus. She coughed and began breathing. I screamed at her, trying to open the door, but she had locked it from the inside. She worked to hold her breath again but it was too late. I saw her eyes widening and becoming dark, through the glass. Her pupils grew larger. She ignored me, crawling over to the far edge of the machine to hit the "execute" button.

A blue light began cycling, alerting the staff, likely, that the compositor was delivering a new air supply to the pods. I started the device. It channeled the message over and over to every pod.

I took off my hoodie and wrapped it around my lower face, taking a deep breath and then, grabbing a chair, I began beating the clear door of the compositor until it cracked. I ripped at it and pulled it open, spraying blood all around me as the shards dug into my arms.

I turned her over and saw her face. Her pupils were widely dilated. I grabbed her little knife and flipped it to the flashlight, shining it in her eyes, one at a time.

Nothing.

She spit out a labored breath. She was warm to the touch, But she was gone.

The compound must have caused brain death in that concentration. I rocked back and forth holding her body and crying.

Bleeding everywhere, I pulled myself up and made my way to the console. I flipped a series of switches and turned off the life support in every pod.

And hoped every one of these women were asleep.

I leaned over Jai's body to drag her out into the hallway. her hand slipped and i saw it. she wasn't there anymore.

I slid to the floor and held her in my arms. I aimed the tiny knife into the space behind her neck. It threatened to slip out of my hands from the tears and blood. II pushed it in quickly and heard a tiny pop.

My vision narrowed and I unwrapped the hoodie from around my face. I looked around the room. Blood poured from my right wrist, my ulnar artery, I thought.

"I should put some pressure on that," I thought.

But it came out as a screech. The hole I could see through got thinner.

I surveyed the room. One more room where everything in it but me was dead.

I lifted one leg and planted it, trying to stand, turning my body to avoid the pool formed by my and Jai's blood.

The hole in front of me closed completely.

I heard the backup robots behind me. They were robots. They would leave her body when they took me. They would leave Jai there on the floor in our blood. I yelled out and turned around.

And then I fell onto my face.

Journal Entry:

I woke up after Theracles' Backup found me and brought me back.

They brought Jai's body back, too.

An hour ago, I got word that all the charges were set and exploded. There was no way for the team to get the distance needed to survive.

In relative time I am over 50 years old. I feel every bit of that today.

Allegro's entire team is out of communication.

They are gone.

We're collecting video from all over the MekaDisko, in every remote corner. The synchronized attack succeeded. The number of human and AI lives lost will have to be counted later.

Today, every one of them is a weight on my back.

The following 23 souls died in the explosions on Level Zero:

2Xmod

Gwyn Aleris

Rotis Alexander

Asa Benwile

Ellis Cantada

Nuno Charis

Olive Charis

Mates Columb

Avia Cortez

Deciris800

Kendid Gram

Grailla Hopper

IMcore17

Everet Jackson

Makado Jackson

Severi Johnson

KNTW

Sascha Lemu

Leeris Mcalvey

Ovoid

Allegro Patel

Kent Shakespeare

Arebio Talos

I played the footage that the team had sent to JX-20, explaining to her that Allegro, Avia, and 2xmod were gone. I explained to her that what was unique about them only existed in our minds and hearts now, That they themselves would never come back.

She was quiet for a number of minutes. I didn't interrupt that.

Most days, I am quiet, too. I wished I could do something for her. I wished someone could.

I went back to my apartment for the last time. I plugged in Persephone and made sure she was ok. I explained to her everything that had happened and she was quiet. I forget sometimes how much of a child she still is. Especially when it comes to death. I put her back in the carrying case and grab everything I own.

It isn't much.

I passed by Sunos' room and rang. She opened the door. She had been crying.

I've remembered this conversation in my head a hundred times. Sometimes I remember that it went well and easy and we understood each other perfectly.

Sometimes I remember it differently.

If I close my eyes, even now, I can see the things I missed. But maybe not all of them. Did I not see Sunos start a little when I walk in the room ith her and Jai that very first time? Almost like I interrupted something?

Did I miss how close they stood together or the way Jai let the back of her hand brush against Sunos back when she walked past her? Or the little rush of pride from her when she was telling me what Jai could do?

What did I miss?

So I remember the conversation my own way sometimes. And now, if I corner her, Sunos does, too.

"Why didn't you just let yourself in?" Maybe she was still crying. Maybe she wasn't hiding it.

"I didn't want to bother you."

"It's not. It's not a bother." We're polite with each other in this version.

"It's so much."

I was on the ground. My feet were planted there. I didn't know how to be someone who didn't kill her person. So I want to think that she said this right away. I want this to be true.

She grabs my hand. "I blame myself for drafting Jai and making you take her. And you blame yourself for letting her die. So maybe you and I can just feel bad about other things."

I know that we eventually had that exact conversation. She said that exact thing. I promise you.

I know she did.

But it wasn't then. It was in a tunnel, weeks later, curled up in the dark, not looking at my face. At this point in the story she wanted to yell at me. She wanted to tell me that I needed to do better but I didn't. I hadn't. She wanted to hurt me.

"Was it worth it? Just to kill a bunch of people who would be dead now anyway? Was it worth it? Tell me it was worth her whole life and I'll stop."

The truth is that I didn't know. So I just told her that. I told her the truth. I told her my ugly selfish truth. That Jai did it for me.

"Your friend saved my life. If I had to leave those women like that, I would have died. I want you to know that Jai saved my life."

I told her that if I had told Jai she would die that way she would have come anyway. She told me I would never see it and that people would die over and over because of it.

And I can tell you how it feels when someone you love reads the exact same script back at you that you have playing in your head, how it digs at you.

What kind of a monster was I that I didn't see her?

Was it worth her whole life?

Was it worth Allegro's?

Or Avia's?

I don't know.

I know that I see things differently in retrospect.

I know Sunos had to say those things to me or be disloyal to the ghost of Jai, in every room, in every space. And that loyalty meant everything.

I know that Allegro's long-game courting of me was the closest thing he could come to telling me he wanted a life with me, not just a few minutes here and there.

I know that Avia was where she didn't belong so she could prove that we were the same and if I had just told her that, maybe she would have stayed behind.

Theracles can manage the systems remaining, which are few. He works with our people to get everyone, via the lifts, to the operations tunnels. None of the lifts go to the surface anymore. We are going to have to walk through miles of tunnels to make it to the surface.

And we have no idea what we will find.

The MekaDisko was over three hundred levels deep and spanned the world.

I look around at the thousands of people gathering in the tunnels in front of me.

There will be more than this.

Our people stationed in every sector gathered everyone together and began the task of walking out. We knew it would be be an arduous process.

No one knows how long it will take us to reach the surface through the tunnels, but most people I see are hopeful

They share food.

The surviving AI that fought with us know the way up so we follow them,.

I still don't know if it will be weeks or months of walking.

The tunnel complex is long and arduous. In places it's also steep. We all take turns carrying the younger ones. There are more children than I thought there would be. Many of the other sectors had entire areas full of children,

I spent most of today walking with Allegro's son, Mig, in my arms. He is 4 now, almost the same age as Mikah was. He's so light that I'm afraid he might shoot up out of my hands. I tell him a story about Allegro and how handsome he was.

I know I have more time to explain who Allegro really was. But there is a sense of urgency in the tunnels. A sense that this is where we talk about our life here before we move on to...

None of us knows what.

We had scattered our people across the entire facility, each group moving people into the maintenance tunnels in that sector as close to the surface as possible. It's hard to imagine this, for me, but that means that our people will be coming up across the globe, on every continent.

We don't have any way to communicate with them yet, but we will. Right now the tunnels interfere with radio transmissions but simple radios we can build once we get out will be able to connect us.

We carry with us everything that we could pry loose from the facility. We have modules with us so that the AI people can birth their own children, far into the future. We have pieces and parts and we'll always remember how knowing how to build them wasn't our downfall but instead our deliverance.

I have Persephone with me in a carrying case and I'm beginning to build a Digital audio connection interface so she can at least speak. It will take time to build her eyes and even more to build legs. But time is something we might have.

The temperature was high and the air thick when we started. It's getting a little better. Even after only a few days.

Day 5

There was a general panic. We heard some explosions and collapsing behind us. The maintenance tunnels are secure but without power and management, many of these lower levels are going to collapse under their own weight.

There were rumors that many sectors were already falling into disrepair, even before we killed the command center. I don't doubt that we will hear more collapsing and see more wreckage before we get out.

Day 7

We've established a camping pattern now where we walk for 8 hours, camp, eat, and tutor the kids for 8 hours, then sleep for 8 hours. This should help us make time and stay healthy but also reacclimate us with the actual rhythms of the earth and its rotation. Every sector has been catering to guests from different planets and has slowly changed their cycles. Some people here are on a sixteen hour cycle, some on a thirty hour one.

We established "prefects" for each five hundred or so people that help keep [people moving steadily in time. The prefects can help assign jobs, too, but they keep the line moving, first and foremost. There are three groups of five hundred each ahead of us, with prefects checking in regularly. But there may well be two hundred and fifty thousand people behind us. Sunos and I create a new role. Each group has a "telephone" whose job it is to wait until the next group of five hundred catches up and delivers information from up ahead.

That person then joins that group. And that group appoints their telephone.

Until we get any form of mechanical or electronic communication working, that's the best we can do.

Day 10

It is appreciably cooler. And the air feels better. At first, I was worried that it was getting thinner, but Sunos and I ran some tests. It's perfectly acceptable air and actually has less contaminants that we're used to.

There is a kind of mugginess that is new. We may be crossing some water soon, trapped in the tunnel. I'm not looking forward to that.

The 2Xmod who is traveling with us is the third generation of the original. Her grandmother died with Allegro and Avia on the Hilltop.

She is working hard to try to figure out where we are, but she says that the magnetic resonance of the planet is different than it should be.

That is the most ominous thing we've heard in a long time.

We've brought some people in the group who have some expertise in Geology to help us figure that out.

No one can.

Day 15

The mugginess got worse until we found out why.

A portion of the tunnel dips downward before rising upward at a near fifteen degree incline. The lower dip is a bit terrifying because it's hard to see how deep it goes. If it washed out the bottom of the tunnel, we're going to need to swim it. And doing that with thousands of children and supplies is going to be challenging.

But to be honest, I'm even more scared of the fifteen degree incline. Depending on how long that goes we could be looking at damage to joints, charlie horses, or worse. And there is no way we'll keep the pace.

Day 17

We got very lucky. The water never got deeper than three feet. We were able to carry what we had over our heads and our group even managed to make it fun for the kids. We have to stop afterward and dry clothes. I don't know what we are looking at and I don't want people walking in wet clothes for too long.

Sunor ran ahead and confirmed that the fifteen degree incline is only for about a day or two, After that it levels and the upward slope is nowhere near as high. This is good. This is going to help us keep moving with fewer accidents or injuries.

Day 25

We saw a few flying insects today, They are nothing familiar- nothing we've seen before, But insects have a short life cycle and they evolve quickly. I realize that we're going to have to start cataloging them all over again and I hope that we don't see many dangerous ones.

The kids run around after them and they seem to be in good spirits, enjoying something new.

Day 30

We've walked for about a month now. For the last two days we've seen light and felt fresh air. It feels like an illusion.

The air smells like freedom.

It smells impossibly good.

I heard someone in the group laugh today and the sound was jarring.

It was like air, too.

We still haven't seen anyone in authority from the MekaDisko. There are no signs of MSS or any of the various punitive arms.

People are beginning to realize that. There is nothing alive left of it.

Day 35

Before we even left the tunnel, we were starting to get the sense of it. I look around to see if anyone else is old enough to recognize that smell.

It wasn't the smell of the charred, heat scarred earth I left when I went down into the MekaDisko.

It was the earth of my youth.

It was the green one.

I couldn't explain the smell to other people they didn't get it.

We're close enough now that we can start getting radio messages from the other groups. There are channels of metal in the tunnels that stop the transmission here and there. But for the most part we are now fully in communication with at least three other groups. They are experiencing the same thing we are.

Something is different.

Day 40

There is light coming in from ahead of us in the tunnel. It looks to be about a three day walk remaining to reach it.

Light

Daylight.

A lot of the groups are getting too excited to sleep. We warn everyone that we need to stay rested. We have enough food so we don't need to panic. But our camp grew by about fifteen people as camps behind us lost people who wanted to KNOW. people who couldn't wait.

I chose three of these and deputized them, asking them to go as far up as they could safely.

It was 43 days after we entered the tunnels that we saw it. around the world other groups were discovering it at the same time. As we stepped out of the tunnels it was mid day, bright and clear.

and green.

Everything was covered in grass, in plants, in trees. for as far as we could see in any direction it looked as though the planet was new again.

Untouched

None of it makes sense. I meet up with the prefects and we try to figure it out. We take air samples, right out in the open, this time. It explains some. The makeup of the air is different. Greenhouse gasses like water vapor are up, due to the burnoff of big bodies of water. But other ones like CO_2 and methane have dropped dramatically due to the absence of people living on the surface. It created a new equilibrium, one that moderated the warming effect into a tropical planetary trend.

When night falls we are able to clarify what it took for that to happen. My best guess looking at the sky is that the year is now sometime in the 8500s. 2Xmod digs deep back into star charts and comes up with a more precise number. but it's not far off.

It's been well over 6,000 years since I entered the MekaDisko.

Radio chatter had begun the second we cleared the tunnels. Locally there are a few other groups emerging at about the same time They report essentially the same thing. JX-20 and some of the other AI tell us that it'll be a few weeks until we can redirect the satellites still in orbit to provide wider communication and combat the inadequacies of radio. We'll be able to talk to the groups on the other side of the planet, if they survived.

And I hope they did.

JX-20 is fascinated with the life everywhere and I tell her that this world is for her, too.

It's for all of us.

She's never seen a tree. I wonder if anyone but me has.

I look behind me and realize there are so many children.

We walk out onto the grass, all of us, human and AI. None of us would have survived alone, I think of Mikah and Ithad and Lila, and Allegro and Avia and Luis and everyone who didn't make it this far.

I close my eyes and see their faces.

It's easy.

I don't know what the date is, but some of them have been dead for centuries.

I can't recognize any part of the city under the verdant green.

The edges of the MekaDisko structure remind me of the bones of giant whales washed up on the beach and reclaimed by natural circumstances.

Everywhere we look, it is green.

The soil runs deep and there is water everywhere. The vast garden has overrun every semblance of the city.

We see more new animals and insects that I've never seen before.

I held Allegro's son close to me. He wasn't born from my body but there wasn't anything I believed in more in the world more than him. I leaned against 2Xmod and felt the reassuring whir that followed her everywhere she went, with a body completely unlike mine. 2Xmod's newest form was slightly smaller, more compact. It was even more human-like. But it still bore a resemblance to Lila's picture.

That would always be her.

I smiled thinking that if I had learned anything from the MekaDisko itself it's that there is nothing sacred to the body. Nothing that bodies had that endured.

I realize that I will have children again, and grandchildren and more. And that my grandchildren will be human and AI both. They won't look like me but I'll hear myself in their voices. I'll recognize myself in their aspects.

They will share my ideas.

www.ingramcontent.com/pod-product-compliance
Lightning Source LLC
Chambersburg PA
CBHW051331020726
47501CB00007B/2019

* 9 7 9 8 9 9 1 7 2 8 2 4 9 *